Demented

by

Lynfa Moses

Copyright © 2016 Lynfa Moses

All rights reserved, including the right to reproduce this book, or portions thereof in any form. No part of this text may be reproduced, transmitted, downloaded, decompiled, reverse engineered, or stored, in any form or introduced into any information storage and retrieval system, in any form or by any means, whether electronic or mechanical without the express written permission of the author.

This is a work of fiction. Names and characters are the product of the author's imagination and any resemblance to actual persons, living or dead, is entirely coincidental.

ISBN: 978-1-326-88697-4

Contents

Chapter 1 The Wife

Chapter 2 The Mistress

Chapter 3 The Wife and the Young Man

Chapter 4 The Husband

Chapter 5 The Mistress and her Daughter

Chapter 6 The Mistress and her Ex

Chapter 7 The Son

Chapter 8 The Faithful Wife

Chapter 9 The Daughter

Chapter 10 The Son's Partner

Chapter 11 Another Sunday Lunch

Chapter 12 Partner's Parents

Chapter 13 Love Letters

Chapter 14 The Mistress and her Lover

Chapter 15 The Wife's Revenge – Part 1

Chapter 16 The Toyboy

Chapter 17 The Wife's Revenge – Part 2

Chapter 18 The Help

Chapter 19 The Wife and the Social Worker

Chapter 20 The Surrogate

Chapter 21 The Granddaughter

Chapter 22 The New Mother

Chapter 23 The Wedding

Chapter 24 The Morning After

Chapter 25 The Ex and the Wife

Chapter 26 Further Revenge

Chapter 27 A Surprise Visit

Chapter 28 A New Father

Chapter 29 The Wife's Solution

Chapter 1

The Wife

Paula first got the idea at the hairdresser's. It was because she had to wait so long for her appointment. Very irritating, especially as she'd made such an effort to be on time.

The main thing that had stressed her was that her cleaner Mary hadn't turned up to Jack-sit. Mary had rung to say her bus was stuck in traffic. What a feeble excuse; it had happened a few too many times before too. She'd sack Mary if she wasn't so good with Jack.

Paula couldn't leave him on his own, there was no knowing what he'd do. He'd left the gas on last week and, if she didn't have such an acute sense of smell, the whole house could have blown up. The number of times she'd told him not to fiddle with the knobs. Then her neighbour had told her that she'd seen him peeing in the garden. He could have been arrested for indecent exposure and that might have got into the *Richmond Times*. It certainly would have spoiled Paula's chances of chairing her branch of the Mother's Union.

Today he'd been a bit better. He'd gone to the newsagent, which admittedly was only two minutes away, and Mr Khan was always surprisingly nice. Jack had got the *Mail* for her and *The Times* for himself. Not that he read it anymore. She'd thought she could slip out for an hour or so. He'd left her enough times in the past, not knowing where he was, imagining the worst. No thought for her stuck at home with their son. But he'd started pacing around – never a good sign.

She'd considered putting him on the train to Arlene. It was straight through to her place and he always got there. As far as she knew. He'd done it so often in the past, it must be written into his DNA. She'd have to abandon her shopping trip, but her hair couldn't wait. It got so frizzy without regular straightening. She'd have to go on dealing with Jack in her own way.

Paula put on her camel Jaeger coat, walked across the Green and arrived at the salon in time for her appointment. The girl who took her name was texting on her mobile and didn't even look at her. She just nodded to the waiting area as if Paula had come in by chance and was not a regular customer.

Paula breathed deeply trying to calm herself. The magazines were depleted. No *Vogue* or even a *Good Housekeeping*. She picked up a *Hello!* but she never knew who the people were these days unless they were royalty. Sheila, her usual hairdresser, was chatting with some young lad. Paula leaned back on the chair and closed her eyes. She got so tired with Jack keeping her up at night.

At last Sheila called her over and the boy washed her hair. 'Going out tonight?' Sheila asked.

'No,' Paula said and thought about Jack, hoping he was all right. She contemplated the uninspiring evening she would have with him. She'd be trying to follow a television programme and Jack would ask who the characters were and completely misunderstand what was going on. He seemed to forget the beginning before it ended. She would probably just go up to her room to read.

She must have sounded grumpy because Sheila continued talking to the boy over her head. 'Tell me about this site your aunt's been on,' she said.

'Mum was disgusted,' replied the young apprentice. 'She says Aunty Jean's become a cougar.'

'She's just jealous, Alex. She'd probably like a younger man.'

Paula strained to hear over the running water, blow drying and constant ring of the phone.

'What are we doing today then, Paula?' asked Sheila. Paula explained what she wanted but was disappointed not to hear more about Aunty Jean. As Sheila snipped and straightened Paula's auburn tresses, Paula's mind returned to something Jack had said years ago. *Men like younger women and women like older men; it's the natural order of things. Our sex drive is different. It's to do with procreation; women run out of eggs, while men's sperm goes on for ever.* He had droned on about Methuselah and the selfish gene while Paula listened passively, accepting his authority. She hadn't commented that his sex drive was more about lust than procreation.

Alex returned with a sweeping brush and Paula tried to eavesdrop again, though they were now talking very softly.

'Does she, like, do it with them?' Sheila asked.

'I wouldn't have thought so – not at her age. But they take her out. My uncle won't go anywhere.'

'I think she's one of them MILFs,' said Sheila.

Alex laughed so hard he dropped all the hair from his dustpan. 'She hasn't got any children,' and they both dissolved into further giggles.

Paula looked round with her lips set firm. Another of these words young people used which she hadn't come across. Something disgusting no doubt, yet she wanted to know. Anyway, Sheila should have been talking to her. Hairspa was an expensive salon.

'Sorry, Paula, Alex's so funny. His mum tells him everything and his aunt does. Perhaps cos he's gay. They understand us women more, don't you think? You look lovely though. Let me show you the back.'

Paula looked at herself in the mirror. She was always so pale and she looked tired today. Her neck was scrawny. Jack had once said she looked like a plucked turkey. She supposed her hair looked presentable and other people always complemented her on her looks.

Sheila smiled but Paula's face was as fixed as if it had been sprayed by the lacquer Sheila used for her hair. Sheila explained about the dating site for finding young men which Alex's aunt had used. 'Why don't you give it a try? I'm sure you'd easily find a nice young man to take you out. I mean you are so slim and elegant. Not for anything, you know, just as a companion. Since your husband's not so well.'

Paula handed Sheila a smaller than usual tip. 'No. It might suit his aunty but I don't think it would be right for someone like me.' But her mind continued to dwell upon the conversation as she walked across Richmond Green. She'd better hurry. At least she'd told Mary not to bother to come as she was too late. She didn't want her arriving and finding Jack. He was probably fine.

She called out as she opened the door. No response and her heart gave a little flutter. But no, it was all right, he'd dropped off in front of the telly.

She might give this website a try. It fitted in with something that had been brewing in her mind. Her ideas were sketchy but she knew that somehow she would pay Jack back for all the years she had put up with his philandering.

That evening, after she put Jack to bed and gave him his sleeping pills, she started to Google.

There seemed to be masses of sites for internet dating but most were targeted at women younger than her and she almost gave up. She looked up the terms she had overheard in the hairdresser's. Fancy talking about things like that in front of their clients. There were others too, like 'cougar cub' and 'GILF', which she found meant 'Grannies I would like to…' That was absolutely vile. Though there were young grannies. She thought about her son – she doubted she'd ever be a gran.

Sheila hadn't told her the name of the site but then she hadn't asked. She couldn't confess to Sheila that she was interested. She wasn't really anyway. Now what was that word they had used? 'Cougar', that was it and she typed it in. There were images of wild cats plus sites such as *Are you a cougar? How to identify a Cougar?* and *Do you want to date a Cougar?*

At last she found *www.mrsrobinson.com* where many a young man was interested in the more mature woman. She suspected they were gigolos, only interested in money, but there was no exchange of cash, only bodily fluids. She might prefer it if it was the other way round. Alex's aunty may not have been telling the full story.

Mrs Robinson seemed to have a wide choice of men, though you couldn't access all the details until you joined. It was free for women which surprised her. You'd have thought there would be more older women looking for younger men than the other way round. She'd been much younger than Jack. That was the norm surely, even now. Should she do it? Well, it could do no harm – just find out if there was someone out there who would meet her requirements.

They asked her to submit a profile and attach a photograph of herself. She wasn't going to do that – she might get recognised and, anyway, she didn't know how to do it. But how would she describe herself? She wanted to make herself sound desirable. Though when they saw her they might be disappointed so she couldn't exaggerate too much. What type of woman would attract a Mrs. Robinson man? One wearing leopard skin and bling, white stilettos and tattoos, high boots and black leather? That wasn't Paula. At least not yet.

'Slim, attractive, flame-haired,' she started, but on reflection changed it to *'Slim, attractive, auburn haired, sixty year old, wishes to meet younger man for conversation, outings and fun. London based.'* That was quite truthful and wasn't sixty the new forty?

She decided she would give her real Christian name. There were lots of Paulas in London after all.

She filled out the section on hobbies. She tried to sound interesting, but not old fashioned, someone who young men would like to meet. She began with *Film*; well, she had been to the new arts cinema recently with one of her friends from the Mother's Union. What else could she put? *Travel*? They'd gone on some package holidays when James was young but Jack had been on business trips alone mainly. She decided on *Theatre*; that sounded a bit intellectual and not as boring as reading. Lastly *Dancing*; that would show she could move around a bit and she had been a good mover when she was younger. And she was a regular at her Zumba class.

She pressed the send button. The deed was done.

Within minutes she had seven replies. Her fingers shook as she scanned them. She clicked on one: Dean, 38, from East London, *I love older women and you sound just my type. I'm a gym instructor so very fit!!! I'm quite shy with women and want to meet someone confident who will give me a good time. I'm very giving myself too!!! I am certain we can have a grate time. If we click I will be your's for ever.*

Grate time – he can't even spell and his grammar's to pot. She didn't suppose that was the important part but it irritated her.

Another had a picture of a naked torso but with its head cut off. Not like Charles the First, just a bad snapshot. Paula assumed it was because, like her, he wanted to remain anonymous. Brian from Bedfordshire was supposedly thirty-one and his profile was overtly sexual. Her eyes grew wider and her jaw couldn't stretch further as she read his vignette: *I worship pussy – would you like yours to be worshipped? Sexually I am mixed – certainly not vanilla.* What did that mean? Vanilla was a flavour. Then she twigged – or thought she did. *Do you want to be a cowgirl and ride me? Or do you prefer to be ridden?*

She looked at his interests section. *Giving, receiving.* He didn't say what. *Film* – well, at least they had that in common, but she saw the word adult afterwards in brackets. She read on: *Fetish clubs, role playing, anal, oral, rimming, dogging, seagulling, D&B and S&M.*

She stopped. He was only interested in one thing. The only non-sexual activities seemed to be rimming, dogging and seagulling, whatever they were. Dogging couldn't be intercourse with animals, could it? She had no idea about D&B, but S&M – she knew what that was. Not a misprint for M&S unfortunately. Her knickers drawer was full of their stuff.

How could she have thought she might see one of these fellows? They were trash, lowlife, scum! But she wouldn't be contacting them for herself, as such. Her plan was hatching. She needed to be careful but she'd reply to one. That wouldn't commit her to anything. Images of rapists and serial killers came into her mind. She looked at how to remove herself from the site. Then she remembered her mace spray. She could slip that into her handbag and she'd be safe enough. She considered herself a good judge of character, so would soon know if he was a bit dodgy. But perhaps she needed someone dodgy.

She decided on *Hot Rod, 45, from Croydon*. The age gap was less than there was between her and Jack and she had never met anyone from Croydon, so she doubted he would know any of her friends.

His profile said he wanted to meet an older woman as *maturity is magic*. At least he could spell. He found them more interesting and less inhibited. He was into discreet relationships and threesomes. That set her mind racing so hard it gave her palpitations.

She poured herself a gin and slimline tonic to give her Dutch courage. In the time she had been away, someone had winked her, Mrs Robinson said. At least that sounded better than poked, which she had been by *Hot Lips, 28,* from Basingstoke. Hot seemed a favourite epithet.

She clicked on the reply button for Rod and started her response:

Hi Rod, Thank you for your reply. No, that sounded too formal. Delete. *You sound just the sort of man I'd like to meet. Perhaps we could go for a drink. I'm free on Thursday week.* That would give her a bit of time to reconsider.

Was she being too forward? But he had messaged her first. She continued: *I thought we could meet up in Central London.*

Now where could she suggest? Perhaps the South Bank, that sounded quite classy and safe and her overground line went into Waterloo.

I suggest the downstairs bar in the National Theatre – at about 7.30pm.

Perhaps that was a tad staid, but better staid than sorry.

How would they recognise each other? Wear a red carnation? Carry a copy of the *Times*? She'd tell him she'd be wearing her silk cream jacket. She was sure he could find something distinctive to wear – he'd probably done this sort of thing before. She wouldn't be able to recognise him from that grainy photograph.

What had she done? She'd crossed the Rubicon. No, she could cancel. He didn't know where she lived. Suppose she saw someone she knew? She could hardly introduce him as her toyboy.

What about Jack? She'd have to get Mary in; she didn't care if her daughter was in labour. Though using Arlene might be better for this outing; then she wouldn't have to explain where she was going. Mary was so nosey.

Paula got very impatient with Jack these days. Now she wanted him out of her way, not like in the past. If only he had wanted her then as much as he needed her now. All those bogus business trips. Jack had given her forty years of misery. Well, perhaps not quite forty. When they were first married, she'd been blissfully happy. They'd made such a handsome couple, Jack so distinguished and she, by his side, a fresh young wife. Except she was pregnant. He hadn't really taken care of her even then.

Yes, she would go through with it. It would serve him right. She checked her emails. A response from Rod – did these people live on Mrs Robinson? *Fantastic,* it said, *I'm sure I'll spot you!!! See you soon xxxx*

Chapter 2

The Mistress

Arlene peered through the window into the fog, opened the front door and looked up and down the dark street – no one. She wondered how long it was since he rang; it must have been a good two hours. She didn't bother to get changed these days for his visits. The black negligée seemed superfluous.

'I'm on my way darling,' he'd said. One of his tricks: call everyone darling.

Out of habit she tried his mobile. She didn't expect an answer.

Perhaps she should ring Paula. They were not really on speaking terms, though Paula must know about Jack's little outings and Arlene suspected she encouraged him to visit. But contact seemed a step too far. She might have to mention the dreaded money. She needed to talk to Jack about that – if it was one of his better days.

Arlene poured herself another glass of Chardonnay and lowered herself into her Parker Knoll armchair. She was a touch arthritic now and had put on weight.

She was anxious, couldn't settle. She decided to look for the agreement Jack had signed about the loan. She searched in her roll-top desk, which she had bought with her first pay packet after getting a post at the local polytechnic. There were gas bills, old cheque books, letters and black and white photographs of her and Karen. No sign of the contract. She came across a copy of an old journal, her first published work, 'Feminism and monogamous relationships, a radical critique'. Ironic, considering the situation she was in now and had been for the last thirty years.

The bell rang and she hurried to the door. Jack stood there bedraggled, shivering, wearing his old Burberry. He had looked so good in it a few years ago. 'Sorry, must have caught the wrong train. Got confused at that station, you know W-W-W…'

'Waterloo? You must have gone too far.'

'Yes, had to show the man the paper with your address on.'

Paula left that in his pocket now, or even put it there. She'd been doing that for a while. Arlene was glad, but was it caring or complicity?

'The man?'

'The man.'

'The guard? He helped you?' Jack didn't reply and Arlene knew better than to question him too much. 'Well, you're here now, sit down. I'll get you a warm drink.'

'Warm drink?' He looked blank. 'Yes, a whisky.'

'Should you? With your medication?' She poured him a Bell's. She wasn't going to waste the single malt as she was sure he could no longer taste the difference. Her brow furrowed, but any ill-effects weren't her problem. She wasn't his carer. But that was *exactly* what she was – a carer with benefits. He took the drink and tapped his fingers, looking at his watch.

'You've only just arrived.' She tried to keep the irritation out of her voice.

'Paula,' he said and she waited for him to continue. But he was addressing her; he thought she was his wife. How could he? Arlene was dumpy and dark, though now grey. Very different from Paula, who was auburn and fragile. At least Paula had been; it was years since Arlene had seen her and then only from a distance.

There was no point in getting angry with Jack. He couldn't help it. He was tired and agitated after getting lost. She would talk to him about old times. That sometimes calmed him down, even brought back the old Jack, the one with wit and charm and a sense of humour.

'I was looking through my desk and came across an old copy of *Sociology Today*,' she said. No response. 'There was an article based on the paper I gave at that conference where we met.'

A flicker of memory. 'I remember. I came.' At least he knew who she was now.

'I'd gone to bed early.' She recalled that she'd been avoiding the wandering hands of an eminent professor. It was the only occasion that he'd paid her any attention. At that time of night the size of her breasts was of more interest to him than the length of her publication list. 'You came with a bottle of champagne and two glasses.'

Jack closed his eyes and concentrated. 'Yes, I'd seen you somewhere.'

'We'd met in the bar. You were with your business friends, all in Burton suits, and I was with the university crowd.'

'You didn't want to know me.'

She wondered how he could have thought that. She must have appeared a lot more confident than she felt. 'Not true, but we hadn't seen each other for a while. You came over a few times just after I split up with Dave.'

'Dave?'

'You remember Dave?' Jack had been a friend of her ex for a long time though it was a while since they'd seen each other, as far as she knew.

Jack hesitated and took another slurp of whisky.

'You worked with Dave. We came down from Stockport. He joined your company. You were his boss. He left me for his secretary.'

'Yes, what's her name?'

She had buried the name deeply and didn't want to search for it. 'Not sure. I don't think it lasted long.'

Jack frowned and screwed up his eyes. 'Sylvia,' he said triumphantly.

'I think you're right,' and she was pleased it meant nothing now; but why should it after all these years? When she thought back, it was a good job Dave had left her.

'She was a slut. How could he have left you for her?'

Arlene smiled. 'I'm not sure why Dave married me, to be honest. He always said I wasn't a looker. Perhaps it was because I wouldn't have sex with him until we were engaged. Called me a cock teaser. But I was traditional, the sixties didn't swing in Stockport. Who said, if you remember the sixties, you weren't there? Well, I was there and I remember them only too well.'

'But you'd changed a lot when I met up with you again – the little northern caterpillar had become a London butterfly.'

By the time she'd got together with Jack, she was indeed a different woman. The sixties had ended and the seventies had come and gone. Arlene had struggled through university as a single parent, taken part in the women's movement and developed a career.

'That's so poetic, Jack.' He smiled, looking pleased. 'You were always good with words and you were really interested in my research. Though that night I think you used it as a seduction technique.'

'Mongomy?'

'It was about capitalism and how monogamy shores it up. You know, to do with the inheritance of wealth, the rich in particular knowing who their progeny are. But you took advantage of the fact I was criticising monogamy.'

He laughed and seemed to be his old self again. She remembered how he had kissed her and gently unzipped her skirt. She hadn't resisted and returned his kiss with passion. She remembered she'd been wearing a new black bra and some lacy knickers to match. She wondered why; she couldn't have thought she'd make a conquest. That wasn't her way. Anyway, she hadn't shaved her legs. Feminists in those days didn't do that but she was embarrassed by the dark hairs showing. Not that Jack noticed. Even with her unsightly stretch marks, she allowed him to undress her. Though she'd known him for years, ever since Dave worked for him, this was the start of their affair.

Perhaps it would have been better if she'd refused him, as thirty years later it was still going on. She continued to be the other woman. Her daughter didn't know, nor her grandson, Simon. He would be horrified at the thought.

'Two old wrinklies,' she could hear him say. In her mind's eye she saw Simon's face grimacing as he imagined their ageing flesh and pale gnarled limbs entwined, her sagging breasts, Jack's thinning body hair.

'You never told me for ages you had remarried. I thought you were divorced from your second wife when we first got together.' She still needed to justify the affair to herself.

'Well, I thought you wouldn't have me, I suppose.'

'Remember the arguments we used to have about Maggie Thatcher?'

'Great woman, none around like her now,' he said, gulping down his whisky, as if in imitation of Dennis.

Arlene knew that he wasn't really aware who was around now. They could no longer discuss current affairs. 'That's why I never introduced you to my friends, especially the ones from work. They hardly spoke to you if you weren't a Marxist, let alone an admirer of Mrs Thatcher!' Jack had all the rewards, not her or his wife. 'But I could never meet your friends because of Paula, could I?' she said.

His face became pale with a vacant stare in his eyes. She took the glass from him in case it fell to the ground. She decided to plough on. 'You know, when I came across the journal with my paper in, I was looking for the contract you gave me.'

'Paula will be waiting for me to come back from the golf club.'

'No, Jack, she knows you're here these days.' Paula must surely know after all these years. She put him on the train and she couldn't think he was away on business. Arlene would prefer if it was out in the open, not hidden, like in the past. 'Jack, the contract, the one you signed when I loaned you that money. I asked you to talk to Paula about it.'

'About what?'

'The money. Have you told her about the money?'

'I haven't got any money. Paula's taken all my money.' His whole body seemed to crumple and his eyes looked haunted.

'Oh, never mind,' Arlene said and began to unlace his shoes, unfasten his tie and loosen his belt. 'You need a shower.'

He had been so clean, spick and span. Now personal hygiene was a problem. He agreed to shower and emerged fresh from the bathroom, wearing the black silk pyjamas she kept for him. She corrected the buttons on his jacket and pulled the cord tighter on his trousers. He had lost so much weight that his bones were rising out of his flesh. But he was still handsome, at least in her eyes. His grey hair was flecked with white, his features were even and his long face ended in a strong stubborn jaw. Though look a little further and you could see the stoop, the translucent skin, and, worst of all, that blank stare.

'Come to bed,' she said. He must be tired after the journey and the whisky should help him sleep. He sometimes paced around; no wonder Paula wanted the odd night off.

'Must play, now I'm at the club. I've still got my swing,' he said.

Dementia and a bit on the side was not a good recipe. She should have seen it coming, the forgetting, repeating things, even the time he'd had an erection and then asked what he should do with it. She had thought it was a joke but it was more a case of the flesh being willing but the mind being weak. Was there a male equivalent of a cock teaser? She doubted it.

'No, you're not going to play golf now, it's too late. Let's go to bed.' She led him to her room and they slipped into the sheets. She remembered the old excitement; the anticipation of the night, the guilty pleasure; now she was relieved as they fell asleep side by side in a comfortable embrace.

She awoke with a start and felt for Jack. There was an empty space beside her. It was still dark. She wondered if he had got up to use the loo but there were no lights, no sound of the flush, no dripping tap. He'd gone. It felt like a one-night stand, or what that might have felt like if she'd ever had one. She was sure she'd locked the door and he didn't have a key. He could have fallen, hit his head, be lying dead in a pool of blood on the stairs.

She got up and switched on every light in the house but he was nowhere to be seen. Oh no, she'd left the key in the door. How stupid. He must have wandered out.

Once again she scanned the foggy street but there was even less sign of life. What should she do? Call the police? That was the obvious thing, but what was a strange man doing in her house, in black silk pyjamas? She could imagine explaining this to the police or even worse her daughter. 'Just a friend?' they would ask with raised eyebrows. On the other hand, who would think anything else at their time of life? She would have to ring Paula. He might have got back there somehow.

She hesitated to dial the number, thinking how often she had rung, normally at appointed times so that Paula would not pick up the phone. Arlene hung up if Paula answered, leaving her shouting down the receiver, knowing it was her husband's mistress rather than an innocent wrong number. Now she was ringing in the depth of the night with only Paula there.

Arlene put her glasses on and peered at the dialling pad though she knew the number by heart, like a poem she had recited as a child. She pressed the keys and heard the ringing which seemed to go on for ever. She almost gave up in relief.

'Hello,' a voice heavy with sleep answered.

'Sorry to disturb you,' replied Arlene. 'It's about Jack – he seems to have wandered. He got out of the house.'

'Who's speaking?'

'I think you know who I am. It's Arlene. You knew he was here.' Why was she talking like that? The intonation made the statement sound like a question. She doubted Paula would admit that she sent him, even at a time like this.

Silence.

'No,' Paula said at last. 'I wasn't well. I went to bed. I left him safe downstairs. Have you called the police?' Her voice became shriller, accusing, blaming.

'I thought he might have got back to you. He usually has his address written on a card doesn't he?'

'Well he's not here,' Paula snapped. 'You call the police. I'll get our son to look for him.'

Chapter 3

The Wife and the Young Man

Paula sat up in bed, reeling from the phone call. She knew Jack had gone to Arlene's; she had encouraged him so she could meet her date. She assumed that woman would keep him safe. It wasn't her fault that he'd wandered, was it? It was Arlene who was to blame. If Mary had been able to Jack-sit, none of this would have happened.

Worrying thoughts crept into her mind. He'd been talking about his work lately and the firm had an office off the South Circular. Such a busy road and not that far from Arlene's. My God, he could get run over. No, she would have heard. Someone would surely help an old man, confused and wandering? But then the Social Services would be involved. That wouldn't be good. No, she didn't want them interfering. She had her reputation to think about. How would she explain his getting to Arlene's? He'd been going for years, of course. She'd asked him if his golf club had moved to Putney when she'd discovered where Arlene lived. When he said he was going to play golf, she knew where he was going and didn't expect him home. As he became more confused, she made sure he got on the right train.

They might discover she'd sent him to his mistress so she could meet up with her toyboy. Now *that* would make the local press. She'd told Arlene she'd ring James but she couldn't do that. What could he do anyway? The police would find Jack, she was sure.

She thought about her date. It certainly hadn't been worth endangering Jack's life for. She hadn't meant to do that at all.

Her stomach had been performing somersaults as she got ready to meet Hot Rod. She'd not been out with a man since before Jack. Over forty years. Always the faithful one. She was developing

15

varicose veins so decided to wear her green Hobbs trousers and her new top that showed a little cleavage, if she wore her Wonderbra. She'd told him she would wear her silk jacket and that would cover her arms. Though she was behaving in a manner rather below her station, she was not ready to dress like a chav. And she didn't want to give him ideas. Actually she did, and he probably had them already.

Despite being tall, Paula wore high heels and her feet were aching after walking from Waterloo. She'd forgotten how far it was, though perhaps she was getting a bunion. The painful magic of maturity?

The stark brutalist architecture of the South Bank, naked and thrusting, seemed somehow appropriate for her illicit liaison; it was of her era rather than her date's. She sat down in the Lyttleton theatre bar and looked around anxiously. It was not crowded as the play had just started. Where was he? She couldn't see anyone who resembled her image of Rod. She didn't want to put on her distance glasses so her view was blurry. She decided to take refuge in the Ladies' to check her make-up. Those awful lights; they made the bags under her eyes look really dark and her lines looked like furrows on a ploughed field. This has all been a big mistake. She hoped Rod was myopic as well as *Hot*.

When she emerged, a man was sitting where she'd been and she passed near him to see if he would recognise her. Her walk was tall and confident – no elderly stoop.

'Paula?' a voice said in a South London accent. She looked around. Oh no, was that him? He was not even wearing a jacket and tie. She moved a little closer. His shirt was unbuttoned and hairs were peeping out. At least he wasn't wearing a medallion. But worse still he had a tattoo. He was smiling broadly and patting the space beside him. My God, that must be him and he'd recognized her.

She nodded and held out her recently manicured hand; as he took it, she noticed the tattoo went down to his wrist. She managed a weak smile.

'Drink?' he asked. Perhaps she could say she was unwell and just go. No, she couldn't back out now. She scanned his face – he had that designer-stubble look and rather fetching blue eyes. It was only one date. She didn't have to see him again.

'Please, a dry white wine,' she said. 'Pinot Grigio.'

'Right. Beer man myself, but I'm sure they'll know.'

Paula sat down and, as he got up to go to the bar, she glanced at his overly tight jeans, avoiding staring at his shapely backside. She'd never thought about men's bottoms before but he had rather a nice one. Jack's had virtually disappeared. Her eyes wandered up Rod's body but she realised they didn't have far to go; he must be a good six inches shorter than her. She had always avoided going out with men under six foot. She should have questioned why he hadn't put his height on his profile. But perhaps it wasn't that six inches she should worry about.

He returned with the drinks and sat down close to her. Paula blushed though she hoped her foundation hid her heightened colour. She smoothed her hair, wondering what to say. She had worked out her story: she was divorced, didn't want another long-term relationship, fed up of men her age, etc., etc. She didn't quite know how to start though. A glass of wine might help.

Rod took a few gulps of his pint and stared at her, leering, his arm around the back of her chair, gradually sliding down to her shoulder. 'Nice place,' he said, looking round the bar and the views over the Thames.

'Haven't you been here before?' she asked. Oh no, that sounded condescending. Rod didn't seem to notice and he leaned so close she could smell his after shave.

'Do you know,' he asked, slurring a little, 'I'm really good at working out things about people.'

'What do you mean?' asked Paula. This was not his first pint that night.

'See those two over there,' he said nodding towards a smartly dressed couple. 'Ordered a bottle of bubbly. Celebrating.'

'That's not too difficult to work out.'

'No, but do you know what his present is?'

'I presume the evening at the theatre?'

'Yer, but what else?' The woman stood up to go to the Ladies'. She was wearing a short, clingy, pastel dress. 'Look at her.'

'Very nice I'm sure.'

'No panty line as you girls say – not got any on.'

Paula looked again. 'You might be right, fur coat, no knickers.' Though, without her glasses, she had no idea.

'She's going to let him make her come in the theatre.'

Paula turned to him, her eyes staring, but with a hint of a smile on her face. 'I don't know how you can say that. This is the National, not the back row of the Gaumont.'

'My mum says I was conceived in the heat of the night.'

Paula frowned. 'Isn't that the case with most conceptions?'

'I don't mean like that, it was in the back of the cinema. Odeon in Croydon, I think my mum said. The film was *In the Heat of the Night*. That's why I'm called Rod, after Rod Steiger. You know, the American actor. Quite famous, I think he was.'

'Of course he was famous.' She stopped. Their age gap was showing. 'I wasn't sure if it was your real name.'

'Everything about me is real, unlike a lot of these posh twats in here.' He proceeded to point out breasts that were silicon, faces that had been botoxed, others that had been lifted and had a thorough knowledge of labiaplasty. It was a wonder he didn't ask her if she'd had one of those, or anything else, done.

Paula was fascinated, despite herself. He reminded her of Jack when he was younger. Well in some ways. Jack often told some risqué jokes which sometimes she hadn't understood. Yet Jack was intelligent, well-dressed and tall, unlike… 'How do you know about all these sort of things?' she asked.

'Women are proud of them. I've seen many before and after … you know. Sometimes you can't tell the difference but I always say I can. You can with the boobs. Like caressing bloody lumps of stone – don't know why they pay all that money. Take your own knockers to the knackers, I say.' He laughed loudly and Paula glanced nervously to see if anyone was staring at them.

He started whispering in her ear – but what was that? His tongue shot in and licked her inner ear, like a large, wet cotton bud. She couldn't remember anyone doing that to her since she was a teenager. Actually, it was quite nice. Her delicate blush became a hot red flush and she looked around again to see who might have seen this unsolicited foreplay. This certainly wasn't the place for that sort of thing.

'What about those two over there? Have they had work done?' she asked, trying to get Rod to use his tongue to speak rather than delve. She indicated two rather good-looking men, one smartly but casually dressed in jeans and a linen jacket and the other in a dark business suit.

'I'm not so good on men. Possibly a hair transplant, but they're definitely gay. I've got very good gaydar,' said Rod. 'The one in the suit is trying to get off with the other one. He's a rich bastard and will buy him a meal and drinks to get him into bed.'

Paula was astounded. She never liked to think that normal-looking men were homosexual. He was probably talking absolute bosh. 'Do you really think so?' she asked rather too loudly and she could see the two men looking over to her because she was staring straight at them. She hastily turned away and Rod was at it again, whispering in her ear and sucking her ear lobe. She wondered how he managed to do both simultaneously. And they say men can't multitask.

'Do you know how they do it?'

'I really don't want to know.' My goodness, what would he talk about next? 'Have you used Mrs Robinson before?' she asked moving her head abruptly. She had to extract his probing proboscis from her ear.

'Yes, I met up with Chloe, she was a swinger.' Paula hadn't heard that term but assumed it was a compliment. He whispered again and Paula realised she had broached the wrong subject. 'You know, she had a sort of open marriage and wanted me to swap with her husband and my partner.'

'Your partner?' Paula felt she couldn't do this if he had a wife though why, as she was already betraying Jack, she had no idea. But Jack deserved it and thoughts of Arlene and other women flashed through her mind. She wondered if Jack was all right at Arlene's. If she'd only rung her to remind Arlene to lock the door. But she couldn't have done that. Paula wasn't supposed to know Jack was there.

'Oh, we're not together now. She left me for someone she met on Friends Reunited. She'd gone out with him when she was fourteen – met up again twenty years later and she was off. She didn't do open though, so when I went to Chloe's, we did it while her partner watched. He seemed to get a real kick out of that.' He continued leering and moved his body closer to hers, placing his hand on her thigh. 'Shall we go somewhere else?'

This was progressing much faster than she'd expected. But why hadn't she expected it? He did call himself Hot Rod. She was glad she hadn't worn a skirt but what was this ambivalence about? Her profile on Mrs. Robinson must have given him ideas which the elegant, refined Paula sitting in the National Theatre was not ready for yet. She would have to play the game as she had gone this far, though she hadn't allowed him to get to first base yet. 'Not here,' she whispered, trying to make her voice low and seductive.

'You what?' he said.

'I'd prefer if you came back to mine but not tonight,' she said in a normal tone. 'I've got my son staying. I can't do next weekend but what about the Saturday after?' This would give her time to develop her plan.

Rod's face lit up and he grinned. She gave him her mobile number and he walked her to Waterloo. She felt like a teenager as she avoided his snogs and wandering hands.

'You're not – oh, never mind,' he said.

'Not what?'

'A trans.'

'A what?'

'Nothing, it doesn't matter. Just that they're reluctant for you to go too far. It's okay, don't worry about it. See you a week on Saturday.'

So, with the memory of Rod's tongue almost licking her tonsils as he stood on tiptoe to kiss her goodbye, Paula boarded her train to Richmond. Now she really had crossed the Rubicon.

Chapter 4

The Husband

Jack didn't dress, just put on his coat and wandered out. He soon came to a street. It was quiet, though there were still some cars and the odd drunk walking home from a late night out.

Jack felt an urge to go somewhere, but where, he didn't know. He looked around. He didn't recognize the McDonalds or the Shell garage. He had no idea where he was but continued to walk. He came to a bigger road.

Lights shone in his face and there were loud noises, roars and squeals. Things were hurtling at him as if falling from the sky. He tried to breathe but his lungs wouldn't let him, his throat felt like it was strangling him and he could hear his own heart thumping against his chest. What were all these things coming at him? He was starting to panic but eventually realised the lights were cars or big lorries careering along the road. His sigh of relief penetrated the hostile night air.

He walked and walked until the sky grew light; the pale sun peered myopically through the mist. He saw a common with brightly clad people running and early morning walkers exercising their dogs. He sat down on a bench. A small dog came sniffing at his legs. He'd had a dog when he was young. Looked a bit like this one. It was followed by an older man. The chap looked at him and was putting the dog's lead back on when he said, 'Jack? It's you isn't it?'

Jack looked blank.

'Hello, Jack, it's me. I can't believe I've bumped into you here after all these years.'

Jack continued to stare. What was this chap talking about?

'You look a bit chilly. Come and have a coffee. I live over there.'

'I've got a game of golf arranged,' said Jack.

The man carried on opening and closing his mouth and his words floated in Jack's brain. He looked at the man. He knew him from somewhere.

The man led Jack across the common to a large house. They entered a tiled hall and Jack could hear their footsteps echoing. It was dark and the man pressed a button and some lights went on.

'Are you all right with stairs?'

'I'm a fit man. I've still got my swing,' replied Jack.

Jack struggled up the stairs, followed by the chap and his yapping dog. Half way up the lights went off and Jack stumbled. Somehow the lights came on again and the man led them into a small attic flat.

'This doesn't look right,' said Jack.

'I've lived here for years. I think you even came over once when I first moved in.'

'Need a tea,' said Jack.

'Mind your head, ceiling's a bit low. You sit in the lounge. It's warmer. I'll get you a cuppa straight away.'

The word Jack wanted was like a mosquito buzzing around his mind that he couldn't quite catch. Every time he got near it, it flew away. 'Haven't you got a little room that you go to?' The man looked puzzled and Jack flapped his arms and pointed to his lower half. The man showed him where the toilet was and Jack went in. He struggled to undo his pyjama cord, but then realised there was a hole designed for peeing. Thank God he'd made it. He'd been bursting. Now where was he? He returned to the corridor. There was a door – this must be the way. He opened it but a wet stick jumped out at him, hitting him in the face and a heavy object hurled itself through the air, making a clang as it hit the ground.

'That's my broom cupboard. Oh God, watch that mop and iron,' said the man and led him back to the lounge. Jack looked around, wondering if this was a Home. It looked a bit shabby but Paula might send him to a cheap one, now she had all his money. Yet this fellow looked familiar.

'Sit down Jack,' the man said, ushering him towards the settee. Jack sat down amongst the dog's hairs and stray biscuit crumbs. 'It's good to see you again Jack. How are you doing? Still got your business? Are you still with Paula? God she was a looker.'

What was this man talking about? He squinted his eyes and stared at him hard.

'Don't talk about your mother like that,' said Jack.

'It's Dave. Remember, I was there when you first met Paula. I was best man at your wedding.'

Jack stood up and strode around.

'Calm down mate.' The man tried to guide him back to the sofa, when suddenly Jack felt his body shake and he was crying. What was happening to him? He was like a child again. 'Come on Jack. Have you had a few too many?' The man took hold of his hands. They felt warm. Jack was trembling, he was so cold. The man put on the gas fire and sat him next to it. The heat radiated out, but Jack was shivering uncontrollably. 'You're not well, shall I get a doctor?'

Doctors. He knew about doctors.

'Don't be silly, you can phone your mother. She doesn't know where we are.'

The man laughed but Jack hadn't said anything funny.

'What was your son's name? I met him a few times. Now, I do think I should phone Paula, but let me make your tea.'

The dog jumped up on Jack, wagging his tail and trying to lick his face.

'Get down, Snatch,' said the man, but the dog took no notice.

Jack stroked Snatch's coarse hair and began to feel calmer.

The man went out of the room and returned with two blue striped mugs with drinks in them. 'I've put some sugar in it for you. It'll give you some energy.'

Jack looked at the tea suspiciously, stirred it and took a sip. He spat it out.

'I told you I don't need any pills. I need to get back.' He threw the cup but it didn't go far, ricocheting off the coffee table, the hot drink spilling down his coat. The cup shattered and Snatch started barking and yapping around Jack.

'Christ, Jack, what did you do that for? You'd think I was trying to poison you. Take your coat off, it's all wet. I'll put it to dry.'

Jack tried to undo the buttons on his old brown Burberry but his fingers didn't obey him. He began to pull at them roughly - all these fucking little things he couldn't do. He let the chap help him.

'Good God,' said the man. 'You've only got your pyjamas on.' As he was hanging Jack's coat up, a crumpled piece of paper with some writing on fell out of the pocket. He put on his glasses and peered at it. 'That's Arlene's address,' he said. 'You know Arlene?'

Jack frowned. His thin face was pinched and his cheeks felt hot. Why was this fellow talking about Arlene? Did he know about the affair? He had tried to poison him and now he was accusing him of being unfaithful to Paula. Why had he gone with him? He needed to get out of here.

'Are you still married to Paula, Jack?' Dave said slowly and clearly as if to a child. 'Do you still live with her?'

'I've got to get back to Paula. She thinks I'm playing golf.'

'Jack, you're not well. We'll get you back home. I'll get in touch with Paula and tell her you're here. But I can't understand why you're in your jamas and how come you've got my ex's address in your pocket?'

Jack's mind shut off from the myriad of questions. He wasn't going to tell this fellow anything. Was he the police? Was he anything to do with this money Arlene was always on about?

'Jack, I don't suppose you can tell me how to get in touch with Paula?'

Jack moved nearer to the fire and rubbed his hands together in front of it. He was freezing cold. He had to warm up before he escaped. But he was wary – that man might push him into the fire. He needed his coat too but he couldn't see it – someone must have stolen it.

The man sighed. 'Oh never mind. Let me get you a blanket. You're still freezing. Are you sure I shouldn't call a doctor?'

The odd bloke went out of the room and Jack considered making a run for it. He shouldn't be in this place. He looked around. It did look a bit familiar. Was it the clinic? He hated seeing the doctor who kept asking him questions and getting him to draw things. Those puzzles were getting harder and the list of words to remember much longer. Always tried to trick him, giving him words to remember at the beginning, then asking what they were at the end. He never got them right. Yet all the doctor said was, *That's fine Jack,* and whispered things to Paula.

A doctor came in with a blanket.

'Jack's the name, Jack New. I really don't want to count backwards this time,' he said.

'I'm Dave. We knew each other years ago. I worked in your company. Was at your wedding.'

'I really don't see any point, you know. I've told my wife not to bring me here.'

'Paula didn't bring you Jack. Remember you were wandering on the common.'

'I need to go home now. I've got a game of golf booked.' The man manoeuvred Jack back to the sofa and put a rough blanket over him. It had a funny smell about it. 'Are we going to a wedding?' asked Jack.

'No, Jack, I was talking about ages ago. Your wedding.' said Dave.

'Dave,' said Jack.

Dave looked relieved. 'Must have been a shock seeing me like that after all these years. You got a bit confused didn't you?'

'Red hair, yes, if it's real. She could be wearing a merkin,' said Jack.

'Merkin?' asked Dave. 'I remember now. A prostitute's wig, they wore them over their pubes. First time you met Paula you went on about bloody merkins. I was chatting her mate up. I said Paula'd have to prove to you she was a real red head, in bed. And you said she might be wearing a merkin. Can't believe she married you after that. But you had money.'

'Paula's taken my money. This is a cheap home. I'm not surprised she put me here. She won't spend my money on me.'

'Jack, what are you on about? Are you divorced? Bet she got a good settlement. That's the way with the courts these days, always on the woman's side.'

'I'm a married man.'

'But I still don't know who you're married to. You were on your third when I knew you. Now, you know Arlene, because you've got her address in your pocket. But you can't be married to her or Karen would have told me.'

'I don't know anything about Arlene's money,' said Jack.

Dave sighed. 'Oh never mind. I think you should lie down.'

'No, No.'

'You can't go back out like that, you're not dressed. You'll freeze to death.'

Jack looked down. That man was right. How come he was in his pyjamas? He didn't remember putting them on. It was a trick to keep him in this Home. They must have got together, Paula and Dave, to get him in here. That Dave was always a bastard. He was so tired, that doctor must have drugged him.

'And you'd not fit into any of my clothes. I'm a little squirt compared with you. I could ring Paula to come and get you, if you're still married to her. But I don't have her number. Do you have it Jack?' Silence. 'I don't want to ring Arlene; we've not been in contact for a while. I'll ring Karen. She'll know what to do.'

He tried her mobile. 'Can't get hold of her. I kept in touch with Karen you know. Tried to be a good dad, but Arlene didn't want me to see her.'

'You left Arlene for that slut, Sylvia,' Jack shouted.

'How come you remember that? Bet you remember all those other lovely secretaries too' He gave Jack a big wink. 'You didn't mind the odd slap and tickle with some of them either did you? In the store cupboard? I remember you had a bit of a fling with Lizzie. That was before you split up from wife number two wasn't it? The sixties, those were the days! Women didn't mind a bit of touching up. None of this PC nonsense, sexual harassment and all that. Arlene was always into that sort of stuff.'

'Sex?'

'No, all that women's lib stuff. I bought Karen a doll once, a Barbie. She loved it but Arlene gave me a mouthful. Not giving her the right values or something.'

A stray memory floated through Jack's mind. 'I bought Karen a doll.'

'No Jack, you don't know Karen. She's grown up now; though if you're in touch with Arlene…' His brow became even more furrowed. 'And you had a son, so you wouldn't have bought him a doll!'

Jack felt his eyes heavy, his lids were closing and sleep engulfed him.

Chapter 5

The Mistress and her Daughter

Arlene was exhausted, sitting drinking coffee, feeling helpless. She was tempted to drive around looking for Jack, but feared he might return to find nobody at her house. Her mobile rang. Was it the police or perhaps Paula? She dreaded both.

It was Karen. That could be worse. 'Dad says he's got some strange man called Jack wearing black silk pyjamas fast asleep on his couch, who has your address written on a piece of paper in his pocket.'

Arlene's spirits soared, and her sentences tumbled out. 'That's wonderful. How on earth did he get there? Thank God he's safe. He's not strange –he's Jack – an old friend. I hadn't heard anything from the police. I was so worried. I must phone Paula again.'

'Mum, slow down. What are you talking about? You rang the police about this man? Who's Paula?'

'Jack's wife,' she replied. Why had she said that? She'd kept this hidden for so many years.

'Mum, what's this all about?'

'I'll explain later, must dash. Sorry, I haven't got Dave's address. Can you give it me?'

Arlene realised it wasn't too far. She could drive over there quite quickly and take him back to Richmond. She almost persuaded herself that she needn't phone Paula again. Just pick Jack up and take him back, as if he'd been in her house all along. No, she'd have to tell her he'd been found.

Her fingers shook as she dialled Paula's number to find her rather anxious, but not, it seemed, about Jack. 'That's a relief. Can he keep him for a bit? I'm in rather a rush – getting ready to go out for lunch with my son. I'll come over later.'

'I could take him back to your house, if you want?' suggested Arlene meekly.

'No thank you. I think you've done enough damage. I'll come over. I'll give you my number and you can text me the address. You do have a mobile don't you?'

Arlene was dismissed. God, she might have to meet Paula later. She threw on some clothes and went outside to her small Toyota. As she was getting in, Karen drove up and shouted through the passenger window. 'I wanted to catch you. I was worried.'

'I'm going to Dave's. Paula can't come to fetch Jack yet.'

'I'll take you. You know your driving's getting a bit erratic.'

Arlene shrugged her shoulders. She was too exhausted to argue. Anyway, it might be a good idea to have Karen with her. It was a long time since she'd had any contact with her ex. She climbed into Karen's four by four. Her daughter was looking her up and down. 'What are you wearing?' she said. 'You look like a refugee from Kentucky.'

Arlene doubted that Kentucky had refugees, but could see what Karen meant. She looked down and saw that she'd put on an odd assortment of garments. She was becoming like the woman in the poem who wore purple with a red hat – except in her case it hadn't been deliberate. She must have originally thought her trousers were quite smart, but the check now seemed loud, and they bagged at the knee. She loved her Fair Isle sweater which she had pulled on for the cold, but it did clash badly with her bottom half. She looked at her tall elegant daughter and wondered how she had produced her. 'I was so worried I didn't think what I was putting on.'

'I'm still not sure what you're worried about.' Karen's driving also became erratic as she heard the story. Brakes slammed and gears crunched. 'So, how long have you known him?'

'Oh let me see, must be over forty years. You met him once. I think it was your fifth birthday.'

Karen frowned, but eventually her long-term memory started to work. 'We went to the park, didn't we, with my best friend, Jane.'

'Yes Battersea, I made a cake, ham sandwiches and bought some crisps and chocolate buttons.'

'I wore that pink party dress. I used to love it and you didn't want me to have it because it was too girly.'

'I can't remember that.' Arlene had visions of herself, dressed in a turquoise, crimplene skirt. She had turned the hem up, but this small alteration did not transform it into 1960's chic. It was also rather tight, as she had put on weight since Dave's departure. Her curvy figure had run to fat. She must have looked a sight. 'We went on the bus, me struggling with the old wicker picnic basket.'

'And Jane and I asked if we could go upstairs.'

'And I let you. It was so smoky. We didn't know about passive smoking then.'

Arlene had agreed to meet Jack at the boating lake and she'd spread an old red blanket on the grass nearby. She regretted her decision to wear a skirt, as she sat on the grass trying to look elegant or just decent. She kept straining her neck to see if he was coming. She'd said nothing to Karen in case he stood her up. That sounded like a date, though it really wasn't one. But a tsunami was brewing in her stomach as she waited for him.

At last Jack strode over, carrying a large parcel for Karen and a bottle of Sweet Martini for himself and Arlene. He looked so smart and sophisticated. She got up and they shook hands quite formally, though Jack also gave her a peck on the cheek.

Arlene forgot she was in her daughter's car and her eyes became heavy as if burdened down by her memories.

'Mum, you're not falling asleep are you? I remember. I couldn't understand why he was there and not Dad.'

Indeed, Karen had started to cry as soon as Jack had arrived.

'Daddy,' she cried, 'I want my daddy.'

'You know he can't be here. He's gone away.' Arlene looked at Jack meaningfully. Jack knew Dave was still in London, but didn't give the game away.

'Come and see what your Uncle Jack has brought you,' he said.

Though Karen had not been introduced to her uncle before, the garish pink wrapping paper decorated with roses must have indicated something special for her birthday, and her blubbing subsided. When she opened it, a large doll appeared, with a string protruding out of its back.

Karen was quick to pull the string and a staccato American voice said, 'I love you,' then, 'Can I have a cookie?'

'I bought it on a business trip to the States,' Jack explained. 'I hope she likes it.' Karen and Jane were enthralled and Jack and Arlene talked to the background of giggles and screams from the girls. 'You know I've always had a soft spot for you, Arlene.'

Arlene blushed. 'Have you? That's nice. I'd like us to remain friends. I know you were really Dave's friend. I wanted to explain about what I said to Karen. I've told her he's moved away.'

'He wants to see her. A girl needs her father,' Jack said.

Arlene felt her hackles rising. He had no idea what was best for her daughter. 'I'm sorry Jack, that's none of your business.'

'No, I'm sorry; it wasn't my place.'

'What about your, how is - sorry I've forgotten your wife's name.' This was long before he met Paula. Goodness she had known Jack longer than Paula had – much longer- yet she was still his mistress.

'It's Janice. We're splitting up actually. It's not been working for a while,' Jack replied.

Arlene felt the excitement in her stomach return, but said nothing.

'I wanted to ask you if I could take you to dinner sometime.' She remembered how her heart had thumped so much she imagined he could hear it. But then she'd let him go – though he'd not really pursued her until later.

He was twisting off the Martini top, when there was a scream from Karen, 'Mummy I think Dolly's broken. She's only saying one thing.' Arlene saw the doll's string was hanging down from its back. Karen must have yanked it too hard.

'Where's Daddy?' it kept repeating and Karen joined it in unison, and then burst into loud wails.

'I want my Daddy.'

'I think we'd all better be going,' Arlene said and bundled all the picnic things together.

Karen brought her mother's memories swiftly to a halt as she swerved to miss a cyclist, jolting her mother forward in her seat. 'I remember that awful talking doll, it broke straight away.'

30

'You loved it. You were upset when it stopped working.'

'Never mind the doll. You've not been with him since then?' She was asking the question, but her voice had a ring of incredulity.

'No, no, we didn't see each other for years after that.'

Karen looked accusingly at her mother, 'But you did later and it sounds like he was more than just a friend to you?'

She did not reply, just looked down, examining her liver spots and fiddling with her watch. Was it that obvious to her daughter? Karen's eyes widened and she turned to look at her mother, almost bumping into the car in front as she hadn't noticed it had slowed down.

'So you've been SEEING this Jack for a while. But how come you're friends with his wife then?' asked Karen.

'We're not exactly friends.'

'You've been having an affair haven't you? All this time. I mean with your feminist views. And the way you went on about Dad's affairs – honestly. You brought me up not to pander to men and you've been - well.'

Arlene didn't reply. She could see Karen was shocked and angry. She didn't blame her, but half of her thought it was none of her business. She'd been a good mother, always putting Karen first. Hardly gone out except when Karen was at Dave's which wasn't often. Refused invitations to conferences except that fateful one, so she could be home with Karen. She'd helped her with her exams but hadn't put pressure on her as far as she could remember. She'd brought her daughter up to be her own woman.

They drove on in silence. She wished she hadn't agreed to the lift. It could well get worse when Karen met Jack.

'I'm still trying to get my head around this Mum,' said Karen. 'You were so critical of my boyfriends when you were having an affair with a married man.'

'I don't remember being critical of them. You had so many I can't remember them. I'm very fond of Jeremy and was pleased when you married him.'

Arlene had been glad when Karen had settled down as she'd been through many short-term relationships before him and it might have been true that Arlene had disapproved of some of them.

'What about Mark? Remember when I brought him home? You were horrible.'

Mark had been Karen's boyfriend at university. Karen had thought him so charismatic and charming. 'I thought he didn't treat you well and he was such a chauvinist. I can't believe you're bringing that up after all these years. I thought I was supportive and encouraging,' said Arlene.

'Yes you were - too encouraging in one way certainly. You went on and on about women's *right to choose*, but I didn't have any choice.'

Arlene had heard Karen talk like this before, but not for many years. Something was stressing her and not that she'd found her mother had been having an affair. 'I would have supported you, but Mark didn't want it either.'

'No, not after you went on about how he would have to work part time to look after the child and how poor we'd be and how it would spoil our lives.'

Arlene was convinced she'd said no such thing but perhaps she had. Things had been simpler then, more black and white not fifty shades of uncertainty.

'I just didn't want you to make the same mistake that I did.'

Karen's voice grew louder until she was screaming at her mother. 'So was I a mistake then?'

'Karen, don't be ridiculous. All I meant was that I married your dad before I had finished my education. I really don't know why you're bringing all this up. You're happily married now with a lovely son.'

'Yes, but I took a long-time conceiving. I thought I might not be able to have any children.'

'I don't think this is the time to talk about this. I'm really concerned about Jack.'

'OK, let's talk about you and this awful business with Jack.'

'It's not awful, just a bit tragic, I suppose.'

'What do you mean tragic?'

'Well he's ill, Jack's ill.'

'What do you mean? Is he dying? I'm sorry but, well, he's pretty old – how old is he?'

Arlene had to work it out and when she did, was reluctant to say. 'A bit older than me.'

Karen wrinkled her nose. 'So what's wrong with him?'

'Dementia, you know, Alzheimer's.'

'Mum, I don't know how you could,' as if talking to a naughty school girl. 'That's disgusting.'

Arlene looked at her daughter. Karen's reaction was worse than she'd expected and she blinked to fight off the tears. The traffic ground to a halt and Karen put on the radio. Arlene was glad to listen to some music – no more discussion hopefully. But as soon as the adverts came on Karen switched it off.

'Sorry Mum, I know it's nothing to do with me. It's just a bit of a shock. I'm upset you couldn't have talked to me about it.' Arlene mumbled a reply. 'Can I ask you something, a favour?' Karen said.

Arlene would agree to anything rather than carry on discussing her affair; though how she would explain all this to Dave she didn't know. Then why should she worry, after his behaviour? Perhaps Karen was right, she did like to appear holier than thou, despite being a confirmed atheist.

'Jeremy's business was hit in the recession. I know you don't like him being in finance, but he's been doing really well. Though, recently, he's had a few problems.' Arlene's stomach sank, but she waited for her daughter to continue. 'We're OK, only it's the school fees. I wondered if you could help us out – a loan until things improve a bit. I know you've got savings. We'll pay you back when the company gets back on its feet. '

'There's a perfectly good comprehensive not far. Simon's a bright lad, he'll be fine.'

The hard edge returned to Karen's tone, 'Trust you to say that. Jeremy said to say it was for something else. But I thought you'd be sympathetic. I don't want to move him in his GCSE year. I thought you loved your grandson. He's your only one. Unless there's something else you haven't told me.'

'You're being ridiculous again,' anger crept into Arlene's voice.

'Who's being ridiculous? Putting your principles, your political correctness before your family?'

Arlene hesitated; she didn't want to tell her daughter that she had no idea where the money was. 'I haven't got it anyway.'

'Mum, you told me, the money granny left you. The proceeds from the house.'

Arlene pulled at the bobbles on her jumper and looked out of the window. 'It's tied up, difficult to get at, you know.'

'There are always ways. Jeremy can help sort that out. You're just using it as an excuse.'

'All right, I'll think about it, see if I can get it out. How much are we talking about?'

Karen swallowed as she replied. 'Well £10,000 for the fees, but we had to re-mortgage the house to help the business and they're threatening to foreclose.'

'And you're running round in this thing, it must eat petrol. Besides what it does to the environment.'

'I'm selling it. I've put it on eBay, but it's old, it won't fetch much. I thought you might be able to stretch to lending us fifty grand.'

Arlene gasped and sank back in her seat thinking about her money, the little nest egg she'd loaned Jack. Cash flow problems he'd said. She hadn't needed it at the time. She'd been trying to get it back for years but why hadn't she sorted that out before he had deteriorated this far?

'Sorry to have to ask you, but, please, think about it.'

They sat for a while in silence. Arlene's head was throbbing.

'It'll be strange for you seeing Dad after all these years. Anyway what are you going to do with this Jack when we get there?' Karen asked as she turned left off Clapham Common in totally the wrong gear.

Arlene was flung forward almost hitting the front windscreen. 'Talk about my driving!'

'Can you answer my question?'

'Wait for Paula I expect, she'll be over later. She had something to do.'

'I don't understand, he's not your responsibility.'

'Well I suppose not, but he did wander from my house. Oh, I forgot I've got to text her Dave's address.'

'I'll do it for you.'

'I can manage.'

Karen didn't respond as she parked outside her father's. Arlene swung her legs out of the car, but it was so high off the ground she stepped gingerly onto the running board to get to the pavement. Karen had already marched ahead, her high heels clacking on the tarmac drive.

'Gosh this is grand, does he own all of it?' She wondered why Karen didn't touch Dave for a loan.

'No, his flat's in the attic. Can you manage the stairs?'

'Of course,' she replied and walked more confidently than she felt to meet the man she hadn't seen since her daughter's wedding, who had rescued her lover, lost in the middle of the night.

Chapter 6

The Mistress and her Ex

Jack stirred as he heard a voice. It sounded familiar. He looked up and saw Arlene. Where had she been? What was she doing in this place? What was this place? But everything would be all right now she was here. He looked around – that man was still there. Now who was he? There was someone else too. A woman but he knew it wasn't Paula. He'd better get up and introduce himself. It wasn't polite to sit down when ladies were present.

'Jack New's the name. To whom do I have the pleasure?' He looked at the young woman and offered his hand. She didn't take it so he dropped it to his side.

'Oh Jack, this is my daughter Karen,' said Arlene.

'Hello,' replied Karen.

Jack felt she didn't like him for some reason but he needed to talk to Arlene. She was trying to get him to sit back down on the settee. He supposed that would be all right but was glad when she sat next to him. He leant over and whispered in her ear.

'Arlene, where have you been? Why did you bring me here?'

'No Jack, I didn't bring you here, but you know Dave, you used to work with him.'

'How come you know Jack so well?' Dave asked. 'You'd hardly met him when we were together, at least as far as I knew.'

'Yes, explain it to Dad, Mum,' said a young woman.

He looked at her. Who was that?

'Who's this lovely lady?' Jack asked.

'Karen – Dave's and my daughter. '

Jack frowned and looked around. He suddenly felt frightened. There were too many strangers here. And where was Paula? He'd done something to upset her.

'I think Paula's trying to kill me. She thinks I'm going to take James away. Take him on holiday with you.'

'Who's James?' asked Karen.

'James is Jack and Paula's son,' replied Arlene. 'Jack, how old is James?'

Jack had to think a moment. He was never very good on birthdays but he remembered buying him a bike quite recently. 'Oh, let me see, tennish?'

'No Jack, he must be about forty. You're getting confused. Paula looks after you; she's not trying to kill you.'

'Is that all he is? You know Jack mistook me for him!' said the man.

Jack looked at him. He was still uncertain who he was but Arlene knew him so he's probably okay. Something was bothering him though and he needed to tell Arlene. Something Paula had done to him. He tried to remember. That was it, she'd stopped him from moving, from going out.

'She ties me up, I can't get up. She won't let me go out.' he said.

'I think we should get Social Services in,' said the young woman.

What was she talking about? Social Services? Don't they run Homes? Was she here to put him away? He was starting to dislike this person, but he'd be polite, find out who she was.

'Who's this lovely lady?' he asked.

Arlene turned to Karen and Dave. What was she saying? He strained to hear. 'I don't imagine she does tie him up; but perhaps to stop him wandering? I should have done that last night.' Jack didn't like the sound of that, but what had happened last night? Had he done something to make Arlene cross?

'Yes, you could have played bondage games,' muttered the young woman. 'Haven't you brought his clothes, Mum, or did he come over to you in his pyjamas?'

Arlene looked flummoxed. 'Of course, I wasn't thinking. I should have brought something for him to wear, how silly.'

'Well you could text his wife to bring some. I'm afraid I've no time to get them from yours. I have to collect Simon and Jeremy from the airport; they've been skiing.'

'I thought you had money problems,' Arlene hissed.

'Will you be able to get home all right? Have you got your bus pass?' asked the young woman.

Bus pass? Arlene couldn't have one of those – they're just for old folk, thought Jack.

'I'm not a child,' said Arlene.

'We all forget things. Bye Dad, bye Mr ...er...Jack.'

The young woman left and the man went out of the room. Jack relaxed and stretched his legs out. At last the strangers had gone. Then the man came back in. He did look familiar but Jack wasn't sure who he could be.

'Do you want some breakfast? Slice of toast, marmite you liked, I remember, Jack? What about you, Arlene? Sorry, I'm out of marmalade, that's what you used to like on toast, didn't you?'

How did he know that? But it was true. He loved marmite. Paula hated it. That's what they say, don't they, about marmite? Paula wouldn't even have the jar on the table without its lid on. Made her nauseous she said. But if this man was offering he'd have some.

'Don't worry Dave, just a coffee for me. Milk if you've got it and no sugar. Jack'll probably have a tea.'

'Yes, I'll have two slices of toast please with marmite.'

'Fine,' said the man, 'I've got some milk so you're in luck there. I have to look after myself now, you know.' The man went out of the room and Jack laid his head against Arlene. He closed his eyes and small snippets of memory floated back. Perhaps he did know that man.

The man brought in the breakfast, whistling cheerfully. 'Bit of luck I saw him, wasn't it? You never know what might have happened to him. I mean he must have come along the South Circular- could have been lying dead under some great big lorry. Or cracked his head against a lamp post in the dark. There'd not have been many people walking around at that time to find him.'

'Yes, Dave, I don't think we need go into what might have happened.'

'Didn't seem to know me at first but then we got talking about old times. About when you married Paula, didn't we Jack? How they met and that. He soon got talking then. He remembered when I worked for him in London. That typing pool, a sea of available girls.'

Jack thought about his work. He'd had a company, he knew that. This man had worked for him. Yes, he'd been a bit of a wide boy. That's right it was, what's his name?

'And you certainly took advantage, leaving me for that secretary.'

'It was for the best. I don't think men are meant to be monogamous. You know, plough the fields and scatter.' The man began to laugh.

Jack wondered what was so amusing. He remembered that hymn, sung it at Church. His mum had insisted he went every Sunday. He'd not had a bad voice; now how did it go? Jack started to sing it and now Arlene was laughing.

'Well, you certainly did that Dave. Did you ever have any other children?' she asked.

'No - didn't do much scattering myself. I was always careful or at least they were. Probably knew I wasn't the marrying type.'

Jack wondered whether he'd been the marrying type, but he must have been as he'd had a few wives. Sometimes he couldn't quite remember all of them, but often they seemed clear as day.

'I would have stayed with you, you know,' said the man.

Things began to return to Jack. This man had been married to Arlene and had left her. Dave that was it.

'What do you mean? When I came back from mum's that weekend you'd packed your bags. Karen was only four. I remember saying, *Is this the five year itch?*'

'But I could tell you didn't want me to stay. I would've stayed if you'd asked me.'

'Well, I knew it wasn't working. I certainly didn't want to be on my own with a young child but with some of the things you did…'

'Well I would have seen more of Karen if you'd have let me,' he said.

'I remember saying, *What about Karen?* And you said, *You can keep her.*'

'I didn't mean it. Well you've done OK without me. I hear you've got a smart place in Putney, pretty up market.'

Putney, he knew Putney. That's where his golf club was.

'Only a small terraced house, but it's nice, very central.'

'Well I'm just renting here,' he said.

'I worked hard for my money and my house wasn't that expensive when I bought it.'

Jack watched as Dave and Arlene talked. He wanted to say something but it took such a time for his thoughts to get to his lips and for it to come out properly. Every time he was ready to say something they'd gone off the subject

'Do you know what Jack's been up to since he married Paula? And how come you're in touch with him?'

'Does he take sugar?' she asked.

'Well he's drunk his tea without. How do I know? I haven't seen him for years.' '

'I mean we're talking about Jack as if he's not here.'

He'd have to say something if they thought he wasn't here, but his eyes felt heavy and his lids were closing.

'Don't take me home, I want to stay here and go to sleep.'

'It's all right Jack. You haven't had your tablets; they'll help. You can't stay here; this is Dave's place.'

Jack roused himself. He shouldn't have said he wanted to stay. He still didn't know what this place was. He got up and looked out of the window, then walked into the hall, then back into the lounge.

'I'm afraid Paula's going to be a few hours yet. Is that OK? Do you mind if we stay here? I could take him back on the train, but he's not really dressed and Paula said she would come and get him later.'

'No, it's fine. I'll make us another drink.'

The man went out of the room. Arlene put her arm around Jack and he let her help him back down onto the settee.

'You remember Dave, don't you?'

He did but how was Dave here now? He'd left Arlene, he was pretty sure, a long time ago. Did he know that he and Arlene had been lovers? Dave hadn't wanted her though so he couldn't blame him for stepping into his shoes so to speak.

'Does he know about us?'

'No, not really but it's none of his business.'

'Is he angry with me?'

'I was divorced from him when we got together so don't worry about what Dave thinks.'

Dave returned with three hot drinks. He didn't look cross. He looked as if he was quite pleased with himself. He'd always been a cocky bastard.

'So what's been happening to you over the years, Dave?' asked Arlene. 'I mean Karen tells me a bit, but I think it's probably the censored version.'

'Well, I suppose I was quite a lad, had a pretty good time with the women.'

'Dave, just tell me how you're keeping.'

'You'd like to hear what I've been up to with the ladies, Jack, wouldn't you?'

Jack looked at him. He saw a much older man than Dave. Dave had been dark; this man was grey. This man had problems with his teeth. He remembered his mum had bad teeth and you had to pay a lot for a proper dentist then. Dave – if it was Dave - kept smiling, showing his awful nashers, baring them like a dog.

'Jack are you hearing me?'

'Mum had no teeth. Had the lot taken out – they used to do that in those days.'

The man looked angry, the smile was gone from his face and he started shouting. Jack wasn't sure what he was saying but something about paying for your dentist now and how Jack had lots of money but he didn't. He had the urge to get away and was about to get up when he looked in front of him and saw a big hole like a mine shaft.

'Careful Arlene, don't fall into that.' He pointed at the chasm, he didn't want her falling down there. He peered down it to see how deep it was.

'It's okay Jack. It's just the carpet. You sometimes get confused with big swirls of colour and think they're holes. Look - the dog is walking on it. He's fine.'

Jack looked at the dog. He recognised it. It was Fido, his dog. What was he doing here? What was Dave doing with his dog?

'Here, Fido, come here.' He slapped his thighs and the dog jumped up at him. Jack stroked him. He liked dogs but Paula never let him have one. It was good to see old Fido again.

'He's not Fido. You'll confuse him. He's called Snatch. Remember I was walking him when I rescued you.'

'Go on then, Dave, tell us about your conquests,' said Arlene.

'Well, there was Zandra, met her at a Gentleman's Club.'

'That's a misnomer if ever I heard one.'

'Are you going to interrupt or do you want me to tell you?'

'Sorry, go on tell me, you were always a good story teller.'

Dave carried on. 'You'll be pleased with me, she was a pole dancer, but after we got together she stopped. I didn't like the idea of other men seeing her like that.'

Arlene raised her eyebrows. 'You don't get it, do you? Women shouldn't be controlled by men.'

'She didn't really want to do it; it was only the money. And I supported her and her two kids, though it didn't last long.'

'Well, you never were the faithful type. I remember Jack telling me about a holiday in Ibiza or somewhere and you both had a whale of a time.'

Jack remembered that holiday and how Dave had chatted up this Welsh girl. He remembered that she said she knew Tom Jones. He'd talked to her friend. Then Dave went off with his girl to the beach. Jack's girl had been a bit more reluctant and he thought he'd been getting somewhere when her friend came back to the bar, crying and covered in sand. Both girls went back to their hotel and when Dave returned he seemed angry and pleased with himself at the same time. He'd implied he'd had a shag but he never told Jack what had really happened.

'I've got a good story, well one you'd like better anyway. I got a bit fed up with the women here so I decided to get a girl from overseas, went over to Thailand. Actually, I persuaded Jack to come with me.'

Jack stopped stroking Fido. That was another thing he remembered.

'Thailand. You slept with a lady boy.' Jack laughed and kept repeating it, until Dave snapped at him to be quiet.

'For goodness sake, Dave, Jack isn't well,' said Arlene.

Jack recalled a beautiful young woman this agency had produced as a bride for Dave. Their eyes were popping out of their heads when they saw her but Dave's must have popped out more that night. He started to laugh again and then he heard his laughter turn to sobbing. He was crying like a baby. There was something he knew Paula would be angry about and he didn't like it when she was angry. Arlene put her arm around him and his sobbing grew less. Why did he do these things? He couldn't seem to help it.

'James is gay. I don't mind. Don't tell Paula though. She wouldn't like it.' They both stared at him.

'Jack, do you mean your son James?' she asked gently.

'Yes, James is gay. It's all right, though, isn't it?'

'Well I never,' said Dave.

'What does it matter these days?' Arlene asked.

'Not to me and you perhaps; we're broad minded. But it doesn't sound as if Paula would approve.'

'Don't tell Paula,' repeated Jack. He shouldn't have told Dave. He'd not said anything to Arlene before and yet he told her everything. He felt Arlene's arms around him and he leant against her, enjoying her stroking him as if he was Fido. He felt her move and rise from the sofa. Fido jumped up to take her place and Jack began to stroke him. He could see Arlene looking at a framed photograph on display.

'That's Karen and me,' Dave said

'I don't remember taking that picture,' she said, examining it more closely.

'No, I think it was at my mum's. I've got more,' and he opened a drawer. Lots of photos fell out onto the floor. Dave had always taken photos with his old Brownie. Jack had a better camera, but hadn't bothered much except when he was with Arlene. He'd taken lots of her.

'I used to look at them when you refused me access. You shouldn't have done that. She needed a father.'

'Then why did you leave us?'

'We've been through that. I know I was in the wrong.'

'I moved, you didn't bother to get in touch,' she replied, blushing.

'You never gave me the address. Karen wrote to me. That's how I found out where you were. You told me to fuck off. I was shocked at your language. You only let me see her because Karen rushed out shouting for her daddy.'

43

Arlene sounded doubtful, 'Karen wrote to you? How did she know your address?'

'She wrote to my mum. You didn't stop her seeing her nanna.'

'I always thought Jack had given you our address,' she said.

'Were you in touch with Jack back then?'

'Off and on, he helped out with money when I was going through university.'

What was Arlene talking about? Money always came into things. Paula had taken his money but yes, he had helped Arlene but that was before Paula, before even … He couldn't think, his brain was fucking seizing up.

'Did he now? I never knew that.'

'He told me bits about what you were doing. That was one of the reasons I didn't want you seeing Karen. I didn't want her subjected to a series of different women. I let you see her when I realised how much it meant to her.'

Jack got up. He needed to go. Paula was wanting him home. He knew there was somewhere she had to go. He had to get the train. He made a rush for the door and pushed it but it refused to open. He looked around. There was no other way out. His legs gave way under him and he collapsed back onto the settee.

'Jack what on earth are you doing? Are you going to be all right with him here on your own? But I promised I'd have a pint in The Stag with my mate. I've got a telly if you want to watch it. I'll take Snatch out for a breath of air too. You can pull the door when you leave, it's a Yale.'

'I'll be fine. Jack will calm down. Look he's closing his eyes.'

'Well, good seeing you again after so many years. You still haven't told me what was between you and Jack, but I think I can guess. Karen'll fill me in anyway.'

'I'm sure she will,' replied Arlene.

'I suppose it was tit for tat'

'What do you mean?'

Jack opened his eyes and peered at Dave. He had that cocky look about him again. He felt like punching Dave but he was only a small chap and Jack wasn't the fighting sort. Dave was saying something to Arlene quietly. They probably think he can't hear but he could hear bits. Something about Paula at his wedding. She'd looked lovely and he'd scrubbed up well himself. He'd told her how beautiful she'd looked. Hadn't done that enough really. Paula always needed reassurance about her looks, though she'd always looked great if a bit skinny. He knew Dave fancied her and leered at her at the reception. And he had that look on his face that he'd had on holiday after going to the beach with that girl. He remembered thinking he should have chosen someone else to be his best man. What's he saying now? Paula had the hots for him. Cheeky bastard.

'Get him Fido,' shouted Jack but Dave had got Fido's lead on and was going out of the door. Jack thought about following him but as he struggled up, Arlene came over.

'Don't worry Jack. Dave always exaggerates when it comes to women but he can be a bastard. Paula has always loved you and it's us who have betrayed her.'

Chapter 7

The Son

James felt rather squashed in his smart city suit, his waistcoat buttons straining over his expensive white shirt which hid his hirsute chest. Inside, his heart was pounding and beads of sweat began to trickle down his face as he struggled onto the crowded tube. He knew his mother would be waiting anxiously for him. She'd been so excited when he had asked her to meet him in town. He began to regret his decision to bare all, especially on a weekday lunch time. He might bottle it, but then what would Chris say? James knew it was something he should have told her years ago rather than let her guess. And now there was even more reason to tell her. She must already know, surely?

He was late, but he had to appear calm. He wasn't going to rush through the restaurant. He might knock over a glass. He could be a bit of a bull in a china shop sometimes. He looked around over the heads of the waiters hovering behind each table, solicitously topping up the wine or Perrier. James could see his mother sitting tensely, craning her neck to see if he had arrived, and glancing frequently at her watch. He apologised profusely for being late, but she brushed his words aside and giggled like a schoolgirl. 'Haven't you ordered some wine?' he asked. She seemed as if she'd had a few already but, no, she was just excited to see him. He felt guilty about how little he did see of her. It would be easier when everything was out in the open.

'No' she said 'I'm driving, I have to fetch your father.'

'Don't they have transport from the day centre?'

'I have to fetch him from Dave's. He sort of stayed there last night. Do you remember him, Dad's friend from work? He used to come over when you were little. I think he even took you out to Twickenham to see the rugby once. Your father never liked rugby, so he got Dave to take you.' Paula was speaking quickly, the words tumbling out.

'I think I remember; but I thought they hadn't seen each other for years.'

'They hadn't, they only bumped into each other by accident.'

'And he asked him to stay the night? Where were they? Hampstead Heath or Clapham Common?'

Paula's eyes widened. 'Yes, it was Clapham Common, how did you know?'

'I didn't,' he replied. 'It was a joke. Oh, never mind. Just tell me what happened.'

'No, no,' said Paula. 'You told me on the phone that you've got something to tell me. We don't want to talk about your father.'

James swallowed hard, he wasn't quite ready. He put one hand through his dark wavy hair, while summoning the waiter with his other. 'Let's order first,' he said. 'Anyway, I think I should know about Dad, it's a bit worrying if he's wandering around Clapham Common at night picking up strange men.'

'For goodness sake James. It wasn't like that. Where's that waiter?' She looked around and a young man came hurrying over. 'I think I might have some Pinot after all.'

James ordered a glass of red and a glass of white. 'It sounds like you're not coping. You can pay for more help if you need it.'

'Well, your father's not easy, but I cope. I have done for forty years; I mean he was hardly around when you were little. I'll think about having more carers. Mary's very good with him, I'll employ her more.'

James tensed as he heard the name of her cleaner. That was another confession he had to make. 'So how come he was wandering about at night?' he asked.

Paula hesitated, 'I told you, it wasn't like that; well, I suppose it was. Recently he's been going to see a woman he's known for years, an old friend. To give me a bit of respite, he sometimes stays the night. I thought he'd be safe, but she didn't lock the door and you know how he wanders. You remember the time he insisted on returning home on his own when I was shopping and got terribly lost? We had to call the police. Anyway, we were lucky because he came across Dave and he's with him now.'

The waiter came with the drinks and Paula grasped her glass eagerly.

'Mum, slow down. You let him stay with some strange woman? I'm surprised at you; I mean do you know her?'

Paula glared at her son and her voice became shrill, 'How you can tell me how to look after your father. You don't have him 24/7, do you?'

James didn't want his mother angry before he told her his news. 'Sorry, you're right. It must be hard for you since he got ill.'

'Well actually James, it's always been hard for me. I mean there were many times I never knew where he was when you were young.' She stopped abruptly as the waiter came over to take their food order. James asked for a steak, while Paula ordered a salad and more Pinot Grigio.

'I can't remember that. There were business trips of course. He seemed a pretty good dad to me.'

'You've always thought your father could do no wrong,' she said. 'I assure you he wanted to go to see this woman. He likes going there. He always has.'

James stared at his mother, not knowing what to say.

'Your father was no saint,' she spoke quietly, as if the whole restaurant might be listening. 'It's been going on for years.'

'You mean having an affair?'

She shushed him and he lowered his voice.

'Are you sure?' he asked, but he somehow had always known his father had been seeing someone. He had overheard rows, his mother's silences, Dad slamming the door and walking out. His own angst had felt overwhelming to him at the time and he hadn't delved too deeply into his parents' relationship.

'You've known about this a long time? You don't seem to be too concerned about it.'

'Oh I have been, James. I've just got used to it.'

'And he's still seeing her? That's where he was last night? Don't social services do respite care?'

Paula gave her son the sort of look she'd given him when he was a teenager, but her phone bleeped as she was about to speak.

'You've got a text,' he said. 'Perhaps it's about Dad.'

He reached over to take her phone when Paula grabbed it. As she opened the text, James tried to read it upside down. Paula bent down to get her glasses from her bag but kept her hand on her phone. After she read it, James could see she was trying to suppress a smile.

'Who's Rod? James asked.

Paula flushed. 'Nobody important. A friend's son. I've been giving him some advice about women. Never mind about that now. I'll explain what happened. Let me start from the beginning.'

'I think you'd better,' he said, checking his Blackberry before switching it off.

'Your father was always a bit of a ladies' man,' she continued. 'But I knew he was dedicated to his family – us.'

'Well he had been married before.'

'But he didn't have any children with his previous wives. Having you made all the difference, and I didn't mind his occasional dalliance.'

Paula became silent as the waiter served their meals and brought her another glass of cold white wine. 'I was so young when we married and such an age gap. I let him dominate. I know I should have stood up to him more.'

James had heard his mother complain about his father's dominance many times. 'So, how long was he been seeing this woman?' he interrupted. 'What's her name?'

'Arlene.' She spat it out. Paula stabbed at a cherry tomato as if it had been the cause of Jack's philandering. 'I'm not sure how long. I really don't want to talk about her. How's your steak?'

James mouthed *OK* as he swallowed a rather large piece of his ribeye and began to wonder if it had been going on while he was at home and whether all those business trips had been real. 'I think I met her. Dad introduced me.' He was about to say that he had liked her, but stopped himself.

'Did he?'

James tried to backtrack. 'I bumped into them by accident. He said she was an old friend. I can't really remember, but I think it must have been her.'

'I can't believe he told you about it.'

'No Mum, he didn't. I'm just surprised you didn't tell me.' She had often been very critical of his dad, to get James on her side but hadn't mentioned this betrayal.

'You make it sound as if I'd engineered it all. I assure you I was the innocent party. I don't mind so much now. It does give me a bit of respite. And he's happier there than in a care home. And I have thought about that you know.'

James resisted the temptation to make the obvious quip about extra services; though he imagined the physical side of the affair had been over for years. He felt ashamed he wasn't more shocked or angry with his dad. 'You won't like me saying this Mum, but you've had separate rooms for quite a while. I don't suppose that helped.' As soon as he had said this he realised it sounded like he was blaming his mother; but she didn't explode with anger as James had feared. She was quite calm. That text seemed to have put her in a better mood.

'Well that's only part of a marriage, you know, and not the most important. He was seeing someone else before Arlene. Not long after you were born in fact. You were a big baby, and I suppose I wasn't very responsive when I was pregnant. I can't imagine many women are. And your birth – it took a lot out of me.'

James remembered his mother used to tell him things when he was younger. He had been her confidante, but more about her hair or her dresses, not her sex life! He felt embarrassed but not as embarrassed as he might feel later.

'And I knew I didn't want another baby. I tried the pill; that made me fat. And then there was the AIDS scare and I never knew where your father had been. Not that he was, you know, like that.'

'What do you mean like that?' James tone was sharp.

'Well, you know, gay. I never thought that of him. And of course, he snored and the smell on his breath after he had his nightly whisky. It was like sleeping in a Bell's distillery.'

'OK I get the picture. But Mum, can I ask you something? What do you feel about Dad's illness?'

'What do you mean? How does any wife feel when her husband's got Dementia?' She took a rather large gulp of wine.

'It's just that you seem to be more in control.'

'Well I have to be in control, I mean he can't do anything much for himself. I can't let him out of my sight. Look what happened last night.'

'I'm not sure I understand what exactly did happen last night, but at least he's safe. You're going to stop him going there, lock him in at night.'

'Yes, I'll have to,' she said, but didn't meet his eyes. 'Anyway you said you'd asked me out to lunch to tell me something.' She looked expectantly and it was James' turn to be uncomfortable. How should he start?

'I'm thinking of getting married.'

That was a stupid thing to say but it was true he was, they were.

'James, that's wonderful. Who's the lucky girl?'

James started fiddling with his napkin. 'Well, I have a partner called Chris.' He had used the unisex name in the past when he had not been totally out, but why was he doing this now? He'd been determined to tell her everything today. He was a grown man but still wanted his mother's approval.

'A partner, but why haven't you told me about her before? Why haven't you introduced me?'

Her voice was quiet and James saw a tear forming in the corner of her eye. James wished he'd never started this. He fell silent.

'Are you engaged? I thought it might be that nice girl I met, your work colleague, Jane, no Jenny.'

'Well, Jenny's having our baby.' He knew she couldn't face the real truth yet.

Paula spluttered, choking on her wine, but regained her composure. 'I suppose that's the way people do it nowadays. I mean, not get married just live together. So, are you getting married because of the baby? But I thought you said your fiancé's name was Chris?'

'I didn't use the word fiancé.' It seemed an old-fashioned concept. Would Chris like to be called his fiancé? 'Chris is my partner but Jenny's having our baby. She's a sort of surrogate.'

'Oh has Christine got infertility problems?' She frowned more deeply and sorrow crept into her voice. 'I really can't believe you haven't mentioned her before?'

'Mum, I know you've wondered why all these years I haven't brought any women home to meet you.'

'You did bring some home. I remember when you were in the sixth form.'

She was right. He'd tried to go out with a few girls but it hadn't felt right. He was surprised she'd dredged that up.

'Mum that was yonks ago.'

'I thought perhaps you were ashamed of your Dad?'

'No of course not and anyway he hasn't had Alzheimer's for that long. I assumed you'd guessed.'

'Were you having an affair with a married woman?'

James was becoming frustrated. His mother was playing games with him, deliberately being obtuse. But then what was he being? He would have to spell it out.

'I thought you hadn't met the right one. You know bachelor gay, in the old sense of the word.'

'No, Mum, in the new sense of the word. I am with Christopher and a surrogate is having a baby for us. We're getting married. You can buy that hat, be a granny. I'm sorry I haven't told you all this before, I wanted to, I really don't know why I didn't.'

She stared and her face began to crumple, her mouth opened but no words came out. He knew he had blurted everything out too fast, but he carried on, 'Yes, Mum, I'm gay.'

'But you can't be, you've just had a steak.'

'I thought all those stereotypes had gone. I know you were brought up with Mr Humphries mincing around the shop floor, but this is the twenty-first century you know.' He knew she was struggling to take everything in. 'I want you to meet Chris and come to our wedding. And be a granny to our baby. Mum I want you to be part of it.'

'But a baby, it needs a mother and a father, not two fathers. A real family. Why do you think I stayed with your Dad? To give you a proper family.' She slammed down her cutlery. 'Why didn't you tell me before? Why wasn't I part of the planning? You've just sprung everything on me – now it's all a fait accompli.' She got up and walked out, her lips set firm.

'You won't have a pudding then?' he called into thin air. He switched on his Blackberry and it rang immediately. 'Are you outside?' he replied. 'You may as well come in now.'

Jenny waddled in with Chris. Her bulge seemed to overwhelm the whole of her small frame, like a giant football attached to her front. He could hardly believe it was their baby in there. Her long brown hair was tied back and she wore a multi coloured hand-knitted cardigan over loose cotton trousers. She looked wrong in here; this restaurant with its white table cloths and silver service. It was full of people like him and Paula. Chris on the other hand, tall, fair and casually elegant, fitted in perfectly. Could look right anywhere.

'So Mum was spot on, she didn't want to know,' Jenny said.

'She'll come round,' said James. Well, she might but he doubted it.

'Did you tell her who I was? She's such a snob. She probably didn't like the thought of her cleaner's daughter's eggs.'

'Or my sperm,' said Chris.

'It could be my sperm; we don't know about that yet. I implied it was mine.' He thought with disgust of the time he had slept with Jenny. Just because she wouldn't agree to a syringe or even the good old turkey baster. So the baby had been conceived in an unconventional manner or, more true to say, the conventional manner, but not for surrogates or gay men. James and Chris had taken it in turns to sleep with her at her most fertile times, and after two months she was pregnant.

'Well it must be me she doesn't like,' said Jenny.

'She thinks it's the other Jenny, my colleague. No it's all of it she doesn't like. I shouldn't have told her everything at once. I thought the idea of having a grandchild would soften her up to the whole gay thing.'

'Didn't she have any idea you were gay?' asked Jenny. 'What about your other lovers? Didn't you take any of them home, as friends, like they do in novels?'

He thought of the times he had brought friends home. There had been his rather beautiful Scandinavian friend, Lars, who'd come to stay. Paula had taken quite a shine to him. And that dark eyed Irish lad; she'd said he'd reminded her of George Best. Sometimes her naivety astounded him. And she'd only remembered the girls – amazing. He shook his head.

'Does your Dad know?' asked Jenny.

'Well, he knows I'm gay, at least he did. I told him when he was with it. Told him not to tell Mum for some reason. Wish I hadn't. He may well have forgotten all of it now. Last time I saw him he thought I was a nurse in hospital and gave me this razor ready to shave him. When I did, Mum told me off, as I would confuse him; but he lives in total confusion. It was strange though. When Mum took the razor, he became really frightened and cowered in the corner. But no, he doesn't know about the baby.'

'Shall we order coffee?' asked Chris, looking around for a waiter.

'I know you don't like talking about my dad. You seem to think I'm going to catch it from him, as if it's a disease. You know if we go through with this wedding, it's supposed to be for life! I may get as confused as him or you might, you can't tell.'

'I've read it runs in families,' said Chris.

'I thought you were a graphic designer not a medic.'

'I hope you two aren't having second thoughts. Jack's all right. Mum's really fond of him, but she did say he'd been acting strangely and that Paula needs some extra help,' said Jenny. Chris tried to summon the waiter to bring coffee, but they had stopped hovering.

'I've talked to Mum about having extra help. Oh, but I haven't told you what happened last night,' said James. He then thought better of relaying the whole saga, so outlined the bare facts; saying Jack had been staying at an old friend's. He didn't want Jenny telling all this to her mother.

'A woman was it? Mum said she thought he'd been seeing someone on the side for years – sorry James, didn't you know?'

How come everyone else knew but him? He should have spotted the signs, looked out for his mother more.

'What an old bugger eh!' said Chris.

'I'm not sure that would be an appropriate description of my father's sex life,' said James coldly, but the others laughed.

'I know Jenny can't drink, but I'm going to order a brandy as well if I can ever get a waiter over here,' said Chris.

My God… Chris was taking his generosity for granted. He can't see how upset he was about his mother.

'Sorry, it's only the middle of the week. Some people have to get back to work,' and with that James summoned the waiter for the bill.

Chapter 8

The Faithful Wife

As soon as Paula stormed out of the restaurant she regretted it. She had reverted back to type and even to her it seemed she was playing a part. Her revulsion towards homosexuality – did she really feel that? She knew the bible said that and she still went to church, still in the Mother's Union but if truth were told it was more for the company. Jack was no companion now if he ever had been. No, it was not about her beliefs but because James had not confided in her before. What a rotten mother she must be that her only son had done all this without feeling he could talk to her. Yet when he did, look how she reacted. Her words echoed in her ears and she realised that she sounded like that woman in the twin set, the one she had abandoned. But how could she preach to others about morality?

    She wished she had taken the train, rather than driving after all that wine. She'd only brought the car after that text asking her to bring over some clothes. Why hadn't she accepted Arlene's offer of dropping him over? The old Paula could not accept her husband's mistress coming to their house. But she was lucky not to have been pulled over. That would not fit in with her carefully choreographed image. She really didn't want to meet Arlene, but now may have to stay for some tea as she was so light headed. And make conversation with Dave, someone she'd tried to avoid after the wedding incident.

    She was glad she had her satnav and managed to find a parking spot soon after it announced that she'd reached her destination. She decided to text James before she braved Dave's flat.

    Hi James, she wrote, *I'm so sorry about walking out of the restaurant – it all came as a bit of a shock. I must have sounded so old fashioned to you, but I've got strong views. You know your father used to call me Mary Whitehouse.'* She'd been attempting to lighten it, but James was probably too young to have heard of the television morality campaigner. *I really don't want to row with you and as it seems this is the only way I can have a grandchild, then, of course, I will accept it.*

Love Mum

The last sentence sounded grudging but she'd sent it now. She wished she knew how to do those smiley things which young people put on. My goodness if James only knew what she'd been up to. Thankfully he never would. She got another text from Rod, reminding her how much he was lusting after her. This time it irritated her, though she couldn't help feeling a bit flattered as well. No one had lusted after her for many years. Certainly not Jack.

But what about James? She would ring him and apologise properly. It would go to his answer phone anyway. She was surprised to hear his voice at the end of the line. Now what could she say? She hadn't worked it out.

'Did you get my text?' she asked.

'Yes, I'm glad you've decided to accept your grandchild, but what about Chris as well? We come as a whole package.'

'Yes, yes, I'm sorry. I shouldn't have stormed out of the restaurant. Please, I'd like to meet Christopher. Perhaps the three of us could go out to lunch?'

'I'd like him to meet you and Dad, Mum. Why don't both of you come over for Sunday lunch – I'll cook a joint.'

Paula hesitated. 'I'm not sure your father could manage that. He gets nervous around new people.'

'There's only one new person. He needs to meet him before the wedding.'

Paula couldn't believe he wanted to invite Jack to the wedding. 'He does have the tendency to dribble when he eats.'

As soon as she'd said that she knew James would be cross. But he did and she hated seeing it. Perhaps it was because she harked back to the old Jack, not this one who she didn't recognise sometimes. Though he still recognised her, but for how long?

'Oh Mother! Shall I pick you up – this Sunday - OK?'

'It's fine. I can drive over.' She composed herself as she got out of her white Mini Cooper. At least she had smoothed things over with James. Did she look good enough? She'd had her red hair recently coloured and straightened. She had worn quite well.

The front door was open, so she walked up the dingy stairs to the flat and rang the bell. Arlene opened the door. Paula hadn't met her before and when she saw her she was extremely surprised that Jack had been with her for years. She had no style. She was frumpy and definitely older than her. She felt like Princess Di with Arlene as Camilla, but then remembered what happened to Diana, while Camilla, she was almost the Queen. She looked at Arlene's dumpy figure, and those trousers – they made her look like an American golfer stranded in Gleneagles. And she'd spent all this time worrying about her, thinking that Arlene must be so good looking, much better than her. She'd imagined her with an hour glass figure, large breasted, a bit like Marilyn Monroe. But look at her.

'Thank you for coming, I'm -'

'I know exactly who you are. Is Jack all right?' interrupted Paula.

Arlene flushed. 'Yes he seems fine, a bit tired perhaps,' she said quietly, showing Paula into the lounge where Jack was dozing on the settee. Paula fussed around him and woke him up.

'I've bought a bag of clothes,' she said. 'Jack, why don't you go to the bathroom and change. Do you know where the bathroom is?'

Arlene showed him.

'I like to get him to do these things on his own. He can, you know, just takes him a while,' said Paula. She'd even bought him some slip-on shoes which he could put on himself, but he wouldn't wear them. Just to spite her. Paula sat down gingerly on the settee, wrinkling her nose. The flat had that stale old man smell about it.

Arlene offered her some tea and explained that Dave had gone out. 'Well I'm sorry. It would have been nice to see him after all these years. To be honest it's only now twigged that he's your ex.'

They both sat in silence sipping their tea rather daintily from the chunky mugs. Paula displayed her large diamond engagement ring and gold wedding band on her well-manicured fingers. They shouted out respectability and commitment and the fact that she was the innocent party and Arlene the other woman. She looked at Arlene's stubby hands. Nails short, no jewellery, almost like Mary's hands.

'You must hate me. I know you know about us – Jack and me,' said Arlene, at last breaking the clink of the mugs.

'Well I don't think Jack and you are an *us* are you? His loyalty has always been to his family.' Paula smirked as she said this; but thought that, if he was going to leave her, it would be for Arlene. And she wondered if Jack had told Arlene about how Paula sorted him out now?

'I know it's no use saying that I'm sorry, but I thought he was divorced when we first got together.'

'I always assumed that you didn't care about whether he was married or not,' she said looking directly at Arlene. 'When I found out about you, he said you didn't worry about petty bourgeois rules like monogamy – that you were into open marriage. I thought you were married and that he was your bit on the side. Like you were for him.' Paula remembered she'd rung Jack's secretary to find out where he was and she knew from her tone that he was up to something. They'd had a big row. He'd confessed and apologised, but then tried to justify himself. Arlene was so different, so interesting. Not boring and conventional like her. He said it had just been a fling and he'd finish it, but she knew he never had.

Arlene visibly shrank. 'No' she said, 'I was divorced a while before Jack and I got together. But it's true I never really believed in marriage. You know I was a sociologist. I saw it as a patriarchal male institution.' Arlene flushed and her voice became more strangled as she carried on. 'It's difficult to explain. We used to have discussions about open marriage, communal living and sharing parenthood in a group, but really I was far too conformist to do it in real life. And Jack certainly wouldn't have. It was always one rule for men and another for women with him.'

Paula almost spilt her tea as she slammed down the mug. 'Are you trying to tell me things about my husband you think I don't know?' This woman has the cheek to go on about the things they talked about when she was at home caring for James waiting for Jack to come home. Now she thinks she knows him better than his own wife.

'No, of course not; I was just trying to explain.'

'To justify trying to break up a family. You may not believe in families; but I think they're the bedrock of our civilisation. The values of our society are embedded in the family - husband, wife and children.' She swallowed hard and looked accusingly at Arlene, but she was thinking about James. She accepted Arlene as the third person in her marriage. As long as the sham didn't become public knowledge.

'Well I don't want to get into an argument but I brought up my daughter as a single parent. Children survive without both parents,' countered Arlene.

'Yes but you did have a man around; my husband.' Paula knew she had trumped her then, but this was not a game of cards with Jack the joker in the pack.

'Jack's been a long time. Is he all right?' Paula asked.

'Shall I see how he's getting on?' asked Arlene.

Paula continued drinking her tea. She didn't really want to go into that man's bathroom.

There was a shout from there. 'Where are my chips?' Jack called.

'Is he hungry?' asked Paula. 'Haven't you fed him?'

'He's eaten. I don't think he's hungry,' said Arlene. Paula glared. She'd have to go and find him. She peeped into the bathroom but his voice was coming from the bedroom. She definitely didn't want to venture in there She looked through the door. Jack was trouserless with his shirt buttoned up all wrong. He was searching for something in the bag that she'd brought.

'I can't find my chips,' he repeated.

'Chips,' echoed Paula, 'with salt and vinegar? Oh God I can't bear it.' She'd had enough today, with James' announcement. She couldn't put up with Jack's nonsense.

'He sometimes says chips when he can't think of the right word. Doesn't he do that at home?' asked Arlene.

Paula turned around and came out of the bathroom. 'No - he certainly doesn't,' but then thought, perhaps he does and she hadn't noticed. He sometimes talks such rubbish she switches off. But then Arlene doesn't have him 24/7 does she? 'You see to him then, you seem to know what he's on about.'

Pauline stood outside the door as Arlene got his trousers. She turned away. She couldn't bear to see Arlene helping him. She should be doing that - not his bloody mistress. Yet Jack clung to her. Well, let her do it. Arlene makes him happy, happier than he was with her. She went back to the lounge and soon Jack followed fully dressed. Arlene came in with Paula's bag. She was carrying those awful black pyjamas. She must keep those for him. Paula was about to comment but let it pass. He might need them again.

'Shall I make you some more tea before you go?' Arlene asked.

Paula hesitated but she was still feeling a bit woozy so agreed. As Arlene went into the kitchen, Paula heard a voice. It must be Dave. She should have gone earlier. There was no way of avoiding him now. Oh no, he's got a yappy dog with him. Snatch wagged his tail wildly as they came into the living room.

'Cor Paula, you still look a right picture. Still as lovely as you were at your wedding.'

Paula raised her eyebrows. That man must be totally oblivious or very thick. Snatch jumped up on her, and she shooed him away.

'You've got some pheromones, he's really taken to you,' said Dave.

'He's taken to Jack as well – must be a mixed up little dog,' Arlene said as she returned to the lounge. 'I'm just making some tea.'

Paula looked coldly at Dave, though smiled benignly, ignoring Arlene. 'Well Dave, it's a long time since I saw you. Thank you for saving Jack.' She must steel herself, be nice to him. He could be useful if it didn't work out with Mrs. Robinson. Perhaps even better for Jack.

'Oh no, I wouldn't say I saved him. Well I suppose I did in a way. But it was such a coincidence; hardly recognised him at first in his jim jams,' he laughed. 'I'm still not sure how Arlene fits into the picture though. Are you and Jack still married?'

Jack found his voice. 'I've got to go – time to pack. Come on Dave we're going on holiday. Paula. you have to stay home with James.' He seemed lucid and sure of himself.

'Yes Jack, where shall we go?' he said. 'How about Ibiza – remember we went there once?'

'Dave, don't give him false expectations. They go in for reality therapy at the day centre,' snapped Paula.

'What's that when it's at home?' asked Dave. Jack continued to insist they should pack and go. When Arlene came in with some tea he calmed down, but Paula took out some medication. 'What's that?' Dave asked.

'It's a mild tranquiliser,' she said, slipping it into his tea. I don't want him in a state in the car. He's tried to open the car door before now and I'm driving home on my own with him.'

'Do you want me to come?' asked Dave, leering slightly at Paula. 'I could help get him in and out of your car.'

'Oh no, that's far too much trouble,' said Paula. 'We live right over in Richmond. You could help get him in though, as he seems to want to go on holiday with you! You must come over another time. Jack sometimes likes to remember the old days.'

She smiled at both of them and Arlene took her chance. 'I don't suppose you'll let him come over to me again, but if you did want some time to yourself ...' She tailed off.

Paula was about to refuse curtly, after all it was his mistress asking his wife if she could entertain her husband. Yet she had allowed him to go *to play golf* so many times before, when it suited her. 'You would lock the door this time?'

'Yes and I could pick him up. He seems to find it difficult on the train though it's straight through. It took him hours yesterday.' It was as if they were arranging a child's day out or sleepover.

'I suppose so. I'll make sure he has his medication before he comes,' she said. 'Or you could give it to him before he goes to bed. It helps him sleep. I had a terrible time before I got it – wandering around the house all night, wanting to play golf.'

Paula stood up, leaving her tea with only a sip taken, and picked up her handbag.

'Just one other thing before you go. Jack invested some money for me, quite a substantial sum.' Arlene lowered her voice and Paula thought she didn't want Dave to hear. 'He's no recollection of it though. It seems stupid, I know, but it was to help the company. '

'James and I have Power of Attorney, so you'll have to go through us. Have you got proof of this investment?'

'Yes,' she said. 'He signed something.'

'But was he of sound mind? I could get him to sign anything. I'll have to talk to James. He's a lawyer, he deals with all that side of things.'

A loan? Surely his business never needed a loan? And he talked to Arlene about it rather than her. She was his wife. He should have discussed things with her - not his frigging mistress. She obviously wasn't worth anyone discussing things with. Though with Jack her role was to spend his money - not make it. She'd never been frugal, but there'd always seemed to be plenty of money and now James dealt with it and said she had no money worries. Arlene must be making this up.

'What's this about money? You gave some money to Jack? We were married and you seem to have done pretty well for yourself. Aren't I entitled to some of it?' Dave asked.

Arlene was open mouthed. 'Dave, you left me high and dry with no maintenance. Now you're asking for a share of my inheritance. The money from the sale of my parents' house when they died.'

'My parents didn't own their home, they lived in a council house. So I got nowt when they died. Anyway I thought Karen said you were a Marxist. He was the one who said *all property is theft,* wasn't he? So you shouldn't really take the money – it's against your principles.'

'I'm not a Marxist and, even if I were, I wouldn't give the money to you,' she raised her eyebrows. 'Karen wants a loan; you surely don't begrudge your daughter, do you?'

'I must go,' interrupted Paula. 'I don't want to get involved in a domestic dispute. We don't even know if this money exists.'

Dave helped Jack up. He was docile now, in a stupor after the tablets. 'Bye Paula. Have a safe journey and let me know when you want me to come over.'

He switched on the lights and showed Paula the way out, while Arlene guided Jack behind them. Paula stepped elegantly into her car. Dave helped Jack into the back and Arlene fastened his belt. Paula pressed the child lock switch, accelerated hard and sped back home with Jack dozing in the back. Her thoughts were jumping between her conversation with James and memories of Dave. Neither were pleasant.

Chapter 9

The Daughter

Karen had vowed never to go to Heathrow again, but she parked her car at Terminal 3. The traffic, the expense, the crowds. There was nothing good to say about it. Of course, the sweet homecoming should have made everything worthwhile. But she had rather enjoyed having the house to herself; no football on the television (Jeremy), no noisy friends (Simon), or constant meals to prepare (Simon and Jeremy).

Perhaps Jeremy would be in a better mood after skiing, a break from his usual business worries. Karen had not approved of the holiday for Simon in the half term before his mock GCSEs. But it may have relieved some of his pent-up testosterone which exploded every so often if he was inactive. It may have done them both good.

She waited at the appropriate place alongside myriads of people holding up cards saying, 'Mr Singh', 'Welcome back Granny' or 'Taxi for Mrs Jones'. She felt naked with just a handbag and the *Telegraph* to read in case of delays. She couldn't stop thinking about her mother and the strange affair she'd been having for years. What a dark horse – and her always taking the moral high ground. How she'd criticised Karen for having a boob job after she'd had Simon. She was surprised Arlene hadn't brought that up when she'd asked her for the loan. Her mother had a good pension so she didn't need the money. It was sensible to give it to her daughter now. Her mother had to die some time, not that Karen wanted that. But presumably she would inherit eventually. The tax man might get it otherwise, though she'd heard her mother argue for an increase in inheritance tax, so perhaps she wouldn't mind that.

Karen decided to give her father a ring to see if this Jack had been deposited back with his wife. 'Hi Dad, it's me. I'm at the airport. Just wondering what's happening?'

'They've only just gone. It was nice to meet up with Paula. I said I'd go over to see her and Jack some time.'

'Paula, oh yes, that's Jack's wife isn't it? Good, you should try to get out more. You only seem to go to the pub.'

'I take Snatch out every morning. Though I don't usually pick up lost men in pyjamas.'

'How long has it been since you saw Mum? You probably haven't seen her since my wedding, have you? Did you know about her and Jack?'

'Never knew anything about it.'

'You're taking the affair very calmly.'

'Nowt to do with me, love. She's a free woman; but never thought she was Jack's type or that she was that keen on men. Perhaps it was just me she wasn't keen on!'

'I'd better go, they'll be here soon.'

'Oh, just a moment love, Arlene's money from her parent's house, Paula's got it. Jack invested it for her and she can't get it back.'

'I don't understand. Mum isn't that stupid as to give her money to someone with Alzheimer's, surely?'

'It seems so, but don't tell her I told you. I said I'd try to get it back for her now I'm friends with Paula. Paula's not exactly your mum's best mate is she?'

'I can't believe I'm talking about OAPs. It sounds like a plot from Dallas or something.'

'At least no one's got shot.'

So that was it. *Difficult to get hold of*, indeed. Her mother had given the money to her lover. Should she ring her? Better not – they'd only get into a row and she didn't want that if she was going to get that loan.

'Mum,' shouted Simon as he trundled his suitcase through the *Nothing to Declare* doors. She hugged Simon though she knew he didn't really like it any more. Jeremy pecked her on the cheek. She was desperate to tell him about Mum. He was always defending her. They got on well despite their different politics.

65

'Where's the car?' Jeremy asked. 'I'm shattered and do you know BA have stopped free alcohol on short haul flights?'

'You'll have to get used to slumming it like the rest of us – cattle class rather than business.'

'Don't rub it in.'

'I talked to Mum. But it's not good news.' She stopped – Simon might overhear. 'I'll tell you later.'

When they had settled in the car and got onto the M25, Karen explained to Jeremy what had happened. Simon couldn't hear as he had his headphones on and he was texting all his friends, 'My God, good for them, hope I'm still at it at their age,' said Jeremy.

'Is that all you've got to say?' asked Karen.

'That's gross. Gran having it off. She can't. She's too old. Aren't grannies supposed to bake cakes and things, not have sex? And the man, did you say he was about eighty? That's ancient. They ought to film themselves for U tube. It'll go viral, as long as everyone's got their sick bags ready.'

'Simon, please don't talk like that about your Granny,' though she couldn't help smiling.

'You were.'

'I was not. I was just telling your father what happened. Don't say anything to her about it.'

'And this money for my fees; I saw that letter from the bursar you know. If I don't do well in my exams it'll be your fault. I thought Granny was paying them.'

'I'm sure there'll be no problem. They'll get paid,' replied Karen.

'But you've just said this old bloke's got her money so we can't have it to pay the fees and I'll have to go to Newlands Comp where no one gets more than 3 Cs.'

'Shut up, Simon,' said Jeremy.

'That's what Mum said. I heard her.'

'I said that's enough. Just listen to your music. Put the volume up.'

'Mum says that'll make me deaf.'

'Tell me about your holiday,' said Karen. No response. Well if they weren't bothered to talk she'd put on some music. She couldn't believe Jeremy didn't seem worried about the money. Karen put on Classic FM rather loudly to drown out the sound of silence.

Later that evening Simon was on his IPad in his room; Karen was drinking a glass of wine and Jeremy poured himself a whisky.

'Should I ring Mum?' asked Karen.

'No, it's late and she would have been shattered after last night or rather this morning from what you said. She's probably in bed.'

'We have to do something about the money,' she said 'and you haven't suggested anything.'

'What do you suggest?'

'You think you might blackmail Paula because of what your mother's old demented lover said about his wife tying him up?'

'It sounds crazy put like that. I just thought if we report it to the authorities it would prove that she wasn't a caring wife and perhaps not a fit person to have power of attorney or whatever it's called.' She thought it was a good idea until Jeremy put the dampeners on it.

'I don't suppose they'd care as long as someone's looking after him and it's not the state's responsibility. There's no proof she's tying him up. He might like it anyway!' said Jeremy.

She took another slurp of wine. 'Well, she's not looking after him properly is she? She can't be if she lets him trot over to Putney in his state and at his age. To his mistress. I mean it was a bitter night as well. He could have died of hyperthermia.'

'I thought it was your mum that let him escape?'

'Yes, but he escaped from Paula's first - at least I think so. It's confusing.'

'So how did he get to your mum's?'

'Oh I don't know. But I'll tell you what was interesting, seeing Mum and Dad together after all these years. I wasn't there that long but Dad said they got on really well.'

'Someone new to tell his stories to. He'll have told her the one about the transvestite and the one about the girl from Pontyprid or somewhere.'

'I don't think I've heard that one.'

'I think he keeps that one for the men. He's a bit ashamed of it, at least I hope so. I think he's even told me one about Paula.'

'Oh what's that?'

Jeremy tapped the side of his nose. 'It won't help your cause. Just makes your dad look bad if I remember rightly, though he doesn't tell it quite like that.'

She turned to look accusingly at her husband. He could be such a snob sometimes. Just because Dad was an ordinary bloke. 'You've never liked Dad have you?'

'I get on fine with him; but you don't seem to have got over your Mum throwing him out. Well you say she threw him out. She says he left her. Anyway, he was a bastard to her and you always take his side.'

'You didn't grow up without a father.' Her voice rose several octaves. 'Mum didn't want me to be in touch with him.'

'I know – you've told me. Several times.'

'But all the time she was seeing this Jack. Pretending to be a holier than thou, right on, feminist and there she was betraying her sisters by going out with a married man.'

'It certainly doesn't sound like your mum. Never thought of her being a friend with benefits. You had no inkling?'

Karen frowned, thinking back, had there been clues she missed? 'No, I was glad she never seemed lonely, always busy. I thought it was work stuff or political protests. She was always involved in things like that. I remember her taking me on a Reclaim the Night thing when I was a teenager, after there'd been some rapists around or something. Mum and her friends organised this march to protest saying the men should keep off the streets not the women.'

'Well, they did have a point. Perhaps that was what old Jack was doing - reclaiming the night!'

'And she seemed so anti-men; hair very short, no make-up, wearing dungarees half the time. I had thought she might be gay.'

'You mean before being a lesbian became fashionable and sexy.'

'And all this time she was having it off with......' An image came into her mind of Jack as a drooling, doddery old man talking gibberish, yet sharing her mother's bed.

'You shouldn't be so hard on her; she didn't leave your Dad for him.'

'No but she started seeing him when I was young. She told me about a trip to the park.'

'It's not like your Dad going off with that secretary. I can't understand why you're so upset with her. Because she had an affair with a married man or because you can't imagine her having any physical relationship at her age? Some women like sex.'

'What's that supposed to fucking mean?' She got up to pour herself another glass of Chardonnay. 'It's the money isn't it? You want me to be nice to her because she's got the money. And whose fault is it we're in this fucking mess?'

'Karen, you've had too much wine. You're getting hysterical. '

'You can talk. You've had half that bottle of whisky. We soon won't be able to afford luxuries like alcohol.'

'Your dad's coming to Sunday lunch isn't he? As they got on so well, why don't you invite your mum too. I'm sure she'll love that.'

Karen's eyes lit up.

'It was a joke – that's the way not to get a loan,' said Jeremy.

'No I think that's a great idea but I'm going to ring Social Services as well, whatever you say.'

Chapter 10

The Son's Lover

Christopher had been with James for five years and in all this time he hadn't met James's parents. Today was *Meet the Fockers* day. James was busily preparing Sunday lunch for them. Chris was staring at his large Applemac screen, trying to complete a design for a client, but failing miserably. He was slightly built, with delicate features - he'd always been pretty fabulous even if he said it himself. His eyes were deep set with long dark lashes and features in perfect proportion, but today his beauty was marred by a worried frown. He was nervous about meeting the *in-laws*, especially James' father. He hated the idea of aging, especially the way Jack had become. He loved James' firm bottom, broad chest and muscular frame. Chris imagined him getting older and helpless – his stomach heaved at the thought of it. He wanted to go ahead with the marriage; but he knew he wasn't the sort to wipe his partner's bum rather than fuck it.

'Chris,' James shouted, 'get your arse over here. Can you lay the table? Mum has just rung. They're on their way.'

Chris was glad to leave his work and went into their large open plan kitchen/diner. He put out some heavy grey slate place mats and wine glasses. 'Does your dad use a knife and fork?' he asked, as he fetched the cutlery from the kitchen drawer.

James rolled his eyes. 'Of course,' he said. 'Just treat him like anyone else. He might ask who you are a few times that's all.'

'What about the baby? Do we mention it?'

'Yes, but not that Jenny is the mother. I did invite Jenny to the restaurant but I know now Mum's not ready for that.'

'What if she asks?'

'She won't. Mum doesn't tend to ask direct questions about things like that.'

'I don't suppose she's had much experience of *things like that.*'

'Anything to do with sex is not acceptable conversation. Not at the dinner table anyway.'

Chris wondered what this up tight old cow would be like. 'So shall I pretend we have separate rooms? That's a point – hasn't she been here before? How did you explain the bedroom situation?'

'I just put your stuff in the spare room and said I had a flat mate.'

Chris's eyes narrowed. 'You never told me.'

'She's only been here the once, didn't seem worth mentioning. It's my flat after all.' Chris's worried frown became an angry grimace. They'd met after James had bought the apartment and James paid the hefty mortgage from his salary. Chris was a freelance graphic designer, but work had been slow recently and they mainly relied on James' income. 'Fuck you then – I don't think I'll bother to meet your parents.'

'Chrissie, don't get like that. I'm sorry, anyway you'll have all sorts of rights after we get hooked. I'm not insisting on a pre nup!'

James smiled and Chris's face relaxed. 'Yes, well you do want me to look after the baby don't you?' He was really excited about the birth and had an image of himself working on Photoshop while the baby slept peacefully in its Moses basket, with a brightly coloured mobile dangling above its head.

'Yes, whoever the father is. And you're to let Mum think it's mine.'

'I know.'

The entry phone buzzed and James pressed the reply button. They could see his mother's face on the screen. 'Darling we're here. We're a bit early, but I skipped church this morning and we took a taxi. I couldn't cope with driving.'

'Great, just push on the entry door. You know we're on the third. There's a lift. Shall I come down?'

'No, we're fine.'

Chris escaped into the lounge while James let his parents in. He could hear Paula enthusing over the new kitchen, which he had chosen. James lacked any sense of interior design. He got up. He would feel more in control if he were standing, helping. James ushered them into the sitting room. 'Mum, Dad, this is Christopher, my partner,' said James. Chris was pleased, not friend, flatmate or just his bare name.

'How do you do?' said Paula formally and held out her hand. Jack was quiet but gripped Chris's small hand, giving it such a firm shake it made him wince.

'Pleased to meet you at last. Can I get you both a drink?' Chris asked.

'Jack will have a whisky and I'll have a G&T,' replied Paula.

'Let him answer for himself,' snapped James. 'Dad is it a Scotch you want?'

'Yes please, who did you say the chap in the green shirt is?'

'You see what I mean,' said Paula.

'My partner, Chris,' said James loudly.

'I'm not deaf son.'

Chris busied himself getting the drinks and as he gave Paula her gin he studied her face. 'I'm sure I've met you before somewhere,' he said. 'You look familiar.'

'I doubt it very much. I don't get out much these days.' Paula smiled nervously, as she sat on their white leather sofa. 'Christopher, why don't you sit next to me and tell me about yourself. I really want to get to know you.' She patted the cushion next to her. 'Do you work with James – are you a lawyer as well?'

'Mrs New.'

'Do call me Paula.'

Chris knew she was flirting with him, and he was enjoying it. 'Paula, do I look like a lawyer?'

'They presumably don't go round in pin stripes at the weekend, so you could be.'

'I'm a designer, sorry I've just realised I haven't given your husband his drink.' He knew how to play hard to get. Chris got Jack's whisky and took it to him. Jack was standing, staring out of the window. Chris looked at Jack to see if there was any family resemblance, but could see little. Hopefully other genes hadn't been passed on either. Jack took the drink. 'Jack New,' he whispered. 'Are you the police? I want to report her. She's trying to poison me.'

'Sorry, Mr New, I don't understand. I'm James' partner, Christopher. Would you like to sit down?' James's Dad was fucking demented and paranoid. If he were Paula he'd put him in a Home.

'What are you saying, Jack?' Paula asked. 'He hasn't had his medication. I'll give him a tranquilliser.'

James entered the room. 'No Mum, he'll fall asleep over dinner, if you give him one of those. He's OK. We're going to eat in five minutes.' James had cooked a traditional Sunday lunch – roast beef and Yorkshire pudding, roast parsnips, roast potatoes and gravy.

They all took their places around the glass table in the kitchen. Paula had a small helping of everything, but Jack ate heartily.

'How do gay marriages work?' asked Paula. 'Your father doesn't have to give you away or anything, does he?' Chris thought it would be better if James gave Jack away, but remained silent. He poured himself another glass of red wine.

'You're knocking it back,' said James. 'No, it's like a registry office, you can do what you want. Like a normal marriage, Mum, as you would say. We haven't set the date yet; we are waiting for the baby to come as it's so soon.'

Chris decided to pay James back for the wine crack. Had he said it because it's expensive wine? He was such a tight arse. Or did he think Chris was becoming an alcoholic? He shouldn't have said that in front of his parents. 'Yes, we wouldn't want Jenny to go into labour just as we're toasting the grooms would we? I think you know Jenny, she's Mary's daughter.'

'Mary?' said Paula puzzled, and then her face changed from bafflement through comprehension to disgust. 'You mean my help's daughter? My grandchild is going to have half Mary's genes?'

'You shit,' said James quietly. 'Well a quarter to be more precise. I presume Jenny wasn't a virgin birth.'

'Paula,' said Chris, 'Jenny's beautiful and smart. Anyway my, I mean James's genes will more than make up for it I'm sure.' Having spilt the beans or rather the eggs, he had to do something to mollify James and he was rewarded by a grateful smile.

'But Mary will be the other granny. Does she know about it?'

'I don't know,' said James.

'Well I won't tell her I know. I'll wait until she says something to me. But Jenny is always miscarrying. I'm sorry to say boys, but she probably won't go full term. But if she does, she would be the mother and could decide not to go through with it – and take my grandchild!'

'It's OK Paula. Surrogates don't have any rights. We will legally adopt the child once it's born,' said Chris.

'That's not how it works. They do have legal rights and we don't adopt as such. But we trust Jenny and she's given up all the others,' said James.

'Others? You mean she's done it before. All those miscarriages and still births? I kept giving Mary chocolates and flowers for her and there was Jenny really spitting them out like a -'

'Thai prostitute with ping pong balls,' came Jack's voice from across the table. They all stared at him. He might be mental but that's fucking hilarious, thought Chris, holding his hand over his mouth to suppress his laughter. 'I went to one of those shows once. Sorry, who's this young man?' he said to James. James was laughing too much to reply,

'Mum, you don't have to worry about Jenny. Surrogacy is common and at least we know her.'

'It certainly is common,' she replied. 'Couldn't you have adopted a child from China or somewhere like Madonna or Mia Farrow?'

'Perhaps, but then it wouldn't be my natural baby.'

James gave Chris a hard stare and Chris decided to leave that revelation until later. He was sure it was his.

Paula swallowed hard. 'I've always wanted a grandchild. But Jenny, really James, I thought you could choose things now and make designer babies.'

'You're thinking of sperm banks and artificial insemination. The surrogate mother's role is a bit harder so there's not such a wide choice,' James replied.

'Well you seem to have chosen the Pound Shop rather than Harrods.'

'Mother, how can you say that? This is your grandchild you're talking about.' His voice sounded shocked.

'Elton John has a son by surrogacy,' said Chris, trying to lighten the atmosphere, though livid beneath the breezy tone. How could that bitch say these things about Jenny?

'I'm sorry James,' said Paula, 'I didn't mean that; but are you sure she won't change her mind? You said she had rights so she could.'

'Well it seems as if you want her to. But yes in theory; though six weeks after the birth we can make it legally binding.'

'Six weeks? You mean she's got all that time to change her mind. I might be visiting my grandchild at my cleaner's daughter's house!'

'She won't change her mind. We have a contract with her now which she has signed; though it's not actually legally binding.'

'What? Why did we bother with it then?' asked Chris, suddenly becoming a little concerned. James was meant to have sorted out all that legal stuff.

'For goodness sake, shall we change the subject? Who's the lawyer here?' asked James.

'Well actually there was something I wanted to ask you about the law. If your Dad has signed something, saying he has got someone else's money, is that legally binding?' asked Paula.

'What are you talking about Mum?'

Chris decided to go into the kitchen to clear up. James was pissed off with him so a clean kitchen might take some sting out of their inevitable row once the in-laws had gone. After loading the dishwasher he popped his head round the door. 'Shall I take the pudding and coffee into the lounge?' he asked.

When Chris said *pudding* Jack looked up. What the fuck was he going to do?

'Arlene made spotted dick.'

'Did she now? I'm afraid we're out of spotted dick. Who's Arlene?' asked Chris.

'Oh I thought James would have told you. My husband has had a bit on the side for years. Now we're practically family, it's best you know all the skeletons in the cupboard. Not that I'd describe Arlene as a skeleton.'

'So have you looked for this contract? Dad, did you sign something for Arlene?' asked James.

'For goodness sake, why are you asking him? He hasn't got a copy or I'd have found it by now. I think you should write to her for it, officially. I'll find out her address for you.'

'Fine,' replied James.

'I'll help you with the dessert and coffee, Chris. You can have some time with your father.' Paula went into the kitchen with Chris, repeating her admiration for the black granite work surfaces and white Italian tiled floor. 'Have you got things for the baby?' she asked. 'Would you like me to get you a cot or a pram or something?' Chris didn't reply but was staring hard at Paula. 'Do you know the-?'

'No, we don't,' he interrupted.

'How did you know what I was going to ask? So you don't know if you want pink or blue for the nursery. People seem to know that in advance these days.'

'Sorry, that's what I thought you meant. Everyone asks that, no we elected not to know. James wants a surprise.' Thank the fuck she didn't ask if James was the father, he'd probably have let the cat out of the bag.

He was still examining Paula's features. Wait a minute. He did know her. 'I remember,' he said. 'I've got a really good memory for faces. I saw you at the National Theatre. You were with a bloke, quite young, didn't seem your type.' Paula stared at Chris and opened her mouth to speak, but the words became strangled in her throat. 'Seemed you'd been to the Pound Shop to get him. I remember you were both staring at us. I thought you were homophobic.'

'No, Christopher, you've got it all wrong, you really have. I was there waiting for a friend and this young man started talking to me. I didn't know him from Adam. I couldn't ignore him. I didn't want to appear rude.'

'No, not your style is it, rudeness?'

'I know I've been rather outspoken today. All this has been a shock. But really James couldn't have a nicer partner.'

Her voice was gushing, but Chris carried on. 'We watched you, you know. You seemed very intimate with this young man you'd hardly met.'

'You won't say anything to James, will you? He wouldn't understand. He worships his dad, always has done. I did arrange to meet the young man there. Can you imagine what it's like being with Jack all the time? I need some companionship but I must confess he wasn't what I expected. I certainly haven't seen him since and won't be seeing him ever again.'

'I'm not here to judge you, Mrs New,' Chris became serious. 'But you seem to be judging us and poor Jenny.'

Paula's eyes narrowed. 'What about you?' she asked. 'Who was your friend? Does James know about him? You seemed pretty friendly.'

James wouldn't be happy if he knew Chris had met up with Adrian. He'd never got on with him and had no idea they'd been back in touch. And Paula would tell him if he didn't keep on the right side of her. He wasn't going to tell her anything. 'He was just a friend.'

'Did James know you were out with him?'

'We're not in each other's pockets you know.'

'I'm sure you aren't; but if you keep quiet about me, then I'll do the same for you.'

'Okay, mum's the word then – for both of us,' he said, pouring out the coffee.

Chapter 11

Another Sunday Lunch

Karen was preparing the organic pork she'd bought to please her mother. Not that Mum would be able to tell and the price was extortionate. She could have just pretended, which she would have to do with the veg. The organic stuff was so dirty – she really didn't have the time to peel and scrub. She'd even done crackling – her father loved that. The knife slipped as she was chopping the apples for the sauce, almost slicing through her index finger. Stupid - she had a jar in the fridge. She hoped her mum would be impressed.

The Archers omnibus didn't calm her. Jeremy was right. It was a ridiculous plan and worse, she hadn't even told Mum that Dad was going to be here. Was she trying to get her parents back together again, like she did throughout her childhood? She should have grown out of that by now. Mum sounded so pleased to be asked to lunch that Karen felt guilty. Even Dad was dubious about meeting up, but promised to be on his best behaviour. No sexist comments or risqué jokes.

She jumped at the bell. Mum was at the door apologising for being early. She had put on quite a good dress, made her look a bit slimmer. And some make up – quite unusual. Karen kissed her briefly. They went into the lounge and Arlene sank into the large leather sofa.

'Can I help?' she asked, as she handed Karen a bottle of Cabernet Sauvignon. 'I won't have a drink, I'm driving.'

Karen refused help but offered her mother a coffee, as she'd made a fresh pot. She gave her the Sunday paper to read. 'Jeremy's just fetching Simon from football.' She didn't add that he was picking up Dad on the way back. Perhaps she should. She wouldn't put it past Mum to walk out when she saw him. In some ways, she wouldn't blame her if she did. Though since he'd rescued Jack, she might still be grateful.

Karen walked back into the kitchen. She took a slurp of wine and returned to the sitting room with a coffee.

'Mum,' she said, smiling, 'have you recovered from your shock?'

'Which one? Losing Jack or seeing Dave?'

Karen frowned. 'Dad really appreciated seeing you after all these years. He said you looked really well.'

'I expect it'll be quite a few years before I see him again. Perhaps if I'm alive when Simon gets married.'

Karen thought about ringing Jeremy to cancel Dad when she heard a car come into the drive. Could she run out and get him to take her dad back?

'I know I should have warned you but I've asked Dad over today,' she said. 'I wanted Simon to see his grandparents together.'

Arlene stared at her daughter but remained seated. Karen could see a hurt look in her mother's eyes. This made her feel worse than if she'd shouted and raved, but then she didn't remember her mum ever doing that.

'You will stay? I'm sorry, I should have asked you.'

Simon burst into the room in his Nike track suit and sweaty football socks.

'I'm starving Mum. When's lunch? Hi Gran.'

Jeremy followed with Dave in tow. 'Simon, shower. Dave what do you want to drink? Arlene – oh you've got a coffee.'

Dave sat opposite Arlene and gave her a nod and lukewarm smile. 'Have you got a beer?' Dave asked. Jeremy nodded.

Karen was left with her parents, undiluted. 'I know this is difficult for you both. I just thought that after what happened with Jack it might be good to discuss, you know, things.'

'Karen, I'm a seventy year old woman. I make my own decisions. I'm not in my second childhood. I don't need your approval for my actions or my ex-husband's. I don't know what there is to discuss.'

'That wasn't what I meant. Let's have a nice lunch and Simon can tell you about his skiing trip.'

Karen escaped to the kitchen to put the finishing touches to the roast and make the gravy. They must have had Sunday lunches together as a family but she couldn't recall them. She remembered her mum had taken her to museums and galleries on a Sunday, while she preferred to be out with her mates, watching telly or listening to pop music. Dad had let her do what she wanted whenever he had her and they'd often ended up watching a video with a take away. Now she tried to wean Simon away from Grand Theft Auto or Angry Birds or whatever was the latest thing. A bit like her mum. But at least she wasn't having an affair, she'd kept a stable home for Simon.

She returned to the lounge to find them all with various parts of the paper. It probably pained Mum to be reading the Sunday Telegraph so she was doing the crossword. Simon ran downstairs, glowing from the shower and Karen called them all to lunch.

They sat around the table in the dining room and Karen brought in the roast. Simon took large helpings of everything and wolfed his food down. Jeremy talked to Dave about football while the women sat in silence. Karen rushed back and forth to the kitchen, clearing unnecessarily, between gulps of wine and limited food. Arlene cut her lunch up but most of it remained on the plate.

'Sit down, Karen, everyone's got what they need,' Arlene said. 'I want to say something.'

They stopped eating and cutlery was laid gently on their plates. Karen opened her mouth to try to silence her mum but Arlene's look silenced her instead. All eyes were turned to her mother. Karen wondered if this was what it had been like when Arlene was lecturing, something she could never imagine her doing.

'I know you found it hard when Dave and I split up, Karen,' she started.

'Should Simon be hearing this?' asked Karen.

'I think he should. Some of it may have an effect on him. The split was hard for me too. I was lonely but as you know I immersed myself in study, got my degree and got a job at the polytechnic. It wasn't until after you left to go to university that I found companionship - love even- with Jack. His marriage was not a happy one, though I have felt a lot of guilt about that part.'

Karen thought back. Was that true? She remembered meeting him a few times in her childhood but her mum had so rarely left her and she hadn't gone to her dad's much. If her mum had been having an affair, she would have encouraged her to stay over with her dad. But she had positively discouraged it so it must have started later on. Still, she was almost fifty so her mum's affair could have been going on for thirty years. Longer than most marriages.

Arlene looked around as if she was expecting one of her family to jump in with a comment. Karen did not disappoint. 'But Mum, now that he's, well, you know...'

'I don't intend to give up on him because he's ill. I will continue to see him and I hope he can now become part of our family in some way. I'm glad it's out in the open; no longer my dirty little secret.'

They all sat waiting for her to continue but Arlene picked up her knife and fork and started to eat. At least she just talked about splitting, not putting all the blame on Dad, thought Karen. She couldn't believe they were supposed to welcome Jack into their family. He would never remember who any of them were for a start. As long as he remembered the money. That was the most important thing. She wanted to mention it but she wasn't supposed to say that Dad had told her about the loan.

'Lovely pork,' said Dave and Karen gave him a grateful smile. She wished he'd say something about the money - the neon £ sign in the room.

'Gran,' said Simon, 'I'm sorry you've lost all your money and can't pay my fees. You won't have to move out of your house, will you? Mum says we might.'

'Simon,' said Jeremy, 'this isn't the time to bring this up. Gran's not losing her house and neither are we.'

'What's this all about?' asked Dave.

Arlene slowly finished her mouthful of food. 'I was getting onto that. I did let Jack invest my money for me but it's perfectly safe. I'll give you a loan as soon as I get it back.'

'But Mum said you don't think I should go to private school. Mum said you don't believe in them.'

'Simon, shut up,' said Karen.

'It's a perfectly reasonable comment. I know your mum thinks I'm a hard bitten Marxist Feminist but actually I'm a faint hearted feminist, as they say, and middle of the road politically. I won't let your education suffer if I can help it. Sometimes the personal is the political and sometimes it isn't.'

Simon frowned. 'Not sure I follow. Can I play on my X box until pudding?'

'But does Jack even remember investing it for you? I don't know why you didn't ask Jeremy. He'd have sorted a bond or something for you,' said Karen. 'I'm not worried for us, but for you. You don't want to lose all that money.' She blushed slightly as she said it and looked apologetically at Dave.

'I've said it's safe. I have a contract. I'm sure Paula will sort it out. I'm going to have Jack over again soon – give her a break.'

They all stared at Arlene in disbelief. Karen forced herself to remain quiet and poured herself another glass of wine.

'I'm going over to see Paula as well, so between us I'm sure we can sort it, love,' said Dave, smacking his lips as he sucked the tasty pork fat off the crackling.

'Is that wise?' asked Arlene. She had a strange look on her face. Did she know something Karen didn't?

'What's the matter, Mum?'

Arlene didn't reply and went soon after the meal. Jeremy drove Dave home.

'That went well then, money's all sorted,' Jeremy said to Karen's back when he returned home. She was unloading the dishwasher and turned round clutching a plate. She had a great urge to throw it at her husband. That would wipe the smirk off his face. But it was her good china so she put it down and breathed deeply.

'I've found the son on Facebook,' she said. 'I'm going to ring him. At least I'm trying to do something. You're doing fuck all'

Chapter 12

The Parents

Chris continued drinking after Sunday lunch while James drove his parents back to Richmond. Such a good fucking son unlike him. He couldn't remember the last time he had spoken to his parents, let alone seen them. He knew they wouldn't want to see him. They regarded him as a sodomite, the sperm of Satan, but there was a void there which he couldn't see being filled by Paula and Jack. He'd asked to go back with James to see their house but James had refused. As if he'd wanted to keep his childhood separate but then Chris hadn't told him much about his.

The landline rang. Strange – no-one rang them on that these days. A woman's voice asked for James. 'Sorry,' he said. 'He's out. I'm his partner, can I help?'

'It's regarding some money James' father invested for my mother. You know he's ill of course and he can't remember anything about it. Mrs New was going to sort it out, but to tell you the truth she's not being that helpful and I understand that James has Power of Attorney.'

Chris's brain took a while to work out what this woman was going on about. He realised he should at least find out her identity but she must have been reading his mind.

'My name is Karen Carr, I'm Arlene Porter's daughter. She's a friend of Jack's.'

Chris's thoughts clicked into gear.

'Sorry,' he said. 'Not sure I can help. Let's hope Paula's not gone and given it to her young lover.' He couldn't tell James, but the more people who knew about Paula the better, fucking snob. She was only pretending to be okay about him and James, he was sure, and her attitude towards Jenny and the baby – that really was gross.

'Sorry,' said Karen. 'I'm not sure I heard you correctly.'

'You did,' said Chris. 'I'll tell James you called. I'm sure he'll be in contact. Ring back? No really - I'm sure he'll ring you.'

He took Karen's number but thought he'd better not give it to James. In fact, he wouldn't mention any of it to him.

When James returned, his features looked stern. What was the matter with him? He'd cleared everything up, only the roasting pan was left soaking.

'Mum told me she'd seen you with some bloke at the National a couple of weeks ago. What the fuck do you think you were doing? From what she said it sounded like it was Adrian.'

So much for *mum's the word*, Chris thought. Even through the cloud of Chianti, his mind told him to bluff it out.

'Yes, I was going to tell you. He said he had some work for me. We met up with this other guy as well but he must have gone when I saw your mum. I didn't want to tell you until the work had come through. You know what Adie's like with his promises. Did Paula tell you who she was with though?'

James eyes narrowed as he looked at Chris. 'You said you wouldn't meet up with him after last time.'

Chris remembered how he'd gone back to Adrian's flat for drinks and a little coke. Things had got out of hand, so to speak. James had heard about it somehow – the community leaks badly. Nothing like that happened this time but he doubted James would believe it. He also had something else to tell James regarding Adie.

'Calm down, let me get you a drink.'

'That's your answer to everything, isn't it?' replied James.

Chris's voice was slurred and he knew he'd had a lot of wine but why shouldn't he? James was always harking on about it as if he had a problem. It hadn't affected his looks or his performance so why should James be worried? All these comments did was really piss him off.

'Actually I asked Adrian to be Best Man. Said you'd be delighted. Said you were so secure in our relationship that you'd got over all that jealousy nonsense. But it seems you haven't.'

Chris sat down and poured himself another glass of wine, draining the bottle. James hadn't taken his coat off and was still standing staring at Chris. Chris hated silence. He always had some music on while he was working and saying nothing was James' tactic when they had a row.

'Anyway did Paula tell you about the young man she was with? Looked a bit of a chav to me.' This might get James to talk.

'She did tell me, yes – unlike you. It was her friend's son. She's told me about him before. He seems to confide in her about his relationships.'

Chris spluttered into his wine and some of it splashed onto the front of his shirt. He debated whether to run and sponge it off but had to refute Paula's bare faced lies first. He started to giggle. It was so ridiculous - yet James seemed to believe her.

'I think Paula may have been telling some porkie pies there. Fuck it – do you snog your friend's son? If she's got friends with sons like that, then why the fuck is she so against Jenny?'

'We're talking about you,' replied James, 'not Mum.'

The phone rang again and James answered. 'Sorry, who did you say you spoke to?'

There was a long silence and Chris could see James's face going through the colours of the Photoshop wheel eventually landing on puce.

'I'll call you later,' James said and slammed down the receiver.

'I've not had a chance to tell you - that bitch rang. Just after some money. Said I didn't know anything about it.'

'You told her that my mum had a young lover – you're the fucking bitch.' James went into their bedroom and slammed the door.

Chris wanted to make up with him. James was his rock, his stability. He was his first real love though he'd started his gay career pretty early. He remembered he'd been attracted to another boy in the choir. It had been a bit like fucking Brokeback Mountain, looks across the stalls, holding hands in the pews. Chris must have been about twelve and his voice was starting to break. He knew he'd soon be out of the choir. He decided to make the first move. His parents always had a meeting after Church on a Sunday and he'd suggested the boy came over for tea. Chris tried to remember his name. Leroy – that was it. Black as the ace of fucking spades. There were lots of black kids in the evangelical church his parents attended. At least they hadn't been racist.

They had gone back to his house. Leroy was a big boy in all senses. He told him he'd been with a few boys, while the furthest Chris had got was masturbating to his Boy George poster. Leroy soon unzipped himself. Chris was eager and was so engrossed in sucking him off that he didn't hear his parents return. He remembered sucking Leroy's dick like it was a stick of seaside rock with Gay right through the middle. The bedroom door opened and he heard his mother scream. He was not sure what she saw but he almost bit the top of Leroy's prick in his haste to get off. He was never allowed to attend choir again and was lectured on the gay plague and unnatural practices. But once he'd had a taste of it there was no stopping him. Eventually they threw him out.

He pimped his way through art school and cruised into his graphic jobs, sleeping with designers to get work. He was so fucking gorgeous that men flocked to him. But James was his first long term partner. Adrian and Chris had an open relationship but he promised to be faithful to James. And he had, apart from that one slip.

He couldn't let Paula drive them apart. He would go to see her, call in on her when she wasn't expecting him. He wanted to see where she lived. He could always assess his enemy better when he saw them on their own territory. She was such a fucking hypocrite. It was probably better to be like his parents – at least they believed what they said. Though that meant he would never see them again and they would never have the joy of seeing his child.

He needed to make it up with James. He was such a stubborn bastard that he might cancel the wedding and Chris couldn't afford to look after the baby on his own.

He stripped down to his boxers and slipped into bed beside James. He blew gently into his ear and licked his lobe. Good sign – no resistance. He made his way down James' body, licking, kissing and gently nibbling him. He sucked his nipples until they were hard, then made his way down the bed feeling for James' dick. It was hard already. Chris wrapped his lips over his teeth and let his tongue play on the head. He opened his mouth and did what he did best until James groaned with pleasure.

'OK – let's move on. Life's too short,' said James. 'And Adrian can be your best man.'

Chris wrapped his limbs around James' body and fell fast asleep.

Chapter 13

Love Letters

Jack was at the Day Centre so Paula had a few hours to spare. She'd considered going to Dickens and Jones to look for a new outfit for the wedding but it was tipping down and quite chilly. And she'd have to change. She'd only pulled on her pink tracksuit she used for the gym. She opened Jack's door. She was considering doing his room up but wondered if it was worth the hassle as only Jack used it. Perhaps she'd turn it into the spare room as it had such a nice view over the garden.

They had slept separately for a long time though Jack had visiting rights which he'd used only sparingly. Didn't need to she supposed. And she'd been glad or so she'd said. She'd somehow grown into this ice maiden – could you be an ice maiden at sixty?

She'd been having doubts about her plans. Had she really invited Hot Rod to her home? It was becoming too real, too close. Her thoughts of revenge were entangled with her frustration with Jack's condition. He couldn't help it and yet at times Paula thought he was doing it deliberately, even forgetting who she was or, worse, confusing her with bloody Arlene.

Jack's room was messy though Mary had cleaned last week. Papers spilling from the desk, clothes piled on the floor and various cups and glasses littered around the room. She looked at his bureau, perhaps she'd find the contract that woman was on about. She noticed some things had fallen behind it. She tried to push it – not too heavy. As she moved it away from the wall she gingerly picked up an old tie, some dusty cufflinks, an envelope full of photos and a small container, like a casket.

She sat on Jack's bed and laid the pictures out. Some of Jack at work, a few of him with his parents but most were of a woman on her own. She put on her glasses and examined them more carefully. My God, it was Arlene. She didn't look much better when she was younger. Arlene at the beach, Arlene in the country, Arlene in a church. Arlene on a bike. There were more photos of Arlene than there ever were of her. She could hardly remember going for trips with Jack and, if they did, he never had his camera with him. There were some of James, of course, but few of them as a family. Wait, what was this one – a bedroom but it was her bedroom or their bedroom as it had been then. Good God. They'd had it off in her bed. She had a desire to tear up the photos but then she might need them. Some of those photos must be thirty years old. He'd been with her when James was ten. And she'd been stuck at home with their son or used as arm candy – no, not really, just a dutiful wife, at his side at corporate events while Arlene was available to take out, have fun and shag. It was as if Jack had two wives

She picked up the box. It was wooden and there was a lock. She shook it. It felt full but there was no jangling of coins or jewellery. She hunted frantically through the bureau and found a collection of keys in a small drawer. Suitcase keys, padlocks, old car keys, window locks and all sorts. She'd never find the right one. It might contain that contract. If so, she'd rip it up.

With shaking hands she tried each key, twiddling them around in the lock, getting more and more frustrated as it refused to open. She flung it on the floor and went downstairs to the kitchen. A cup of camomile might calm her down and help her stomach. A wave of nausea swept through her and she rushed to the loo. She'd had no breakfast so she only vomited bile, like she'd done when she was pregnant. She drank a glass of water and sat down on the kitchen chair, her legs feeling limp.

Thoughts that she'd suppressed for years were flying across her brain - creating images of a young Jack enjoying himself with Arlene. The doorbell rang. Strange, she wasn't expecting anyone. She unlocked her door but kept the chain on and peeped through.

'Hi Paula,' said Chris. 'Can I have a word?'

Paula looked again and her eyes widened. What was he doing here? It must be about what she said to James yesterday. She thought James might have kept it under his hat. She had no makeup on, totally naked. 'I'm in the middle of something,' she said. How could she possibly let him in?

'Please,' said Chris, 'it's important.'

He might be able to open that box. He was a man after all - even though he was gay. She took the chain off and led him to the kitchen. She glanced at herself in the hall mirror. She supposed she didn't look too bad. She'd keep the kitchen blinds shut so the sun wouldn't illuminate her wrinkles.

'Coffee?' she asked and poured one from the percolator. It shouldn't be too bad though it was an hour since she'd had her breakfast cup.

'Being mum again? We had an agreement and then you blabbed to James. What the fuck were you playing at?'

Paula was standing with her back to him, getting the milk from the fridge. What could she say? She wasn't sure why she'd told James. 'You haven't been here before, have you? You know I brought James up here. It was his family home. It's a bit big now but I have so many memories, I wouldn't want to move away.'

'Please don't change the subject, Paula.'

She turned around and looked at Chris directly. She bet that Chris had told James about Hot Rod when he knew his secret was out. As they say, attack is the best form of defence.

'So you haven't told James who I was with?'

'Only after you'd betrayed me.'

'That's the point isn't it? I told James about the young man anyway. For me it didn't matter. For you it was a betrayal. My concern was you being unfaithful to James. Christopher, I was worried about you two staying together with a baby. I want you to be a stable family unit to bring it up. I know James loves you so much.' She handed him his coffee.

'It seems to me you were trying to break us up,' Chris sighed and shook his head. 'But you haven't. I've told James all about it and Adrian - the man you saw me with - is going to be our best man.' Paula forced a smile but her mind was racing, thinking about her own plan. 'But Paula, just in case you want to interfere some more,

I've found out about you and Mrs Robinson. Google's a wonderful thing. I might just tell James about it and who else? You're a big church goer aren't you? I'm sure the vicar would be very interested.'

How did he find that out? Oh God, she didn't understand the bloody internet. Yet how could he condemn her? She was sure he'd had loads of lovers. But there was no point in making an enemy of her future son-in-law. She probably wouldn't go through with her plan anyway and Hot Rod would be history.

'Would you like to look around? See James' old bedroom. It's still got lots of his stuff in it.' She could see Chris was interested and she showed him upstairs. James' old room actually bore little resemblance to the one he'd slept in when he was young as Paula had restyled it completely.

'You know I had no idea James thought he was gay.'

'He didn't think it, he was. God you really make me angry.'

My goodness, so pedantic. He must know what she meant.

'Christopher, I'm sorry. I realise that now. I think I've adjusted well to all the surprises I've had.' She took him back downstairs. 'Please, do come into the sitting room. I'd like your advice as a designer. I'm planning to redecorate.'

'I'm a graphic - not an interior designer.' His voice sent an icy blast into the expensively heated room. 'I think I'd better make a move now.'

'You think you've made some pretty good moves, don't you? But Christopher, this isn't a game. I'm not good on the internet and was just experimenting so I hope you won't share this silly Mrs Robinson thing. Before you go, are you any good with tools?'

Chris raised his eyebrows. Paula opened a kitchen drawer and took out a file.

'Just a moment,' she said and brought down the wooden box from Jack's room.

'I can't find the key and there are some papers in here I need. Could you see if you could file the hinges or something for me?' Do gay men respond to helpless females?

Chris looked at it dubiously but took the file from Paula and, using the end more like a lever, easily removed the lid. Paula realised she could have done that. Now Chris had to go. She didn't want him knowing any more of her secrets. Though these were Jack's and she would share them with James if needed and in her own time. Chris left quickly after her effusive thanks and cold hug.

The casket contained hand written letters and, skimming to the end of the first one, she saw it was from Arlene. She started to read it and her breathing became shallower and shallower.

Dear Jack,

The flowers you sent me are so beautiful. You didn't have to apologise though. The quarrel was all my fault. I know you can't see more of me and you have to stay with Paula while James is still at home.

I will come to Florence on that trip if you think it'll be safe. I've never been and have always wanted to go to the Uffizi. I like the sound of the four poster too! I'll meet you at Gatwick at 7pm on Thursday. The flight back is Sunday night isn't it as I've got tutorials booked on Monday?

Love,
Arlene xxxx

Have to stay with Paula while James is at home?. Had he planned to leave her when James left? The bastard. And now she was looking after him. She had this empty shell of a man while Arlene had taken him in his prime. Why hadn't she seen these letters when they came? She looked at the address. That she-devil had sent it to Jack at work. A trip to Florence. She tried to remember if he'd mentioned a business trip there. They'd all seemed to be to boring places and she couldn't have gone anyway when she had James. Flowers too. When had he given her flowers? She thought back. Yes he had bought her flowers and jewellery and perfume – all guilt.

And a four-poster bed. They'd usually had a twin room in hotels. But that had probably been her choice. This had been more than an affair. He did, does, love Arlene more than her. Why didn't he leave her then after James left home? She'd made it too easy for him. He went off whenever he wanted. Had the best of both worlds and, if they'd divorced, she'd have taken him for all he'd got. He knew that. She smiled. Now she did have control of his money but that wasn't sufficient payback.

She opened another and inside was a lock of hair, dark hair, Arlene's hair. She thought of her own red curls. She'd often been compared with a Titian or Pre-Raphaelite painting, yet he'd never asked for a single hair from her head but then had she offered one? Her eyes filled with tears. She blinked them away. Could things have been different if she'd been more tender and loving? She supposed she'd never been the romantic type but nor had Jack, at least not with her.

Dear Jack,

I've missed you over Christmas. I was with Karen though and it was lovely seeing little Simon. But I am looking forward to seeing you at New Year. Are you sure that you can get out of going to Paula's mum? I don't want to make things hard for you.

She remembered that. Her mum had been unwell and he said he had too much work on, couldn't be of much help blah blah blah. She'd been very understanding as far as she remembered. She must have suspected something. Could that have been the time they did it in her bed? Her head was thumping. She felt as if she had a migraine coming on. These revelations had opened up the wound of this affair. It was red and raw again.

Thank you so much for the lovely handbag. The leather is so soft. It must have been very expensive. You really shouldn't spend that much on me. But you do know my taste- in everything!!

I'm sure James loved having you there for Xmas and hope it wasn't too awful for you.

Love,

Arlene xxxx

Paula threw down the letter. *Too awful* indeed. They'd had a lovely Christmas, entertained, had fabulous food and drink. But they'd rowed too. Jack never seemed satisfied to be with just her, as if he was chained up in their lovely house and Paula was the jailor. He escaped then to Arlene as he did now. And she was giving it her blessing, perhaps she always had. She read more and her anger turned to distress and back again.

This was a fat one – a card. She ripped it open, discarding the envelope on the floor. A sixtieth birthday card. It looked like something from a Boy's Own Annual with a boat and a train on it and *Happy 60th* in gold glitter. There was a note written inside it.

Happy Birthday Jack,

I'm sure the party will go well. You'll just have to be on your best behaviour with the vicar there – not too much whisky. I've decided not to go to Greenham with my women's group, to be with you. I didn't tell them why though! I've got a birthday surprise waiting for you here which doesn't involve tea and cakes.

Love,

Arlene xxxx

She felt faint. Her life was stripped bare and laid out for someone else to see, to mock. Women's group? Greenham Common? Jack had been so anti protests. She must have argued with him. They'd discussed politics while Paula'd accepted what he said or hadn't been really interested. That's why he loved Arlene.

The things Jack had told that woman about their marriage. She thought back – the birthday party had not been what Jack would have chosen. Reverend Peters had insisted on doing tea at the vicarage with women from the Mother's Union and their husbands. He hadn't wanted to go but she'd insisted. He must have told that woman about the whisky that he kept pouring into his tea from his pocket flask. Paula hadn't drunk much in those days and had been furious with Jack for bringing the whisky. Jack had refused the sherry they'd brought in specially and been rude to Mrs. Peters, when all she'd done was ask him if he was retiring. When they returned home they had such a row and he stormed off – probably to frigging Arlene's.

It was like someone had read her secret diary and then shown it to her enemy. How many years had he kept these letters? Treasured them. Kept them in a locked casket. Almost a fairy tale. Like the four-poster bed and lock of hair.

Well, she would show him. She knew how her Hot Rod plan could work. She'd seen something in a film once, in a police station. She went into her room and switched on her computer. Fury speeded up her brain though her fingers shook as she tapped on the keys. She found it and ordered it - amazing the things you can get online. She took several deep breaths and, as she composed her plan, she became more composed herself.

She returned to Jack's room to check out the space. Now she'd moved the bureau, she could see it was the perfect place to put the mirror – just behind her bedroom wall. She had a good builder too. She was sure she could get him to do it by Saturday. If not, she'd have to postpone Hot Rod. And that new print she'd bought would come in handy. It was large, so could cover it when it wasn't needed. She already knew where to get the pills. She couldn't believe they were available in Boots. What was the world coming to?

She would make him feel what she'd felt, what she felt now. The ice maiden had turned into the Snow Queen but this time she would win.

Chapter 14

The Mistress and her Lover

Arlene decided to ring Paula soon after Jack's night of wandering. The more helpful she could be to Paula, the more likely she would get her money back. Though a mistress asking a wife for the loan of her husband may seem a step too far for many.

However, Paula agreed and asked her to have him on Friday night and keep him the next day as she had some appointments. Arlene drove over to Richmond, feeling cheerful. Her dark secret was out, lightening her burden of guilt. A problem shared is a problem halved. Perhaps this applied to secrets as well.

She'd been to the house before. She'd eaten in their kitchen, sat in their lounge, been upstairs in their bedroom. Paula had been away somewhere with James. Her guilt enveloped her as she remembered the illicit sex in the marital bed. A taboo they shouldn't have broken. Guilt should mean that she repented her behaviour but, though she couldn't say *Je Ne Regrette Rien,* she wouldn't be without her years with Jack. Such excitement when Jack made love to her in Paula's and his double bed, the silk sheets soft against her skin and the deep pile between her toes, as she padded over the carpet. It was so luxurious and thrilling, keeping the curtains closed in case the neighbours saw, jumping at the sound of the doorbell or phone.

She recalled something else she'd done. For this she did feel remorse. After she'd found out where they lived, she watched their house like a stalker. She saw Jack in the garden or occasionally going to Waitrose with Paula. She followed him from a distance, as he took James out, and sometimes she followed Paula. It was easier when Jack wasn't there as she knew Paula wouldn't recognise her. She once browsed in a dress shop where Paula was choosing some clothes. Every time she did this she was ashamed but it had become an addiction. Was it jealousy which had made her act like that? Jealous that Paula had Jack all the time, jealous of her conventional marriage, her money, her lifestyle. This phase had thankfully been short lived, and now she couldn't remember how she'd stopped or whether her jealousy had dissipated after seeing Paula's unfulfilled life. Despite having Jack as her husband or because?

She shuddered to think what Paula would say if she knew. Now she had Paula's permission to love and care for Jack, perhaps Paula wouldn't worry what had happened in the past. She suspected that Paula's deadly sin was her pride and, as long as that wasn't punctured, she would be happy.

Arlene's hand shook as she rang the doorbell of the large detached Georgian house. Paula opened the door, dressed in a pink tracksuit. 'I'm taking the opportunity to go to the gym,' she said, making Arlene feel fat and unfit. 'Come in a moment while I get his medication.' She led Arlene into her modern fitted kitchen with green quartz work surfaces and handed her a bejewelled pill box, containing one small blue diamond shaped tablet. 'Give him half, an hour before bed. It will help him sleep. If there are problems give him the other half. I don't want any of the issues we had last time.'

Arlene flushed. 'Of course not,' she said. 'I'll be careful.' She had been about to ask what the pills were; but this admonishment stopped her in her tracks. Jack came downstairs looking perplexed but beamed when he saw Arlene.

'I've packed his bag. Can you return him about six tomorrow evening?' said Paula, and handed him a small leather hold all. She swiftly showed them to the door, dismissing Arlene's goodbyes.

Arlene helped Jack into his seat belt as he seemed to find even that simple task confusing. 'These bloody things. They make them so complicated these days.'

'Don't worry about it – it's done now,' she said. 'We'll soon be at my house. I've cooked a nice meal; I hope you're hungry.'

'Always hungry,' he said. 'Paula tells me I forget that I've eaten but I think she's trying to starve me.'

'Well, you do forget things Jack. And you did wander out last time you were at mine. You remember when you met up with Dave?'

'Yes, Dave, of course I remember Dave – your ex. He was my friend.'

'That's right, we have a daughter, Karen. You met her. I don't think you'd seen her since she was tiny.'

'So how old is she now – a teenager?'

'Oh Jack, do you think I look like a mother of a teenager?'

'What's wrong with that? You're still beautiful anyway!'

'Oh Jack, that's lovely,' she said. Perhaps the benefit of Alzheimer's was forgetting the years, the time which had worn away her youth. He saw only what was now in the past.

When they arrived, Jack seemed much less anxious than he'd been on the last visit. 'I think the train journey here stressed you out last time,' she said.

'Yes, I hate those things. You know, what are they called? Channels?'

Arlene looked puzzled, thinking of the BBC or Sky, then smiled, 'You mean stations, like Waterloo?'

'Yes', said Jack, as he struggled out of his seat belt. As soon as they entered the house, Jack sat down at the kitchen table.

'I've made a lovely fish stew, it's in the oven. Take your coat off, Jack, and I'll make us a drink first. What would you like?'

Jack managed to take his coat off and Arlene guided him into the lounge. He looked at the photographs Arlene had above the fireplace. 'You don't look at the mantelpiece when you're stoking the fire,' he said.

'Dave used to say that. I hate that expression. I hope that's not what you think.'

'Never used to stoke the fire much with Paula,' he said.

'But you could admire the mantelpiece. I'm sure she was lovely when she was younger. She's still very attractive.'

'She was always cold, frigid I'd say. And much too skinny, not like you.'

Arlene was never sure why she had a need to defend Paula. Guilt? 'Perhaps it was because you were having an affair with me and I bet there were others before. You led her a merry dance and your other wives too.'

'Well one of them left me for someone else.'

'You mean Georgina? The one who was…'

'A lesbian, yes, should have realised. Looked like that actress you know – foreign, the one who was in that film. Blue.'

'Not a blue film surely?'

'Things with wings.'

'Oh you mean the Blue Angel with Marlene Dietrich. Did she look like her? She must have been beautiful.' Arlene again began to wonder why Jack had chosen her, even as only a mistress.

'Yes, that's it. Well I wouldn't say she was the spitting image but she definitely played two ways.'

'That was unusual in those days. Was she really bisexual?'

'Not sure she knew until she married me. Then she realised women were a better bet. She was a teacher and her headmistress seduced her. Mother of one of the kids found them one day in flagrante in the stationery cupboard. I don't think she could believe her eyes.'

'You've not told me this before.'

'It caused a scandal. Children being corrupted you know. Both sacked but they went off together. Left me on my tod.'

Arlene went to the kitchen and returned with two glasses of Chardonnay. 'Perhaps that was Paula's problem – prefers women?' she suggested, though she doubted it.

'No, never really wanted to be touched. She used to have everything perfect. Nothing out of place and my body beside her caused the sheets to rumple, even that was too much.'

'Well, you did have James so it must have been consummated.'

Jack continued in full flow. 'Sex was a weapon with her. *Jack, can I get that dress from Dickens and Jones*? Then she'd start caressing me. And, if I'd say we couldn't afford it, she'd turn over and there'd be no oats for me. Then I'd agree and she'd lie back and think of England – or probably what shoes she would get to go with the frock.'

'But why did she have to ask you to get a dress?' She thought of the feminist mantra. *Marriage is legalised prostitution.* She'd believed that back then in the eighties.

'That's how it was in those days. Now I have to ask her for everything. You know she's stolen my money.'

'Not quite stolen Jack, she has Power of Attorney along with James. You were getting confused. You used to forget which bank you were with and you could never remember your pin number.'

She couldn't believe she was supporting Paula who was refusing to give her back her own money! Though she'd been a fool to lend it. She remembered the stew and went to check it. She called Jack to the dining room while she fetched the dishes from the kitchen. The pungent garlic and the aroma of the prawns and monkfish, combined with Jack's lucidity, gave her a spring in her step. That didn't happen often these days as her arthritic hip was quite painful – no there was little springing now.

She noticed the pill box on the table and wondered if there were any instructions with the tablets. Now what had Paula said to do? Was he supposed to take it with food? She remembered something about an hour before something. Paula had said to cut it in half which she did with difficulty. She went back into the dining room.

'I think Paula said you had to take this before bed. Do you need to take it with dinner?'

'Oh I don't know – she drugs me. She's changed you know. She ties me up.'

Arlene frowned. 'Are you sure? If she does, it's probably to stop you from wandering. You know what happened here.'

'You don't believe me, do you? You're just like Paula.'

Jack banged his fist on the table, almost spilling the hot tureen of stew onto the polished wood. His body sagged and his eyes filled with tears.

'It's OK Jack, I do believe you. Don't think about Paula, you're with me tonight. Why don't you take your medication? It'll calm you.'

Jack obediently swallowed the pill and started eating his stew and mashed potatoes. He ate fast. Food was just fuel rather than something to savour and enjoy. Arlene recalled the time he used to love her food. 'Do you remember how you used to enjoy the boeuf bourguignon and coq au vin I used to make for you?'

'I always had to come over here for a good meal. Paula only gave me salad.'

'We used to eat the main course and then you'd say I was the perfect dessert and we'd go upstairs.'

'Or on the kitchen table,' replied Jack.

'Yes,' she replied, blushing at the uncomfortable memory, despite the passing years. 'I had a bad back for weeks afterwards.' She looked at his expression; it had changed from a worried frown through confusion to a broad grin.

'It felt great. You were very naughty. You weren't wearing any knickers through dinner. I only realised when you were getting the pudding out of the oven.'

She remembered that. It had been fun, getting him excited and her as well. Now what had she cooked? 'No wonder I'm so fat. Was there a hot pudding?'

'Well *you* certainly were. I think you'd made a spotted dick – one of my favourites. Paula would never let me have it and certainly wouldn't have mine!'

'It was supposed to be a joke.'

Jack became animated. 'You were wearing a short dress. With stockings and suspenders. Really turned me on. You bent over and I could see the tops of your stockings and a glimpse of your bum. Your delicious fanny was there for my taking.'

She flushed. 'Was I really? How could I have called myself a feminist while I was doing that in my private life? I was obviously a post-feminist before the term was invented!'

'Never mind your feminism. I know the spotted dick was forgotten – substituted by mine!'

'Well no hot steamed pudding tonight. I've made us Eton Mess. Not quite my principles but...'

'You're my pudding,' he shouted and got up from the table. Arlene could see there was a large bulge in his trousers – he must be completely erect. 'Percy doesn't need any coaxing tonight,' he said. They had christened his member Percy when they'd first become lovers but they hadn't used that term for years. Now Percy was behaving like an adolescent on a hot date.

'Jack, I've not finished my meal. You go up and get changed. I'll come in a minute.'

He seemed to have difficulty mounting the stairs, and started tugging at his pants and unzipping his fly. God she'd not seen him like that for years. What had come over him? 'My cock's stuck, can't walk. Let's use the kitchen table again.'

'Don't be silly Jack. My back wouldn't stand it. It was bad enough at fifty, let alone seventy. I only agreed to it because it seemed to excite you. I think you're excited enough tonight.' She went to help him up the stairs, but he fell onto her, rubbing himself against her thighs. 'Come on, I'll help you into the bedroom,' she said as she struggled from under his six-foot frame.

He managed to get himself into the bedroom with his trousers at half-mast and Percy looking over the top of his boxers, stiff and proud. Reluctantly he let Arlene help him remove his shoes and socks, having failed to kick them off. Jack got onto the king size bed. *(Why are you getting this huge bed Mum,* Karen had asked, *it dominates the room).* Arlene could have replied that it dominated her life because at that time it did.

They had christened her clitoris, Clarrisa, to match Percy. She wondered why they had chosen that name with echoes of a type of STD. More innocent times? Now he seemed to have forgotten all the foreplay. He used to lick and suck Arlene's nipples, tenderly coaxing out Clarissa, when she hid from his wandering fingers, then going down on her, his tongue gentle and probing.

Percy was jabbing wildly, even when Arlene was removing her knickers and unclipping her bra. She tried to make him stop thrusting and caress her gently. 'Clarissa's not quite ready,' she whispered, hoping that would bring back memories of times lost. She took his hand and rubbed herself with it and gradually some feeling and desire returned, though not sufficient to match his. She decided to go on top of him. She might then have more control of the thrust. He enjoyed this as her large breasts flopped onto his chest; their going south did not matter to him. His erection was firm and she had to work hard to make him ejaculate. Percy kept standing like a young man, not like Jack had been for many years. Desire seemed to be running through his veins. At last he filled her and she dismounted with relief, crawling over to her bedside table for some tissues.

She slipped on her blue dressing gown and gave Jack the duvet to cover up his nakedness. 'I'll go down and get us the pudding. Would you like it in bed?' He didn't answer and Arlene hoped he would fall asleep after that exertion and the medication, so she left him and went downstairs.

As she was clearing away she put the radio on so the sound of Jack coming into the kitchen was drowned by the strains of Carmina Burana. He lifted her dressing gown, as she was loading the dishwasher, to reveal her ample white behind. 'Percy's ready,' he said.

Arlene jumped, startled, just as Jack was about to enter her from the back. 'Jack, we've just made love,' she said. Had he forgotten? Even if his mind had, his body surely hadn't? He was stark naked and she saw Percy was standing like a soldier on duty ready to salute royalty. Her vagina was sore from the previous encounter. Could she persuade him to go back to bed? No, he had to be satisfied somehow. She could never refuse him anything. She would have to use her mouth. Her knees wouldn't cope with kneeling on the kitchen tiles, so she manoeuvred him into the sitting room. The curtains were wide open and she rushed to pull the cord in case the neighbours were looking. As she did so Jack fell onto her, knocking over the television.

She got him to sit on the settee and kneeled in front of him, put her lips round Percy and moving her head up and down eventually made him come. She suppressed her gagging reflex but withdrew before he spurted, hoping her new cream sofa would not be affected. Well if sperm did stain, it was at least the right colour.

Perhaps he would now go to sleep, but to be on the safe side she decided to give him the other half tablet. He had become docile after Paula had medicated him when they were at Dave's. She went into the kitchen and dissolved it in some water. 'Jack, take this,' she said. 'It'll help you sleep.' He was happy to oblige and he lay back on the sofa. Arlene went upstairs for a pillow and duvet. She continued to clear up, and then tried to resurrect the television. Jack was still lying down but awake. 'Don't tie me up,' he said.

'Of course not, I've locked the door. Anyway, you don't want to go anywhere tonight do you? You must be exhausted. I'm sure Percy is!' That reminder seemed to trigger something in Jack and he pulled off the duvet to reveal himself. Percy was literally up for it again. 'No Jack, not a third time. I can't … I really can't.' She wished there were the equivalent of vibrators for men but presumably that was what a man's hand is for? 'You'll have to do it yourself.' He looked puzzled, but he must still know how to masturbate. That's an instinct, though she knew it hadn't been for her. Or at least behaviour learned at an early age - so not forgotten quickly; but so was tying laces and he'd forgotten how to do that!

'You'll have to wank,' she screamed. As she placed his hand around Percy, Jack grasped both the concept and his appendage. Thank God. Arlene turned away and decided to go to the other bedroom to sleep, hopefully on her own.

Chapter 15

The Wife's Revenge – Part 1

Paula couldn't stop thinking about her plan. So many things could go wrong. She looked at herself in the long mirror in her bedroom. She turned sideways. She decided to take off all her clothes and see what a man would see. She shut the curtains but it was still quite bright. At least it would be darker than this but not much. Her breasts were small so at least they didn't sag but her chest bone looked concave, hollow and her legs were painfully thin. Jack had always complained she was too skinny and she'd longed for bigger boobs when she was younger. Thought that might have kept Jack with her. But she was still as nature had made her, never being brave enough to contemplate plastic surgery. And she was so pale. She could do something about that but having scrutinized her body it might take her a while to look her best.

While Jack was staying with Arlene, she would begin her preparations. She knew what to wear on the outside, she had no problem there, but underneath was different. She hadn't been naked in front of a man, even Jack, for many years. She had always looked better with her clothes on. She was sure that Hot Rod would be put off by her scrawny arms, incipient varicose veins and wrinkled neck. But she knew that he only wanted one thing and if he could get that he wouldn't complain. She needed to keep him at bay long enough for her plan to work.

She hastily dressed and made her way to the beauty salon. She went there a lot. Facials relaxed her and today she had made an appointment to have her legs waxed.

'Going away, are you, Mrs New? You don't usually bother in the winter,' said Sharon.

'Oh, yes,' replied Paula.

'Anywhere nice?'

'Barbados.' It was the only warm place she could think of quickly. Jack had whisked her away there on their honeymoon. They stayed in an all-inclusive resort on a white coral beach. She'd been so excited about going to the Caribbean for the first time. Her friends and relatives were green with envy. She stayed in the shade a lot, looking pale and mysterious under a large cream hat and brightly patterned turquoise sarong. Jack acquired a deep tan and frolicked in the sea with the stunning local girls. She loved to watch him, waiting for the glorious warm evenings when she could emerge from under her umbrella and drink sundowners - a rum punch for him and a pina colada for her. Even then he would chat to the other guests, especially the women. She'd never been enough for him on her own.

She remembered using a Lady Shave for her legs and her bikini line. Waxing hadn't been on her radar back then.

'You'll need a Bikini Wax for the beach. Or why not go the whole hog and get a Brazilian?' said Sharon. Paula had heard of them, though she wasn't very clear what they were. She daren't ask – she'd sound so stupid and unworldly. Perhaps she was – Jack was always telling her *she wasn't the sharpest tool in the box* or some such phrase. A wax down there might make her hotter for Hot Rod so she agreed. 'I'll get Monique then – she does them.'

Paula was led into a private room and asked to remove her bottom half. It felt like she was seeing her gynaecologist or having a cervical smear, except she was given a G String to put on rather than a hospital gown. She was beginning to regret her decision to go for the extreme wax; but she'd often had her legs done so this shouldn't be very different. Monique came in and Paula was glad it wasn't Sharon who usually did her legs. Somehow it seemed easier to bare all in front of someone you didn't know. Did this auger well for Hot Rod? After all, he was practically a stranger.

'I'm just going to trim you first', she said and she snipped away at Paula's pubes. 'Can you do a frog for me?' Paula gave her a puzzled look. 'Oh, is it your first time? I mean splay your legs. I know – we'll do one leg at a time. Don't usually have more mature clients.' She got Paula to put one foot onto her knee and she sprinkled her inner thigh with talcum powder.

'What's that for?' asked Paula to cover her embarrassment. She avoided looking at her own private parts. This morning was probably the first time she'd looked at herself completely starkers – well, since forever. She'd never been one for having the light on in the bedroom. She hadn't really wanted to look at Jack after the first initial curious peek.

'It makes it less painful. Didn't Sharon tell you it hurts? No worse than the dentist though, or having a baby. Not that I'd know about that. Just going on what my ladies say.' Paula had a caesarean with James. *Too posh to push,* as her mother had said later, when that phrase had been invented so Paula was also ignorant of the pain of childbirth. Monique continued, putting a wooden spatula into a pot of hot wax and spread it oozing and dripping onto Paula's crotch like putting honey or golden syrup onto soft white Mother's Pride. This felt quite nice, not too hot, but gently warming. She put some cloth onto the wax and pressed firmly. All the untidy pubic hairs were caught up into the wax strip and Monique gave a sharp tug. Paula emitted a piercing scream through her gritted teeth as the little follicles were stretched and the hairs dragged out by their roots. Her flesh smarted and stung. Talk about a burning bush!

'Sorry, soon be over,' said Monique as she continued administering wax strips until Paula's pubes were just one straight neat line. 'Do you want them dyed? Though yours have stayed quite ginger haven't they?'

'Auburn, yes.'

'Or I could do a heart for you. Some girls like that.'

'No thank you.' She was about to get up and thankfully closed her legs.

'I haven't done your crack yet,' said Monique.

'Sorry? What did you say?' Paula asked sharply.

'Your backside.'

'I haven't got any hairs there,' she said, with her lip curled upwards, in a grimace of disgust.

'Oh you'd be surprised. Some people have quite a forest. Turn over I'll have a look.' She pulled back the thong with a twang and pulled Paula's buttocks apart. 'Sorry, just a few. Do you want me to do them? It's not as painful as the front.'

Paula had googled *rimming,* a common interest of Mrs Robinson's men, so she agreed. At last she was fully waxed. Hot Rod had better be worth this pain.

As she was getting dressed, Monique called after her, 'I forgot to tell you, we've got a vajazzle on special offer. It wouldn't take long.'

'No thank you.' Paula had no idea what it was but was sure it would hurt.

Next the all-over tan. As she was planning to expose her whole body after years of covering it up, she would go for the bronzed look.

The tanning assistant recited her colour choices in a monotone. 'You can have the Golden Kiss, Blonde Bombshell, Caramel, Decadent Dark, Basic Bronze or Chocolate? We've got a chart here but I'd have thought you're a Golden Kiss.' It was like she was choosing paint though they didn't offer you gloss, emulsion or non-drip. She chose as she was advised and the bored assistant gave her a hairnet and demonstrated how to use the booth.

Barrier cream was applied to the hands and feet. 'You don't want orange palms,' she was told. Paula thought she didn't want an orange body either but decided to go through with it and hope she only came out golden. 'If you want an all over, take your clothes off, or you can leave on your bra and knickers. It does wash out.'

Paula decided on the Full Monty and cautiously entered the booth. A disembodied computerised voice with an American accent gave her instructions. It was like having a female Stephen Hawking in with her. She was relieved it talked, as she had left her reading glasses in her handbag and didn't want to come out Decadent Chocolate or whatever. She pressed the green knob as told and a cold film squirted out. She screamed as it hit the recently exposed area around her Mount of Venus. She posed to get all her limbs covered and turned around for her back. Eventually it stopped and, after some more knob pressing, she was being dried. It felt a bit like the Dyson machines in the Ladies in Debenhams.

She emerged, transformed into a Californian beach babe. Well perhaps not quite that, but a lot better. She hoped she didn't look like those awful women from Essex or Liverpool. No, it was quite subtle. The lingering fake tan smell would fade before this evening - she was sure. But her body felt sticky as she struggled back into her clothes.

Paula looked calm and refreshed when she opened the door to Arlene and Jack later that day. They would have no idea what she'd been up to or what she planned. She was casually dressed, for Paula, in her designer jeans and a pink cashmere sweater. 'Goodness, you look a bit exhausted. I hope he didn't keep you up all night.'

'Well, he was a bit restless. Are you sure those pills you gave me were tranquilisers? They seemed to make him rather lively.'

'They're the ones the doctor gave me. They don't always work. Jack seems quite well though.' Jack walked into the sitting room and sat on his usual chair.

'Yes, he's forgotten what happened last night. But I do think you should check out those tablets. They had a strange effect on him.'

'I'll see the GP soon for his check-up. I'll ask for something stronger.'

'That's not quite what I meant.'

'Anyway, I can't stand here talking all evening. I'm sure you have better things to do. But I must thank you for having him and oh, by the way, I had a word with my son and he's going to write to you about the money.'

That should shut her up about the tablets. They must have worked. Well that's what mistresses are for - aren't they? Perhaps it would have been better in a four poster.

'Thank you,' said Arlene, 'he's eaten a big lunch so he probably won't be hungry.'

Paula just nodded and shut the door, while checking her phone, to see Rod's latest text, *Lusting after your luscious body. See u later xx.* That wouldn't be how she would describe it but she was feeling a lot more confident than earlier. She heard Jack call out.

'Shall I put the television on for you? There's motor racing I think,' she replied. He still enjoyed watching sport and was pleased to sit while Paula got him a whisky, laced with a tranquiliser. The other pill was for later.

She went upstairs and admired her golden tan in the full-length mirror while deciding on her underwear. She did have a new red bra and knickers from Janet Reger. But red has connotations. The scarlet woman, red light district and, of course, danger. No, it would have to be black. She took out her padded bra with the lace trim and the see-through silk French knickers. She had considered buying a thong but they looked like they would get stuck in her *crack* as the beautician had delicately referred to it.

She decided on a slinky black dress, which hugged her hips but could be taken off easily. It had the advantage of not creasing as she couldn't imagine she would have time to hang it up or fold it with Hot Rod around. It had slits in the sides to show off her now brown or, rather, golden shapely legs. She didn't look too bad at all. She carefully applied her make up and went downstairs.

She dimmed all the lights until Jack complained he couldn't see. Now was the time to get Jack upstairs. He was getting drowsy but not so bad that he couldn't walk, or she would never manage to put him to bed

She tried her persuasive approach and for once it worked. 'Let me take you up to your room, you can sit in your massage chair for a bit, it'll soothe your back.' She helped Jack upstairs and sat him in his chair. It vibrated slightly and Jack enjoyed sitting in it, looking out of the window into the garden, listening to music or the birds. 'I'll get you another whisky,' she said. It was time for the other pill and she put the Viagra into his drink. Jack sipped it slowly. Paula hoped it wouldn't stop him falling asleep.

Paula brought up some strong twine that her gardener used for the runner beans. She needed something tougher than her silk scarf this time. She wasn't just going to the hairdresser's. He was pretty drowsy so didn't complain when she tied his wrists to the chair and rotated it round so that it faced the picture on the wall. She took down the Pollock to reveal the mirror. She put on Classic FM very loudly. Everything was ready except her mind.

Chapter 16

The Toy-boy

'Rodney,' his mother shouted, 'Will you be wanting tea tonight?'
'No, Mum, I'm going out'.
'Good, then I'll do faggots for your Dad. I know you don't like them.'
Rod couldn't believe his mother had said that; but then women of her age didn't - how old was his mum? Not much older than Paula.
Rod had come across faggots when he was working out his sexuality. He'd got married, had a kid, so he knew he preferred women. Though he never had much luck with them and it hadn't improved since his wife left. He was sure they didn't fancy him because he was short. He'd been bullied at school and called a Hobbit. Hated school. Left as soon as he could. But he still got wound up about his size - well not his size. That was fine. But his height. He liked to meet women when he was sitting down so it was good that Paula walked over to him. He wished they'd talked more before he'd got up to buy them a drink. But he'd needed more alcohol to give him Dutch courage. He'd gone on Mrs Robinson as he thought older women might want a fling. He didn't want to get tied down again. His wife had cleaned him out. She'd got the house he'd bought and he was still paying the mortgage. Couldn't afford to rent anything, not in London. Had to move back to his mum and dad's.
She'd even told people about their sex life and now his mates shunned him and their wives called him a *perv*. Still, Paula might be into that sort of thing. Posh women often were, or so he'd heard. And she was in pretty good shape for her age.

He showered, shaved and trimmed his pubes. He'd once been told that he was back in the seventies down there. Though he wasn't sure what that meant, he knew it wasn't a compliment! He was quite a hairy man and lots of women were turned on by his manly chest. But his lower half did tend to be a bit wild. He'd read how to manage it on the internet so he pruned his ragged bush!

He put on his Paul Smith shirt and Levis – a casual look, but classy. Paula was an upmarket bird so he had to look the part. He decided to clean his shoes – older women often look for that sort of thing. Though he didn't intend to keep them, or anything else, on for long. He cleaned his teeth, remembered the mouthwash and slapped on the *Old Spice* Aunty Phyllis had given him for Christmas. Not trendy but he figured it might bring back memories for Paula.

Now he had to get his things ready but what could he carry them in? He didn't want to take his rucksack, made him look like a teenager. Nor a suitcase, it would look like he was staying for a week - and eventually decided on the sports bag he used for the gym.

'Ooh you look nice,' said his mother. 'Sure you don't want any tea? I could do you a nice chop. Have you got a date?'

'No, Mum, I'm just seeing some friends and we'll have a burger or something.' Paula had texted him to say she had a meal for him. That was a surprise, he thought he'd have to take her out. He'd need to get a bottle of wine and perhaps some flowers.

'You're not going to the gym are you?'

'No, I might stay over at Jake's – just taking my sleeping bag.'

'Ok, then I won't worry if you're not back.'

'Don't ring me.' His mother had the habit of embarrassing him with several calls in the middle of his nights out.

He put on his leather coat and left for the train. He wasn't sure what he would talk to Paula about when they were alone. It had been easy at the theatre with all the other people to comment on, and he'd had a bit to drink, always helped relax him. But he didn't want to be too relaxed tonight – might affect his performance! They probably didn't have much in common. He picked up a *Metro* to see if there was anything interesting or amusing he could try to remember and bring up in conversation. It was full of murders and rapes, not the best topics. He doubted she was interested in sport and she may not keep up with the soaps or pop star gossip. He was becoming nervous, and tried to stave off one of his panic attacks. He breathed deeply and calmed himself by thinking how he could let her take the lead. Mature women often liked to be dominant and then that might continue in the bedroom.

When he got to Richmond he realised that he hadn't got wine or flowers. Thankfully there was a supermarket open. He was in luck, the flowers were reduced and there was a special offer on Asti Spumante. He purchased a faded bunch of red roses and a bottle of *dolce* sparkling wine.

He couldn't find Paula's house but when he did he let out a gasp. Bet this is worth a few bob. Her husband must have done well. Must have got a good settlement in the divorce, like his Julie. Women always do well out of marriage.

Paula came to the door. She looked pretty damn sexy. He could feel his throat constricting, not another panic attack. He breathed deeply and began to relax.

'You look fantastic,' he said, and kissed her on both cheeks, continental style. Rod thought she looked pleased with the flowers and wine; but he was over-awed by the beautiful furnishings and stylish design of her house. 'Shall I take my shoes off?' he asked politely as he noticed she was in bare feet. He realised he had already trailed dirt onto her beige carpet and felt like a naughty child. 'Sorry,' he said, indicating the mud, 'You'll have to give me a smacked bottom for that.' She laughed, but he knew he should have removed his shoes. He saw she had noticed his bag. 'I've just brought a few things to show you, but they're for later,' giving her a meaningful wink.

'I'll put your Asti in the fridge,' she said. 'I've got a cold, dry one to start with.'

'Well I'm sure I can hot it up.' Rod noticed her grimace, but in his experience women often pretend not to enjoy sexy remarks, while it got them excited inside. He decided not to add *and make it wet*, which had been on the tip of his tongue. Rod was anticipating a good evening and couldn't wait to get Paula into the bedroom. He was sure that is what she wanted too, why else had she invited him over and worn that sexy number? Split up to her fanny? He couldn't disappoint her could he?

'I've sent out for an Indian – is that OK?'

'Yes, I've always liked threesomes. Sorry, couldn't resist, the old ones are always the best.' He almost said *especially in women*, but realised that might not go down well.

'I love Indian food,' he clarified, and Paula poured them both some Prosecco. She sat next to him on the sofa and he moved closer towards her.

'Olive?' she asked and Rod took one. He hated them but ate it to appear more sophisticated. 'Or I've got some nuts if you prefer.'

'I thought I was the only one with nuts, sorry, no olives are fine.' His jokes always went downhill when he had sex in the front of his mind. He must calm down and take things more slowly. However, his hands seemed to have a will of their own, as they began to work their way up Paula's legs and start to caress her inner thighs. She did not resist so he nuzzled her ear. She liked that last time. He pulled her face towards him, placed his lips against hers and pushed his tongue into her mouth. Just as Rod was beginning the full French, he heard a car draw up.

'Saved by the bell,' he joked. The take away delivery man was at the door. She took the food into the kitchen. Rod followed her in and saw the table was laid and candles lit in the centre.

'Shall I dish you some out?' she asked, heaping rice, chicken tika masala and aloo gobi onto her square white plates. 'I've bought you some Tiger beer,' she said, pouring him a glass.

'You know how to treat a man,' he said, hoping the food would restrain his desire and subdue his overactive loins for a little while. The smell of the curry had made him hungry for food as well as sex. Rod shovelled his food in, while Paula only picked at her small portion. 'Not hungry, or do you want to leave it until later?' he asked. 'You haven't shown me the rest of your house yet.'

Rod heard a shout which seemed to come from upstairs. Paula frowned. 'It's only the TV upstairs. I must have left it on. I'll turn it off. Why don't you go into the sitting room and put on some music? I've got loads of CDs. Pick something you like.'

Rod chose an Ella Fitzgerald album. He thought she would like that and her husky voice might put Paula in the mood. It must have been the right choice, as when Paula came down she increased the volume.

'Can I use the bathroom?' he said, as he realised he needed to get his equipment upstairs before they got down to anything. She showed him the downstairs toilet but he managed to get his bag and creep upstairs while she cleared some of the Indian. He opened one door and saw a large king size bed with voluminous pillows and a frilly valance. This must be her room so he deposited his bag in the corner. There was some music coming from the next room – some classical stuff. He would play some of his favourites later. But something else too. He could hear a sound like a low moaning. It wasn't the telly. He tried the door of the next room and came face to face with an old bloke sleeping in a chair. Bloody hell – he was tied to it. He hastily shut the door. Then opened it a crack and peeped in to check if he'd imagined it. He could hear the man snoring so he must be alive. Was she into threesomes? Maybe she'd wake him up later to join in.

But then his chest began to tighten, perhaps she was the black widow or a praying mantis who killed her mate, just as they were copulating - or was it after? He couldn't remember. His heart started to pound and his breathing quickened. He tried to slow it down and breathe more deeply.

'I've got some ice cream for pudding but only vanilla,' came a shout from downstairs.

This calmed him. He was nobody's prey. It was going to be a good night.

'No thanks, I'm not partial to vanilla. And I can see you're not,' he replied.

Chapter 17

The Wife's Revenge –art 2

Paula didn't quite hear Rod's reply and she was beginning to get cold feet about the whole thing. How could she ever have thought he was witty, like Jack had been? And bringing half dead flowers and worst of all sweet cheap fizz!

Still he wasn't here for his personality or her pleasure. She didn't expect to enjoy it – at least not in a physical sense. At least she had plenty of KY Jelly.

When Paula realised he had gone upstairs she became concerned he would discover her secret, like Mr Rochester's mad wife in the attic. She thought the best thing was to join him and take him to her bedroom. More alcohol first though. She took up a bottle of red and two large wine glasses and stopped him as he was coming down the stairs. 'Why don't you go back, and I'll come up.'

Rod smiled. 'Which room?' he asked.

She indicated her bedroom and while Rod went in, she locked Jack's door, just in case. This made her feel braver- she could do it. As soon as she entered her room, she lay on her bed and pulled Rod on top of her. She ground her knee into his groin and rubbed herself against him. It was a long time since she'd touched a man *down there*, but he should have been aroused by now. He might need more titillating. She should have given him a few of the pills. She began to unbutton his shirt. She made sure she positioned herself so that she could be seen in the mirror.

'Shall I turn the lights off?' he asked.

'Well actually I prefer them on,' she said. 'I like to see us doing it in the mirror.' She continued to divest him of his shirt and Levis. Eventually he was down to his pale blue Calvin Kleins. He grabbed her wrists and stopped her undressing him further. Not that she was going to anyway. She wondered if she'd been too eager, but he was Hot Rod after all, much more used to this sort of thing than her.

He got up and went over to his bag. He took out a black latex skirt and military jacket.

'Would you mind slipping these on?' he asked.

Goodness he must be into role playing – this might be more fun than she had thought.

She heard a groan. 'Would you put some music on?' she said. 'I think I'll try these on in the bathroom.' She went to check on Jack, but he seemed to be dozing in the chair. She shook him roughly.

She went into the bathroom and tried on the tight black skirt made of shiny black material. It only just covered her bum. Jack had tried to get her to indulge in fantasy games, like doctors and nurses, when they had first married. She had of course refused, the whole idea of it had embarrassed, even disgusted her. She smiled as she looked in the mirror at herself in the tight jacket. It had epaulets with large silver buttons on the shoulders; long zips went up each sleeve and diagonally across her chest. Her waist was clinched in by a large belt with a huge silver buckle.

When she returned to the bedroom she saw Rod had also transformed himself. He was wearing a black leather collar with large silver studs. His hairy chest and colourful tattoos were fully displayed. One looked like a large golden eagle and he was wearing some tight black leather shorts, with braces.

She gasped though the sound was drowned by the loud classical music that was coming from somewhere - was it Rod's phone? She wasn't sure what it was playing or how. Jack had been the classics fan – she preferred Radio 2. It was stirring rather than romantic, but it would certainly drown out any extraneous noises and keep Jack awake. Thank goodness she lived in a detached house.

'Fantastic Frau Viplash,' Rod said which confused Paula. He held up a pair of black leather boots which laced up the front. They had extremely high heels and Paula wondered if she was to wear them or him? If she did, their height difference would be huge!

'I vill try zem on you? Please sit here,' and he indicated some cushions he had placed on the floor in front of him. Paula sat on the floor and he pulled her legs onto his lap. She was glad she'd been going to the gym but knew she couldn't keep up this position for long. He kissed her toes, licking and sucking each one and making a loud slurping noise. She hoped her tan wouldn't come off on his tongue. He took the boots and slipped them on her feet, and laced up the fronts. Thankfully they fitted, though Paula was no Cinderella or Rod, Prince Charming.

'Can I get up now?' she asked.

'Just a moment,' he said, and produced a peaked hat and two swastikas with Velcro on the back which he attached to each arm. Of course the music is Wagner and that's why he's putting on that silly accent. Well, if Prince Harry can do it! He helped her up and she decided to look at herself fully in the mirror. What would Jack think? She hoped he could see her through his *mirror.*

'You're into S & M?' Rod said, suddenly out of character. 'I know you like tying people up,' he said. Paula went pale under her golden kiss tan. 'Vill you tie me up?

Paula was astounded. This was better than she thought. If she was in control she might not need the Brazilian after all. He handed her a pair of handcuffs and what looked like a riding crop. He then lay on his back; his arms spread eagled, waiting expectantly for Paula to attach his wrists to the bedstead. When Rod turned over, Paula saw his lederhosen had a large circular opening, which now framed his pink buttocks. She took the handcuffs and clipped his wrists to the bed very efficiently, as if she'd been a jailer in another life.

'Please Frau Viplash,' he continued. His German accent reverted to South London when the words contained no w's to change to v's. 'I deserve to be punished. I need a good thrashing.'

Paula decided to enter into the spirit of it. She was having a spring awakening in the autumn of her years. 'Ya,' she said. 'You have been a very bad boy. I vill spank you until you beg for mercy.'

'Ya, but my legs zey need to be tied or I could kick you. I forgot – zee equipment is in my bag. I beg you to get it.' Paula got up, displaying herself in the mirror, as she retrieved the leather ankle cuffs from his bottomless bag. They were like small belts with brass chains as if chosen to match her bedstead. She fastened them around his ankles and hooked the chains onto the brass poles on the footboard. They were rather tight but Rod seemed to groan with pleasure rather than pain.

As he lay on his front, arms and legs outstretched, Paula thought she must be in a play. She'd always been good at amateur dramatics, a leading light in her school theatre club. She raised the crop, bending over so her naked buttocks were visible in the mirror behind her. She flicked her wrist and struck his bare behind with the twelve leather tails.

He cried out and she whacked him again and again, harder and harder, enjoying the sound of the leather against bare flesh. 'Please, no more, no more,' shouted Rod. But this was all in the fantasy game, wasn't it? He really wanted more. The German accent had disappeared so she stopped and looked at his bottom. The red welts were only too real.

She felt a warm tingly feeling in her groin. 'My pussy is vet,' she said. 'I vant you to stroke her. I vill untie you, so that you can turn over.' Rod lay still as she undid his shackles turned him over and then moaned ecstatically as she restrained him once again. 'If you do not satisfy me, I von't spank you again.' She looked at his shorts, but there was no customary bulge. Were they too tight? Should she loosen them to allow his thingy to come up for air?

'I think I deserve to have my collar tightened,' he said. She examined the spiked collar around his neck – it looked pretty snug. Surely she would strangle him? She yanked it one more notch and then undid the belt on his lederhosen, which seemed to be holding his desire in check. She didn't want a dead Rod on her hands; though a stiff one might come in useful.

Suddenly the music stopped and she heard Jack shouting from next door. Rod did not seem in the least surprised. 'Iz zat your uzzer prisoner?' he asked. 'I sink vee should bring him in to join zee fun.'

'Ya, you may be right,' replied Paula. 'Vait a moment – I vill get him myself.' As Rod was still shackled to the bed he couldn't really help her.

Paula unlocked Jack's room and he started shouting, 'You've got a man in there. I can see you.' He looked at Paula's clothes and saw the swastikas. 'My God Paula, I know you're right wing, but not - what do you call them - National Front.'

119

She ignored him, got one of her silk scarves and tied it around his mouth. She looked at his trousers, yes, he was definitely aroused. She would frustrate him a little longer. She pushed the chair on its castors into her room and positioned him with Rod in full view. The sight of a young man shackled to the bed in lederhosen silenced Jack more than the Gucci scarf but his eyes blazed with fury as well as astonishment.

'He vill just vatch us,' said Frau Viplash. 'Zat is his punishment.' Rod looked at Jack tied to his chair and laughed. Paula supposed he was used to this sort of thing. She could dim the lights as she didn't need the two-way mirror anymore. She had not enjoyed the harsh lighting at the start but by now she was past worrying about her body.

Paula decided to use the leather tails in a different way. She swung her crop between the two men, tickling and teasing their cocks. Jack was already erect and, as if competing with the older stud, Rod's followed suit.

'You vill undo me with your teeth,' she said and lowered herself over Rod so his mouth could reach the zip across her chest. My God she was getting into the swing of things now. She flashed her breasts at Jack. It must be a while since he'd seen those - let alone touched them. Not that she was going to let him do that tonight. He'd always preferred Arlene's more ample ones anyway. She undid Rod's shorts and looked at his gigantic thingie. She didn't want that inside her, she decided, despite or perhaps because of all those pelvic floor exercises. She looked at his mouth, his tongue was hanging out and he was licking his lips.

She positioned herself so she could see Jack and, displaying her Brazilian, sat on Rod's face. 'Ya, zat is good,' she said. 'Make my pussy purr.' As his long tongue darted in and out she watched Jack, his face becoming redder and redder. She still had her crop and beat Rod harder and harder across the chest, as he licked her. She began to moan softly, then a little louder, eventually reaching a crescendo. Her body shook and shudders ran deep inside her, making her wail like a stray Tom rather than a female pussy.

As she screeched her arms flayed wildly and her crop hit Rod which made him come, like spontaneous combustion, the milky fluid spurting out, running down his black shorts and onto her clean silk sheets.

She looked over to Jack but saw he had slumped in his chair. Had his heart given out? She began to get worried, climbed off the bed and tottered over to him. She hastily removed the silk gag. He opened his eyes and looked pleadingly at her. 'Please Paula, help Percy.'

Paula had no idea what he was talking about. She looked at him, an old confused man, so different from the philandering Jack, the controlling dominant man he had been. She started to feel sorry for him but then hardened her heart. Jack had only been watching her doing the same sort of things he must have been doing over forty years of marriage. She had sat at home alone while he had been having it off with any slutty secretary or shop girl and, of course, Arlene. She smiled and with her skirt rucked up and her jacket undone, she wheeled him back to his bedroom, still wearing her sexy Jack boots and cap.

'Heil Hitler,' said Rod as she returned to her room. With a withering look she unshackled him, packed up the costumes and equipment and dispatched him home. She changed her sheets and went to bed.

Chapter 18

The Help

Mary had her own key, so let herself into the house. She couldn't hear anything but the car was there, so they must be in. 'It's only me,' she shouted upstairs and started making herself her customary cup of tea. 'Can I get you or Jack a cuppa?' she called, louder this time.

She heard Paula shouting from upstairs. It sounded like she was still in bed. That was unusual. She was usually up and about. 'Thanks Mary. We've both slept in this morning, I'm afraid. Jack'll have a tea but I'll just have hot water and lemon.'

Paula came downstairs in her silk Chinese dressing gown.

'I heard what happened. Jenny told me.'

'What do you mean what happened?' asked Paula.

'She'd seen your James. I can't believe Jack was wandering around all night. How is he?'

'Oh, yes, that seems a while ago now but I haven't seen you, have I? Yes, he's fine. But how's Jenny? She must be due soon?'

'She's fine, blooming you know,' replied Mary. Mary knew that it was James or his friend's baby and was dying to tell Paula that they would both soon be grandmas. She didn't approve of this surrogacy thing but, if Jenny gave it to James, then she might get to see her grandchild. Not like all the others. 'You look well, though, Paula; is that a tan you've got?'

'I do hope she goes full term this time; she's had so many miscarriages and still births. I've never known anyone have so many,' continued Paula.

Mary looked at Paula, wondering if she knew something. She'd not usually been that interested in Jenny. It would have been better not to tell her she was pregnant but she couldn't resist and what if Paula was to see her? She could hardly explain Jenny's weight gain by her missing a few Slimming World classes. 'Oh I think she will this time,' Mary's voice was confident.

'How come Jenny saw James? They don't exactly mix in the same circles. I mean surely Jenny isn't out much now, with her being so far gone?'

Mary knew she shouldn't have said they'd met up. 'Not sure. I think Jenny were up in town – has to go up to St Thomas's for check-ups you know - after all them problems she's had.'

'But I had lunch with him last Sunday. He didn't say anything. Anyway, do give Jenny my love.'

'Oh yes, I will. I'll just get Jack that tea. The kettle's boiled for your lemon what not.'

Mary almost ran upstairs. Paula must know something. Give Jenny her love indeed!

She found Jack in his pyjamas, sitting on the edge of his bed, staring at the large picture on the wall. That was new. Paula must have just bought it, probably cost a fortune. Mary wasn't keen on all those swirls. She preferred a proper painting that looked like something. 'Do you like that picture?' she asked him.

'No,' he said, 'Take it down.'

Mary would have liked to but Paula'd only just had it put up.

'We'll have a word with Paula,' she replied. 'I've brought you a nice cup of tea. Two sugars, just as you like it.' She put the tea down on the bedside table, but as she bent over he grabbed at her sizeable rump and squeezed her bottom hard. She jumped up, spilling the hot tea over the carpet and the sheets. When she turned around he lunged at her and grabbed her breast. Mary screamed and pushed him down onto the bed.

Paula rushed upstairs. She must have heard. Mary wouldn't have mentioned it otherwise. She didn't want to get Jack into trouble.

'What on earth is going on?' Paula asked.

'I think Jack's got a bit over excited,' said Mary. 'He sort of touched me up. It's okay though. He doesn't know what he's doing. He probably thought I were you.'

'I hardly think so. I mean, I'm sure he got confused.'

Mary was used to Paula and rarely took offence. 'I think some of that hot tea went on his hands. I'll take him into the bathroom and run his hands under the cold tap. They say that's good for burns, though I always put a bit of butter on them with the kids.'

Paula returned to her bedroom. When she emerged she was fully dressed ready to go out.

'Are you all right to have him here while you clean? I've got a meeting. But they'll collect him for the day centre later. He'll have his lunch there.'

Mary didn't mind. She usually liked having a bit of a chat with Jack. 'Well I won't get on so fast you know.'

Mary knew that Paula wasn't that happy with her cleaning as she'd seen her wipe her finger on the top of the pictures or other hard to reach places. Paula was so particular. She only kept her on because she was good with Jack.

'And watch him in the kitchen, he tried to put the toast in the CD player the other day,' said Paula

'Okay,' said Mary.

'And don't forget to do Jack's bedroom, It may be a bit dusty after the work. And be careful with that picture. It's a Pollock print you know.' Paula shouted as she left the house.

Bollocks more like, thought Mary. 'Yes it's a mess now, not like it used to be,' she replied. Jack had been so neat and organised, but now she had to sort out the piles of clothes and papers that were strewn around. Paula must hate it, she thought. Mary fetched the duster and the all-purpose spray polish and started on Jack's room while he was in the bathroom. The new picture was at an angle and, as she straightened it, she felt the wall underneath. It was glass – the painting was covering over something. She took it down and behind it was a sort of mirror - or more like a window looking though into Paula's bedroom. How strange, perhaps Paula takes the picture down at night, so that she can see if Jack's all right. Was that the work she'd had done? She'd been a bit mysterious about that.

She was tempted to go into Paula's room to see if she could see into Jack's but knew that Paula had recently had a lock fitted. Jack had been wandering in at night and disturbing her. It had seemed a bit cruel, but then she didn't have him twenty-four- seven, so who was she to judge? Anyway, the door was locked. Recently Paula had wanted to do her own room.

Jack returned to the bedroom as Mary was putting the picture back. 'I don't want it in here.' He was distressed and repeated, 'I don't want it here,' several times.

'It's okay Jack. It's just so Paula can see you're all right.' This seemed to make him more unhappy, so Mary led him downstairs and put on a CD of Englebert Humperdinck. 'I've put on some music. You like that, don't you?' Music calmed him. 'I'll make you some more tea before the day centre people come,' she said and went into the kitchen.

Mary decided to phone Jenny, while the kettle boiled, to tell her how odd Paula was that morning. 'She wouldn't say anything and seemed a bit suspicious about you seeing James.'

'Don't you go and tell her anything about you know what.'

'No but I'm sure she knows something. Do you think James has told her it's yours?'

Jenny was sure he hadn't.

'Well I don't think she'll like sharing a grandchild with me. But how am I going to keep it to myself if she brings it here when I'm cleaning?' Mary knew that would be impossible for her and suspected Jenny knew that as well.

'Well at least leave it until she's accepted it, and then she won't reject it, even if she finds out it's the local lap dancer's eggs.'

For a moment Mary could only think of chickens or boxes of free range, until she realised what Jenny was talking about. She didn't like to think of babies as the combination of sperm and an egg. 'Well I hope that's the last one of these you'll do,' she said.

'I only did this because I knew them and they said I didn't have to have those syringes.' She stopped suddenly.

'How did you do it then?'

'Well, as nature intended.'

Mary frowned, 'Oh. I thought they were, well, you know.'

'Gay? Yes they are, but it doesn't mean they can't do it.'

'I know that. I just thought they may not want a woman.'

'Well they both seemed all right. Perhaps they both got it up and thought of England.'

Mary laughed but was uncomfortable about the idea of her daughter *doing it* with two men in quick succession, especially when one was Paula's son. Mind she'd been a one when she was young until she fell pregnant with Jenny. She'd been a bit of a hippy too but it had been trendy back then. She couldn't understand Jenny's new age ways or whatever you called them. 'So you slept with both of them? You won't know which one's it is then?'

'Well no, not yet anyway. I suppose they may get a DNA test sometime.'

'So I may be the only real granny out of Paula and me,' she sounded delighted, but at the same time full of trepidation. 'Does Paula know?'

'She thinks it's James'. Don't tell her anything different. In fact, don't say anything at all.'

'No - mum's the word.' She laughed at her little joke, but felt anything but cheerful. Paula would be so cross if she knew.

She realised Jack had come into the room, still in his vest and pants, and wondered how long he'd been there and how much he'd understood. 'They'll be coming for you soon,' she said.

Jack looked puzzled. 'Who,' he asked, 'the Germans?'

'No, Jack, the war's long over. The Greenway Centre people. You know they give you a nice lunch. Didn't you say they're putting on a tea dance for you as well today?' This cheered Jack up, and he took Mary in his arms and waltzed her around the room just as Englebert was singing:

'I had the last waltz with you
Two lonely people together,
I fell in love with you
The last waltz should last for ever.'

He continued until Mary pulled herself away and sat down. 'Come on, you'll have to get dressed. You can't go to a dance like that.' He was still holding her hand and she looked at his wrists. What were those marks on them? 'How did you do this?' she asked, as she looked at the red and purple bruising.

'Cuffs,' he said.

'Is your shirt too small for you?' She knew old people bruised easily but surely that couldn't be the cause?

She went to fetch a shirt and helped him put it on. The cuffs seemed to button up easily. She thought she would ask at the Day Centre but then wondered if they were tying him up there. She'd read about these homes and places that didn't look after old people properly. She'd have to talk to Paula.

'Well Mary – I'll say goodbye. Can you see my clubs?' asked Jack suddenly, still in his y-fronts.

'Where are you going? You'll not need them at the Greenway.'

'No - I don't think I'm playing golf today. But I've still got my swing you know.'

'You'll need to get dressed first,' she said.

By the time the bell rang and the care assistant was at the door to collect Jack, he was ready and they had no problem getting him into the minibus.

Mary returned inside and began to ponder on Jack's bruises as she made herself a weak instant coffee. She cleaned for Sally as well, who used to be quite high up in Social Services and decided to ring her for advice. 'It's only me, Mary, it's all right I can still come next week. I just want to ask you something.' She proceeded to outline the situation.

'Well,' said Sally. 'It could be serious. It may even be Paula that's causing the bruising. I think you should get the authorities to investigate.'

'What? I should report Paula? But I wouldn't want Paula to know it was me that was worried. I'm sure she isn't hurting him.'

'Do you want me to report it? I promise I won't say I got it from you. Just that it was an anonymous source. I know the person in charge of elder abuse.' Sally's voice was calm and reassuring but worried thoughts whirred around Mary's brain. Paula would know it was her. Who else could it be? Paula would sack her. Her grandchild being at Paula's and her not there to clean and help with it was too awful to think about.

'You have to tell someone or let me,' repeated Sally.

'What will they do?'

'Send someone round to investigate. They won't put Paula in jail or anything. They'll probably offer Paula some help if they think she's struggling to care for Jack.' Sally made it all sound all right so Mary agreed. She was very fond of Jack even though she knew he'd

127

led Paula a merry dance when he was younger. He'd been a proper Jack the lad. But he'd always been nice to Mary, treated her respectfully, not like some of her other employers. He'd have a laugh and a gossip with her. Helpful too. He'd mended the vacuum cleaner and not told Paula that Mary had broken it by letting the bag get too full. She supposed she should have realised the problem when the carpet was dirtier after she'd cleaned it than it had been before. But she'd been young and had only just started charring.

Now poor Jack couldn't mend anything, couldn't do much at all. It was sad. Yet she felt Paula wasn't upset about it. She'd been more cheerful in the last few years than Mary had remembered her. As Jack became scruffy and more confused, Paula had become smarter, trendier, as if she was having a new lease of life, despite Jack being such a burden. But Sally was right, she'd have to tell someone about those bruises.

Chapter 19

The Wife and the Social Worker

As she was going upstairs to look at the internet, the doorbell rang, and she saw the image of two women through the frosted glass door. 'If you're selling something I'm not interested,' she called, opening the door slightly, but keeping the chain on.

'We're here from Social Services. You are Mrs New, aren't you? We've come about your husband,' the older one said, flashing an official looking identity card.

Social Services. What had they come about? They can't know about the other night. Paula reluctantly opened the door and ushered them into the lounge. 'Did you want to see Jack?' she asked. 'I'm afraid he's resting.'

'Could my colleague just see him? She won't disturb him. This is Jane Thomas, the community nurse, and I'm Phyllis Green, social worker with the adult team.'

'I suppose so but I really don't know why you've come. He goes to the day centre and then I pay for other help. He's fine.'

'Should I make my own way up?' asked Jane. Paula agreed - then wondered if there were any pictures of half-naked men on the open Mrs Robinson site as her door was open and the computer was in view.

Paula could see Phyllis looking around the room which contained an elegant chaise longue, a comfortable leather sofa and armchair in ivory and a spotless beige carpet. What was she thinking? 'I suppose most of your work isn't in this area is it? I mean you probably visit the council estates more, don't you?' This had somehow come out all wrong. It sounded as if she was prejudiced, so she backtracked. 'I mean they'll have more problems that you'd have to deal with.'

'I suppose they do, but you never know what goes on behind closed doors,' replied Phyllis.

Paula hoped her make-up hid the shade of white her face had become. 'Shall I make you some tea?' she asked.

'That would be lovely – both milk, no sugar.'

Paula returned with a tray on which there was a teapot and three white bone china cups and saucers, a matching sugar basin and milk jug. By this time Jane had arrived back downstairs and the two women stopped talking as Paula entered the room. 'Did you find Jack was all right? He does hallucinate at times – gets quite disturbed. He's even accused me of having affairs!' Paula's laughter sounded unconvincing even to herself.

'He didn't wake up,' Jane replied, but looked at her colleague and again Paula's heart skipped a beat.

'Did you know you are entitled to a carer's assessment in your own right?' asked Phyllis, taking out a large complicated looking form and pen.

'Carer?' repeated Paula, 'I'm not a carer, I'm his wife. I will always be his wife. Do you think it's *till dementia we do part*? Well it's not for me. That is what wives do – care for their husbands in sickness and in health. Do you have a husband?'

She looked at Phyllis's round face which was, it appeared to Paula, a make-up free zone and doubted whether she'd ever attracted a man.

'Divorced, but I do care for my elderly father so I can empathise with you.'

'I'm not sure you can,' replied Paula. That sounded defensive. She should be more conciliatory, win their sympathy.

'I do know it's hard work, but there's support out there for you, you know. How long has Jack been diagnosed with Alzheimer's?' Phyllis's lips were smiling, but Paula was suspicious.

'Well I'm not sure when he was actually diagnosed. Perhaps only a couple of years.'

'But it's often a slow build up, isn't it?' said Phyllis, in the same friendly tone, which Paula disliked more and more by the second.

She felt she should divulge some things to these officials, even if it wasn't what they wanted to know. 'Yes, he had been forgetting things for a while, glasses, keys, the usual. He's older than me so I just thought it was the aging process. But then he started losing his way. Once we were driving over to my mother's in Bristol. He always drove. Knew the way exactly, but that time he got completely lost. I hadn't been feeling too well, closed my eyes, and when I woke up I saw the Severn Bridge looming in front of me. He had seemed really confused as if he had forgotten where he was going. My mother had moved from Cardiff years before.'

'What's he like on direction now? Can he find his way around? Does he go out on his own at all?' Paula hesitated. 'Do you find that Jack wanders, Mrs New?' asked Phyllis.

'Call me Paula. I do actually. I have to be careful about locking the door now at night. He used to go to fetch *The Times* in the morning but he can't even do that now. Why are you asking?'

'We did have a report from the police about him wandering; but not from here. I thought they might have got the address wrong. They don't always get the correct information.'

Paula looked down and started fiddling with her teaspoon. That's not so bad if they're only here about the wandering. She had been worried about them finding out about that, but so much had happened since then, that was small fry. And anyway it hadn't been her fault. 'No – he was staying with an old friend. She forgot to lock the door. I called my son and he found him thankfully unharmed. But I was livid with her. I won't trust her to help out again. I always bolt the door here now.'

'Is that all you do Paula, lock the door?' asked Jane.

Paula wondered if they were playing good cop/bad cop. She hesitated. Had Mary said something? Did they mean the tranquillisers? The GP had given them to her, so they couldn't be illegal. 'Well I do have some medication to calm him down. He gets so agitated you know.'

'So that's all you use?' repeated Jane.

Before Paula could reply, good cop Phyllis came to her rescue. 'Do you mind if I ask you whether you had a good relationship with Jack before he became ill?' asked Phyllis

'What do you mean?' asked Paula.

'Well, sometimes if a man's been violent or oppressive in a marriage, as he loses his power over her, the wife may try to get her own back.'

'I really don't know what you're talking about.'

'Paula – I'm trying to help you here. My colleague has seen signs of elder abuse. His wrists are bruised as if he's been tied up. It looks as if he's been struggling to get free.'

'I'll have to stop him going to that Day Centre,' Paula knew that this wouldn't wash but couldn't think of a better story.

'We will of course investigate that possibility, but he's with about thirty other people and several staff there.'

'What about the bus home? The driver may tie him in?' She was clutching at straws while drowning in her cesspit of lies.

'I think that's highly unlikely. They do have seatbelts in the mini bus,' said Jane. 'Haven't you noticed his wrists? We would like to take him to your GP to examine him for other signs,'

'No, you can't do that. We've been with Dr Fredrick for twenty years.'

'We may have to Paula. I know how difficult it is to be a carer. Do you tie him up to give you a bit of peace? It can be so wearing. My dad follows me around all the time,' said Phyllis.

Paula started to cry. 'I'm sorry – he can be violent. He was always a difficult man but I stayed with him.'

'He used to hit you Paula, didn't he? I know how you feel. I left my husband because of domestic violence.'

She gazed directly at Phyllis. 'Yes, I thought he might stop when he was ill but he didn't. He was just more erratic. He would have dreams or hallucinations that I had been with other men. He would wake up and come into my room and sometimes pull me out. Drag me by my hair. One night I just tied him up when he was asleep. Only with string. Good knots I suppose, I was a girl guide. So that he couldn't get up in the middle of the night and attack me. He struggled though, when he did wake up. Caused those bruises and he wet the bed. I had my punishment. I haven't done it since. I've had a lock put on my door. That's really helped. Now you know. What are you going to do about it?' She burst into loud sobbing.

Jane had been silent throughout the confession; but then said, 'Paula, would you mind if I examined Jack more fully?' Paula agreed. There couldn't be any other marks on him, could there?

The three of them went up together. Jack was awake when they entered the room. 'I want to live with Arlene,' he said. 'She doesn't want me,' indicating towards Paula. 'She's got another man. A Nazi.'

'You see what I mean,' said Paula. 'Hallucinating. He gets so jealous.'

'I'm concerned for your safety Paula. Who's Arlene?' asked Phyllis.

'Well, I didn't want to tell you but he did have an affair. Long over now and the woman was called Arlene. I took him back because I loved him and for our son's sake.'

'How are you feeling Jack?' asked Jane.

'Who are you? Why are you in my house?'

'Jack, I'm a nurse'

'I didn't ask you to come. Get out.'

At least Jack was showing he could be difficult. Sometimes he can appear so charming.

'I'm so sorry. You can see what I have to put up with,' said Paula in a loud stage whisper.

'We're a bit worried about you. Can I just see your chest Jack?' asked Jane. Jack suddenly whipped off his pyjama jacket and trousers revealing his pale torso, flaccid penis and thin grey pubic hair.

'Jack, for goodness sake. The curtains are wide open,' said Paula.

'What do you care? I've seen you cavorting through my window.'

'It's OK Jack, let me help you back into your clothes,' said Jane. 'No there don't seem to be any other signs,' she added to Phyllis. 'We'll go downstairs now, Jack, and talk to Paula. Goodbye.'

'Will I be taken to court?' asked Paula when they were back sitting in the comfortable armchairs.

'We could take legal action under the Care Act, Paula, to remove Jack. But I think you have suffered enough over the years. I don't think he has the mental capacity to make decisions for himself, so if you want to go on caring for him he's probably better off here than in an institution. But as I said there's help out there for you.'

Paula tried to hide her relief. They'd believed her.

'Oh I can't thank you enough. I really am so sorry for what I did, but I was at the end of my tether. But can I ask you something? Why did you come today? Was it because of the police report or did the Day Centre notice anything? I really can't face them again if they reported me.'

'No, it wasn't them. We had two calls, both anonymous, apart from the police report.' Paula couldn't believe it. One must be Mary. But the other? Surely not Hot Rod?

'We'll have to ask the Day Centre to keep an eye on him, though, Paula. Monitor how things are going. Also I could get a carer in to help with bed times. I'm afraid there would be a charge though, I don't think you would come under our means test threshold.'

Charges were the least of Paula's worries. She had already organised Dave to come around. That might have to be the last time. She may also have to delete Mrs Robinson. 'Yes, I would appreciate that and some respite care might be good.'

'I'll see what I can do. Thank you for being so honest with us Paula. We have another appointment I'm afraid; but I'll look into respite and a care worker for you and give you a ring.'

'I would be so grateful. Thank you.' As she let them out, the tension drained from her body, though she stiffened again as she overheard Jane say something to Phyllis about not following procedure.

Chapter 20

The Surrogate

Jenny was lying back in a hot foam bath, contemplating her swollen stomach. Her normally small breasts were enlarged and blue veins were running down to her engorged nipples. The baby was still but last night it kept kicking her. She'd shown Chris how her stomach jumped when the baby moved when he came with her for check-ups. He'd become really excited, giving her a bit of enthusiasm, which she'd lost. This had to be her last one. She couldn't go through with another pregnancy. Generally she found them easy. That morning sickness which everyone talked about was nothing much and then the next few months she was usually really well. People said she was *glowing*. Even the final few weeks she'd enjoyed. But this time it was hard. She was so tired, very big and she felt like a whale, a sperm whale.

It had been a thrill to pass over the other babies; to see the couple's faces. She had pictures of all her four babies, but they didn't have any contact. Some of the parents wanted them to remain friends but she'd resisted. She'd done her job. She couldn't cope with that. Would they want to contact her when they were older? Did they even know she existed? This one was different though. The other parents had been strangers, but she had known James since she was a child. Mum often had no one to look after her and taken her to the various houses, while she was cleaning. Always a passive child, she'd been happy with her colouring book or watching the telly. James was older and she was scared of him at first. But she remembered him reading her stories or playing hide and seek in the garden, so when he asked her to have their baby she agreed to come out of retirement.

The water was getting cold. She heaved her heavy frame out of the bath and put on the fluffy robe she'd bought with some of her expenses. They'd been generous and Chris always came to the hospital with her. She was proud of her handsome husband.

The doorbell rang. It must be her friend Tessa. She said that she'd come around to watch *Mama Mia*. She was a bit like Meryl Streep with two possible fathers for her child. Though there weren't just two fathers in the film! And Meryl Streep certainly kept her daughter. Tess was very early and she shouted down. 'Wait a minute... I'm just out of the bath.' She slowly manoeuvred down the stairs. No fancy buttons to open the front door. She was surprised to see Chris standing there.

'Sorry to call round. I did text, but you didn't reply.'

'I've been in the bath. Practising for the birthing pool.' He stared and his face had a worried look. 'Joke,' she said.

'I just wanted to talk to you about something. You're the only one who knows both people.'

'Come in. It's blowing a gale out there.' She showed Chris into the narrow galley kitchen. It was difficult for her to turn in it. 'Can I get you a drink?' she asked.

'Great,' said Chris. 'You don't have any red wine, do you?'

'Sorry, dandelion beer? That's as near to alcohol as I've got.'

Chris wrinkled his nose. 'I'll have tea or whatever you're having.'

As she was making two green teas, she heard about their Sunday lunch. 'What's happening between you and your ex?'

'Nothing, we just meet up occasionally. It's just that James gets so jealous and bloody Paula let the cat out of the fucking bag. I just wanted to ask you how I should deal with Paula.'

Jenny raised her eyebrows. 'Really, I hope you two are all right. I don't want my baby going to you if you're going to split up immediately.'

'Your baby?'

'You know what I mean. The baby I'm carrying.'

Jenny had no idea how Chris should deal with Paula. She was tempted to tell him what her mum had said about Jack's bruises, though she'd been sworn to secrecy. No, she'd better not. 'I think it's hilarious. Who'd have thought – Paula with a bit of rough.' She was so patronising to her mum, though she did pay her well and gave her lots of hours. Mary had said Paula seemed cheerful recently. That must be the reason.

'Yes but James won't have anything said against her.'

'He doesn't know about the marks though,' she blurted out. She'd gone and told him. She must be getting more like Mary every day. A real blabber-mouth.

Chris looked puzzled. She explained what she knew. 'So your mum has reported it to the police?'

'No, the Social Services.'

'So what happened?'

'Nothing, really.'

'What you mean nothing?'

'My mother's friend, well, one of the ladies she cleans for, saw the report. Apparently, she admitted it.'

Chris looked confused. 'Admitted what?

'Tying him up. Chris, you're not listening'

'I am. But if she admitted tying him up, why did nothing happen?'

'Well, Mum said that they were going to give Paula more help as they didn't have anywhere to put him if they took him off her, and it would cost too much to take her to court and she'd have a fancy lawyer anyway.'

Chris's features became animated and a broad smile revealed his perfect white teeth. 'So I've got some more on her. I'll get James to see her as she really is.'

'After her saying my baby was from the Pound Shop I feel like -'

'There you go again – *my* baby,' Chris interrupted.

'She makes me so mad. And I can't bear the thought of her being cruel to old Jack.' She remembered how Jack had been kind to her as a child, not that she'd seen much of him, but when she had he'd always told her some silly joke or tickled her and made her laugh.

'Well, that I can understand. Could you imagine having him around all day, not being able to leave the house? It would be like having -'

'A baby?' Jenny suggested.

'That's not fair. They're cute, they learn and develop. For Jack, it's downhill all the way.'

'So you want him tied up or put in some sort of institution until he dies?'

'Stop putting words into my mouth. Look there's no point in us falling out. You've always hated Paula and I do as well. She certainly won't be happy when she finds out the baby's mine.'

'What do you mean *when*? I don't know whose it is.'

'Right, *if*, but I thought you said from the dates it was more likely to be mine.'

'Chris, I really don't know. We can have a test once the baby's born.' She secretly hoped it would be Chris's child, so Paula wouldn't be a granny, or at least not in the biological sense. She was sure James wouldn't mind it not being his. Chris was a different matter. 'Do you have a problem if it's James's?'

'No, of course not, it's just -' His phone sang out *YMCA*. 'Hi, yes, just getting something for dinner, see you soon.'

Jenny was glad he was going. She didn't want to quarrel with him but honestly sometimes she felt they didn't have a clue. Not that she knew what it was like to bring up a child. Sometimes she'd fed them for a few weeks because it was *healthier*. For whom? Not for her. All it did was make her love them more.

'Got to go. James's on the warpath,' and he quickly left.

Jenny hauled herself along the corridor to her bedroom to find some clothes which she could still get on. She was so big she wondered if she had twins. Could the scan have missed one baby, if it was hiding behind the other? That might be the solution, then they could have one each. But they would still both have the same father, wouldn't they? She thought of her cats – one a ginger Tom and one a Tabby. She'd been told they had the same mother but different fathers. But she was no feline producing a rainbow litter or some other biological miracle. No, she just had one baby and she knew the sex, though that was her secret.

Tess eventually arrived bringing with her two bottles of Schlurr. She was a large lady and Jenny thought she looked even bigger this evening. Almost as big as Jenny was. She'd been called Two Ton Tess at school and she was at least that now! 'Off the booze?' asked Jenny. 'I know I can't drink but I don't mind if you have a few.'

'I've got some news. I'm pregnant so I can't drink either. I'm almost five months now, but I didn't realise straight away. You know I'm not very regular, but you can see how big I've got.'

Jenny didn't comment. 'Congratulations,' she said. 'But whose is it?' Tess had split up with her partner, Wayne, and already had two boys by him. 'You didn't tell me you were seeing anyone.' Jenny relied on Tessa to be there for her. Neither had had boyfriends for several years; but while Jenny was happy with that, Tessa always craved love, though only Mr Wrongs seemed to come along.

'I haven't been actually seeing anyone. Wayne came over to see the boys and it just happened. I didn't think I could be, cos he's had the snip.'

'It just happened?'

'Well he asked if he could stay a bit later to watch Match of the Day. His new woman won't let him watch it. We'd had a bit to drink and you know I think he still fancies me, despite going off with that Annie. He even missed the end of the match and it was Chelsea against Everton. He came just as John Terry scored the winning goal.'

Jenny smiled. Trust Tess. She must have done it on purpose. She'd always wanted Wayne back. 'You sound pleased. I assume you're keeping it.'

'Yes, of course. And the best news is – it's a girl. I've just had a scan. We're going to call her Chelsea. You know I think Wayne might come back to me.'

Jenny smiled again, broader this time, thinking of her own baby. 'A girl,' she said. 'Mine's a girl too, but I haven't told the boys.'

'Oh Jenny, why don't you keep her? Chelsea and her could be friends, play together. It may be your last chance to have a baby. And after them four boys too.'

'I can't. I've promised James and Chris. I've signed a contract.'

'You want to though?'

Jenny looked away. 'No, I don't know. I'd have to give all the expenses back too.' She had been thinking about it. Tess was right. It might well be her last chance. But there were practical things. Those stairs down to the front door with the buggy. And her place was too small to keep a child as it grew older. 'But they do seem to be rowing a lot.'

'You could let them have her some weekends like I do with my ex. – well did. It probably won't be like that now. It doesn't seem right to me, a little girl having two dads. A little boy wouldn't be so bad, but a girl, she needs a mother, especially as she's growing up. And think of those nice little dresses we could get for them.'

'Tess, you're beginning to sound like Paula.'

'That snooty cow your mother works for. I've not said anything against you. I think you should keep the baby. I know you're as common as muck, just like me, but I don't mind.' Jenny didn't laugh; the dilemma had stolen her humour.

'But she thinks a child should have a mother and a father, not two fathers.'

'Well she won't mind if you keep her then, will she?'

'Oh Tess, it's not her I'm worried about. I've never gone back on my word before and there are legal issues.'

'But don't you have six weeks or something to decide before they adopt?'

'They don't adopt, they get a parenting order. Wait a minute, I want to google something. I've got an idea which might change my mind.'

Chapter 21

The Granddaughter

James woke with a start as his mobile rang. It was only two o'clock. Was it the baby or had something happened to his dad?

'It's Jenny, my waters have broken. Do you and Chris want to come over? I've rung the midwife, she's on her way.'

'Aren't you in hospital?'

'No, you know I'm having a home birth.'

James didn't remember discussing this – was it something else Chris hadn't told him? 'Isn't that dangerous?' he asked, but Jenny didn't answer.

'Sorry, just had a contraction. It'll be fine. I've had a few you know - babies I mean.' James heard a groan before the phone went dead. He woke Chris, who was lying beside him in drunken ignorance. 'We've got to go – Jenny's in labour. I'd better drive; your veins are pumping red wine.'

Chris struggled up and pulled on his jeans and a jumper. James quickly dressed and went to fetch his MG from the underground car park. 'It won't take long to the hospital,' said Chris. 'Do you want to set the satnav?'

'She's having it at home. Didn't you know either? You've been going with her to check-ups – wasn't the birth ever discussed?'

'Of course. I remember Jenny saying something about....er... not wanting foetal monitoring or epidurals, I don't know. I left that to her. She didn't want much. You know she's into everything natural.'

James was beginning to wonder why he'd left all this to Chris, he should have got more involved. His tone was sharp. 'I know all that. But she doesn't have to have all that high tech stuff in hospital. She surely should have discussed it with us? I mean what if the baby's in distress, needs a doctor not just a midwife. I really don't like the idea – she's putting our baby at risk.'

The MG hurtled through the quiet streets and made its way south of the river to Jenny's apartment in Battersea in record time. The door was opened by a large woman who announced, 'I'm Tess.'

'Are you the midwife?' asked James.

'No, I'm Jenny's friend. Midwife's still on her way – staff shortages. But she'll be a while yet – I mean Jenny, not the midwife. The contractions are still five minutes apart. And I've sorted out the fresh towels and we've got loads of hot water – the emersion's been on ages. I know about this stuff cos I've had two, Wayne's got them tonight, that's why I'm able to be here.'

This woman was talking some strange language which James didn't understand. They walked upstairs. Mary embraced James enthusiastically. 'I've not seen you since you were so high. You have grown, of course you've grown, sorry that was silly. I'm all in a tiz. I've never seen one of the births before – usually the parents are there – well you two are of course. In hospital you're only allowed two watching. At home you can have as many as you like, not that you'd want a crowd I suppose.'

All these women have verbal diarrhoea, he thought, but accepted Mary's hug like a real man. He saw Jenny walking around holding her back, with little clothing on, her bulge dangerously low.

'They say it's better standing up – in my day we had to lie down I remember,' said Mary. 'I do wish that midwife would hurry up and get here. I'll fetch the baby bath in case it's needed.'

'Shall I help?' asked James politely.

'No – I'm fine. It'll be good for me bingo wings.'

James looked at Chris as if for a translation and then to Jenny. 'She means the flab on her arms,' she said before groaning as another contraction overwhelmed her. 'Can you put the TENS pads on my back?' She lay on her front, lifted up her tee shirt and instructed James to put some sticky pads where her bra strap would have been, if she'd been wearing one, and two more just above her bottom.

James did as he was told, but remembered the time he had, possibly, conceived this child. He hadn't been looking forward to it, as he didn't like the idea of women's bits, and had brought a copy of

'Men's Health,' to make him horny, while Jenny had pleasured herself to aid the penetration. In the end he had entered her easily and come quickly, probably much to Jenny's relief. They had been so polite to each other, not like lovers, more like strangers in forced intimacy. Neither had pretended to enjoy it.

'What does this tens thing do?' he asked, after he had struggled to attach it.

'Helps the pain – sends electric pulses through me.'

'Is it safe ... for you?'

'The baby will be fine – I borrowed the equipment from the hospital.'

Well he was glad she was having something but why she couldn't have been in the hospital with a proper doctor he really didn't know.

There was a ring on the bell and Tess brought the midwife upstairs. James thought she looked rather stern – a no-nonsense type. He wondered if she'd approve of there being two fathers. Perhaps he should pretend to be a friend but then he might not be allowed to see the birth.

'Well, quite a crowd,' she said. 'Can I get through? You must be Jenny, and you are?' She looked at James and Chris.

'We're the prospective parents – Jenny's having our baby,' said Chris.

'Well, that isn't on the notes. Have you two ever seen a birth – it isn't red roses and champagne you know though you may see some red.' she said. 'And I won't have time to minister to you – the mother and baby are my concern.'

'And ours,' replied James. What a battle-axe.

'By the way, I'm Virginia. Now dear, let's see how dilated you are. Will you lie down for me, Jenny?' She slipped one of her gloved fingers inside Jenny. 'My, you're almost 10 centimetres – we'd better get a move on. Have you got no mattress protectors? I've some in my car. Boys can you go and get them – it's the little black Polo across the road.' She threw the keys over and James caught them while Chris looked as if he was going to faint.

'Are you all right?' Tess asked him. 'You don't look very well.'

'He's fine,' said James. 'Just being a drama queen!'

When James returned he found Jenny breathing heavily and reciting *Jack and Jill went up the Hill* at each contraction. 'Helps, they say,' said Mary. 'Takes your mind off.' James was unclear why reciting a nursery rhyme would take your mind off having a baby – surely the opposite would be true?

James could see Tess was lusting after Chris. What was it with him and either gender?

'Can I get you some water?' Tess asked. 'You don't have to watch you know.'

Chris looked pale and his voice came out as a soft whisper, 'I'm fine really – I want to see the birth of my child.'

'Oh I thought you didn't know it was yours,' said Tess.

'We don't, he just thinks it's his, it'll be ours anyway,' interrupted James.

'Do you want any Entonox – you know – gas and air?' asked Virginia.

'Oh yes,' chipped in Mary, 'I had some of that with you – like having a few stouts. Much better than *Mary Had a Little Lamb* or whatever.'

Jenny moaned and nodded, agreeing to the pain relief. James gasped as Virginia placed a mask over Jenny's face and pumped some gas from a canister. God, it was like the second world war.

Jenny's legs were now spread apart and Chris's hands were half covering his eyes as if he were a child watching a horror film.

'Do you want to sit up?' Virginia asked Jenny. 'Give her space and put some pillows and that sheet on the floor.' James did as he was told. Jenny got off the bed and squatted on the pillow.

'My God, she's like one of them African women,' said Mary.

'For goodness sake, if you can't say anything sensible, shut up. Its gravity – it helps. Just because you gave birth lying down doesn't mean that's the way we do it now,' said Virginia. 'Push! Come and hold her up. You - I mean.'

She pointed to James. He took off his jacket and went over though he really didn't want to touch Jenny's naked flesh, especially anywhere sexual. He was too frightened of Virginia to refuse, so he went behind her and put his hands under her arms, avoiding touching her breasts.

'Push,' said Virginia. 'You can do it.' Jenny pushed and blew, groaned and swore, grunted and hissed, sang and recited, and cried out for more gas and air as the baby slowly made its way through the birth canal. 'The crown, stop pushing, blow, blow,' shouted Virginia. 'Relax, go limp. Hold her up properly.' James tightened his grip, and looked over to see a head emerging out of Jenny's vagina. The other spectators tried to see but didn't come too close in case of inflaming Virginia's wrath. 'Good, good, push again,' said Virginia.

Tess was leaning over with her arm around Chris. 'Can you see her head?' she asked as the baby's cranium appeared covered in blood, mucous and something that looked like cream cheese. Then quickly, miraculously, a small creature emerged, bright red and screaming with puffy eyes and a cone shaped head.

Jenny collapsed onto the pillow and Virginia put the new arrival to Jenny's breast. Mary and Tess began to cry. Chris closed his eyes and sank into Tess's generous bosom while James stared open mouthed. 'She's beautiful,' said Jenny.

'A girl,' said James, but his daughter wasn't quite as he'd imagined her.

'Do you want to cut the cord?' said Virginia. It was more of an order than a question, so James took the scissors and cut the cord after Virginia had clamped it. It was hard, like gristle, but he managed it. Easier than breaking the tie with his mother. His first thought after she was born was how Paula would react. He was still a mummy's boy.

'Now for the placenta,' said Virginia.

'Didn't they eat them in the old days?' asked Tess. Chris rushed out.

'Can you fill that baby bath with warm water, after he's stopped puking in the bathroom,' Virginia said again to James.

After Virginia cleaned the new arrival and put her into a gown, the baby looked more human. James examined her tiny fingers and toes, her wrinkled skin and her face which looked red and squashed. Yet he felt a bond forming. Chris had regained his composure and held her gingerly in his arms, staring at her.

'Support her head,' barked Virginia, while Jenny lay back on the bed looking exhausted but serene.

'You knew, didn't you?' said Chris.

'What?' asked Jenny, wide eyed.

'The gender, Tess said *her head.*'

'All right, yes, does it matter? I knew you two didn't want to know.'

'But why did you?' asked James, trying to sound calm.

'I just did, that's all,' she replied.

'It's just you've been keeping a lot from us – we didn't even know the birth was to be at home,' said James. Tears welled in Jenny's eyes.

'God, why are you starting on me when I'm exhausted, after all I've been through.' She lay back, closing her eyes with her baby nestling on her breast. James decided not to pursue the matter and got out his Blackberry to ring the office and text his friends. Chris's iPhone had already been working overtime.

'Have you told your mum?' asked Mary when she saw James texting.

'No, not yet and please, Mary, I want to tell them myself.'

'What are you going to call her?' asked Tess. She was talking to Jenny but it was they who would choose the name. She still didn't feel like their baby.

'Will it be something to go with New or...?' asked Mary.

'Well she's just new baby for the moment – we haven't settled that one either yet,' said James.

'What's your surname, Chris?' Tess asked.

'Beard,' said Chris.

'Perfect for the wife of a gay but not a little girl,' said James.

Suddenly the midwife came back in. James had hoped she'd gone.

'I'll be off now. Another delivery. Don't let them bully you my dear. You've got rights you know.' Virginia walked out with Chris mouthing *Cow*, to her retreating back.

James looked at Jenny. 'You don't think that we bully you, do you?' he asked.

Jenny shook her head but she was staring down into her baby's eyes as her minute hands grasped Jenny's hair and she sucked ferociously on her breast. She stroked the baby's arms and legs, as if she was her first child. James could see there was real love in Jenny's eyes though they were still red and tearful. He tried to think what it must be like for her. To go through all that pain and then give up the end result, this perfect little creature. And to them – two blokes who knew fuck all about babies.

Jenny looked up and spoke directly to James. 'You didn't bully me, but I can't I just can't,' she said. 'I'm sorry but I'm keeping her. I'll give you all your expenses back.'

James stared at her and felt like grabbing the baby. She couldn't do that to them. She was a friend. They'd trusted her. This couldn't be happening though in some ways he could see why she'd changed her mind.

'You promised, you can't go back on your word,' said Chris. 'We had an agreement, you signed something. Tell her James.'

Jenny's tears began to flow, as if a tap had suddenly been turned on full. 'I know, but it's my last chance. I couldn't go through this again. You can easily get another surrogate – a posher one with better genes.'

'That was just my mother Jenny. The baby'd have a great home with us and you could keep in touch. You can't afford to keep her on your own.' James' face was dark, while Chris had turned ashen. 'You're upset and tired; you don't have to decide now - you have six weeks before we get a parenting order.'

James carried on trying to mollify her, but was worried that any delay might mean that Jenny would bond more strongly with the baby.

'But you can't,' she said.

'Can't what?'

'Get a parenting order - because the baby has to be conceived by artificial insemination for you to get one. I looked it up online. And anyway, I have to agree to it. Virginia said I had rights and I do.'

James decided not to argue over the legal points now but there must be a way they could keep this baby. 'Look, Jenny, don't decide now. You've been through a lot. We'll go and come back later when you're less tired.' James tried to smile; but he looked longingly at their new baby, blinking away his tears.

They left, leaving Tess and Mary to look after Jenny and baby New. As soon as they reached the car James knew Chris would have a go at him. 'Did you know that when you agreed not to use artificial insemination? I mean you're the smart lawyer,' asked Chris.

' I'm a company lawyer, family law isn't my specialism. But it's irrelevant if she won't agree, she's right there.'

'Nine months and then nothing,' continued Chris, as if it was all James' fault.

'I expect that's what Jenny's thinking.'

'You sound like you're on her side. But you haven't explained why you agreed to natural conception – was it because you want to swing both ways? You remember I didn't want to do it. I think you wanted to see if you could hack it with women. Now we can't get that order.'

James knew this was the opposite of his true feelings but, if Chris thought it, then how well could he know him? Chris had always had a thing about James trying out women. His adolescent fumblings could hardly count. Chris had never been with a woman apart from Jenny - at least that's what he said. He was sure he was gay probably from the womb, but women flock to him. 'I had to steel myself. It was the only way she'd agree to it, you know that. Don't let us fall out, we have to be an united front. The parenting order doesn't really matter, I don't think. We can't push her though, she has to agree.'

'Don't say that word, I've seen enough pushing to last me a lifetime. Can't we get one that's already born from China or Africa or somewhere?'

'We may have to, but that little girl has got half her genes from one of us and I want us to bring her up. So, unless you want to give up, we must get on with our wedding – the courts will look much more favourably on us if we show commitment. You're not going off the idea, are you?'

Chris was silent; but his hand came over and stroked James' leg, moving quickly up to the groin. James smiled a little more contentedly.

Chapter 22

The New Mother

Jenny woke up to the sound of the baby crying pitifully in her basket. Jenny's vagina was sore and her breasts engorged. She was bleeding heavily and her sanitary towel was soaked. The thought of getting up to find a new one or even to get her baby seemed an insurmountable task so, remembering her mother and Tess were still there, she called weakly for them.

Mary was already on her way. 'Oh poor little Baby New. I'll bring her over.'

'Please don't call her that – it's James' name and she's going to be mine. I thought you'd be pleased,' said Jenny sharply. 'Can you see to her? I'm leaking dreadfully.'

Mary picked up her little granddaughter and clutched her to her breast, rocking her until she stopped crying, 'I'm glad, of course. You go to the bathroom, love, and change yourself. I'll bring you a nice cup of tea while you feed her. Tess has just put the kettle on.'

Jenny hauled herself out of bed, still feeling as big as before the baby was born. She needed to pee but she always hated her first one after childbirth. She found some super-sized fresh pads and lowered herself onto the pan, screaming in agony when she managed to get a drop out.

'Jenny, are you all right? I almost dropped this hot kettle with that scream. Is Baby New hurt?' called Tess from the kitchen.

'Not you as well,' shouted Jenny, emerging slowly from the bathroom. They were both at it. 'She's not Baby New, she's a new baby, my new baby!' Mary's mobile rang and Jenny could tell it was Paula.

'Sorry,' said Mary, 'I won't be able to come today. I've had a bad night. But Jack'll be all right, won't he? They've sent that carer in. Clive, yes, he seems ever so nice.'

Jenny could hear Paula's voice chiding Mary. Fancy her mother rabbiting on about Jack now. 'I'm glad James has rung you so you know it's a little girl. She's absolutely beautiful. No, she's fine. She's not what? Jenny, changed her mind? Well, sort of ... yes I suppose so. Yes, she's thinking about keeping her. Can you speak to her? No, she's sleeping at the moment, sorry, I have to go now.'

'You told her, didn't you?' said Jenny.

'I had to, she kept asking about the baby, thought something might be wrong with it. Then she asked if you'd changed your mind. She must have suspected something but James hadn't said anything. I couldn't say no, could I? But have you really changed your mind?'

Mary handed the baby to her daughter who looked at her lovingly. 'Yes, I have.'

Mary frowned. 'But how will you manage? You had that offer of the job in that homopathetic shop didn't you?'

'Homeopathy, yes. I might be able to do that part time,' she said as her baby sucked voraciously.

'And Paula will probably sack me, so I won't be able to help with money, you know.'

'Mum, I've never asked you for money. Anyway, Paula's not the only one you clean for is she?'

'No, but I get more hours looking after her Jack, I'll miss him you know.'

'God - isn't it more important for you to see your grandchild than a demented randy old man?' Jenny could see Mary was upset but so was she and half of her knew Mary had some valid points. This made it more difficult for her to apologise. She was in two minds herself except when she saw that little face. She would struggle financially. She'd been looking forward to working properly, getting out and seeing people. Then she looked down at her baby sucking now more gently on her nipple, her soft skin resting on her breast and her tiny hands clutching at her fresh cotton nightgown and wondered how she could have given the other four up. Why was this one so different?

Mary went into the kitchen but it was Tess who brought her tea. 'What did you say to upset your mum?

'She seems to think I shouldn't keep her.'

Tess looked down at the baby, peaceful in her mother's arms, 'Well they're a nice couple. James was really helpful during the birth and that Chris, he's something else. What a waste.' She put the tea on the bedside table.

'Waste?' Jenny echoed.

'Yes, that he likes men.'

'Tess, we're not talking about his fuckability – we're talking about them caring for my baby. You're the one who said I should keep her.'

Tess shrugged. 'You're right, it would be great for Chelsea to play with your little girl but Chris said they could still play together if he had her!'

Jenny's jaw dropped in disbelief at Tess's gullibility. She took as gospel a spur of the moment remark from the mouth of a handsome man. 'Tess, he's Chris Beard, not Christ with a fucking beard. He'll say anything that sounds right at the time. I honestly don't think he's got a clue how much work it is looking after a baby.' Everyone was against her, yet she was clear in her mind that she wanted to keep her. She drank her tea and finished feeding the baby. 'I'll be fine now. You can both go, I need to sleep.'

A little later she was woken by a constant ringing of the doorbell and she painfully descended the stairs, to find Paula at the door, 'I hope you don't mind but I had to see my grandchild.'

Jenny felt she had to let her in; she might be the baby's granny after all. She wondered if she should tell her the secret of her baby's origins – at the moment they didn't even know if it was James'! She'd be really hacked off that her son had slept with the daughter of a cleaner, not just injected her with his sperm. Paula would prefer her son to have a male lover than a working class one she was sure. Yes, she would tell her. Paula would be pissed off with James too rather than just her. 'Come in,' she said. 'She's asleep at present but you can peep at her I suppose. I need to tell you something first though.'

'I know you've changed your mind,' Paula said quite calmly, which aroused Jenny's suspicions immediately.

'No, well, yes I have. But that's not what I was going to talk to you about.' She led her upstairs into her flat. The door opened straight into her small living room. She wondered what Paula would

151

think of the rich red, orange and turquoise Indian rugs and throws, so different from her style. The lingering whiff of incense couldn't hide the smell of blood, baby milk and sick. Paula would just have to put up with that. Paula lowered herself onto the Futon and smiled.

'You're looking well, it's so tiring giving birth,' Paula said. What had come over her? She sounded like one of the sisterhood. She was up to something.

'Yes, it was quite quick though, compared with some of my others. But I just wanted to say – you keep talking about *your* grandchild.'

Paula looked puzzled. 'Yes, well that will be true even if you keep it.'

'No, Mrs New, me keeping it or not is irrelevant, at least biologically,' replied Jenny.

Paula's frown deepened. 'I don't think I'm following you. Please, do call me Paula, I mean we're almost related now, aren't we?'

Jenny certainly didn't want to be related to Paula but felt she'd had enough rows that day. 'Paula, we don't know if James or Chris is the father.' Paula started and, as Jenny explained the process, Paula's face became more and more pained, as if she were having the contractions Jenny had suffered the previous night. 'We'll have a DNA test, I suppose. I expect they'll still want to know.'

Just then Jenny heard a wail from the bedroom and was glad to leave Paula in stunned silence. Perhaps the presence of the baby would stem the angry vitriol which she was sure would gush from Paula.

When Jenny brought the new baby in, she had stopped crying and opened her bright blue eyes. Paula stared at her with a look which Jenny was unsure was horror or delight.

'Can I hold her?' she asked and held out her arms. 'There's no need for a DNA test. There's no doubt - this is James' little girl and I'm her grandmother.'

It was Jenny's turn to be stunned. She couldn't know. Paula was trying to trick her. Jenny tried to look her in the eye but Paula's gaze was fixed on the baby.

'Now dear, we must talk about who brings her up.'

Chapter 23

The Wedding

Jack got out of bed and tried his door. He rattled the handle, still locked. He called out for help. He tried to find the window or was it a mirror? He was sure he'd seen it the other night but could only see that awful painting. He really didn't like it, seeing different shapes and outlines of faces and ghostly images the more he stared. It gave him funny dreams. He heard someone open his door and a woman came in.

'Why don't you have a bath?' she asked. 'You want to look good for the wedding. I'll run it for you.'

Jack was surprised at her tone and blinked, looking at her again. He thought he might be at Arlene's and occasionally he mixed them up which annoyed both of them, but no, it was Paula. He obediently went into the bathroom and he was desperate for a pee. He even remembered to lift the toilet lid.

Paula wrinkled her nose in disgust. 'You could have waited. Do you want me to help you with your buttons?' He managed to pull off his pyjama top easily. 'Oh, yes, Clive's very helpful, isn't he? I'd forgotten he'd put those poppers on. But wait until I'm out to take everything off.'

Jack struggled a little with the cord on his pyjama trousers but eventually stripped down to his birthday suit and sank into the warm water. Who was this Clive and what was this about a wedding? He thought about his three marriages and the hopes that he'd had. He'd truly gone into each one with noble intentions, to be a good husband and not to stray. But he knew he'd been a bit of a lad. He did have

Arlene still. He'd seen her lately. He couldn't remember what they'd done but it had left him with a warm glow.

Paula opened the door and gave him his towelling robe. 'Put that on to have breakfast, you don't want to put your suit on yet or you'll spill your coffee or something on it.'

'Are we going away? I haven't packed.'

'No, we're going to the wedding. James and Chris are getting married. Remember we went out to get you a new suit? It's this morning at the Orangery, Kensington Palace. They got a cancellation apparently.'

Jack found all this information confusing but recognised some words. 'Doesn't the Queen Mother or Princess Margaret or someone live there?' he asked. 'What wedding are you talking about?'

He knew Paula was getting cross. 'Clive gets you to put things into a diary so you can look at it to see what you're doing each day.' Jack could see her lips opening and closing with sounds emitting but he couldn't make sense of it and his brain closed off.

She retrieved the thin black book from the desk and opened it. Written in Jack's now rather spidery writing was, *James Wedding 11am*. Yes, he understood that and it was his writing.

'See - you've written it here on today's date.' Paula read it out loudly and put the diary into Jack's new suit pocket, along with his reading glasses. 'Now eat your breakfast. We can't be late.'

He sat and ate his toast and marmite. He slapped his lips and the marmite ran down the side of his mouth. Paula left the room. She never seemed to eat with him these days.

'I'll get your suit out and a shirt and tie to match,' he heard her say and before long he was dressed ready to go somewhere.

They got into the taxi and Paula said they were going to see James. He felt very smart in his pencil grey suit from Saville Row and black polished leather shoes.

The Orangery was grand with marble columns and some old fancy carvings but it was crowded with young men dressed in their best clothes. Jack looked around but couldn't see James or anyone he knew. As they went through another door, one of them pinned a carnation onto him and another onto Paula.

'Bride or groom?' he asked. 'Just a joke, you are Mr and Mrs New, aren't you? I have seats for you down the front. With James' aunt.'

'What's he talking about?' asked Paula, as she was being led to her seat. 'You haven't invited Arlene, have you? We're both only children so he hasn't got an aunt.'

The woman sitting on their row turned around and Jack rushed over to kiss her. 'Mary, it's so nice to see you,' he said. 'Paula didn't tell me you were coming to this do.'

'What a surprise,' said Paula.

'Ooh you do look smart Jack and you, Paula, goodness I don't know how you can walk in them shoes. You look the perfect mother of the groom. MOGS they call them, don't they?' said Mary.

Another good-looking man came up to them, this one a little older and balding, but tanned with bright blue eyes that seemed to be staring at Jack. 'I'm the maid of honour,' he said, with a trace of a foreign accent. 'We're just calling me that to distinguish me from Chris's best man. Do you remember me? I've changed a bit since I stayed at your house years ago. Lars, from Norway.'

Paula peered at him but Jack smiled broadly. He looked at his face and an image of a young man with long blonde hair and a wispy beard came into his mind. 'Yes, I remember, I took you both out and taught you to play snooker – you said you'd only played pool. You were pretty good though.'

'Well remembered,' he said. 'You were both very kind to me.' Jack was pleased. He'd remembered something which Paula had forgotten.

'I hope this music isn't too distracting. The Bondage Fairies are a bit loud,' continued Lars.

Paula's smile froze on her lips. 'What did you say?' she asked.

'They're a band - joke name, you know – fairies – gays, bondage – marriage.'

What was that man saying to Paula? She didn't look very happy. But hazy memories of his bound wrists were forming in Jack's mind. He looked at Lars again. He sounded German and he'd seen that German in Paula's room. He must be the same man – the bastard. They must be plotting something together. 'You came to our house, you're German, aren't you? You've been with my wife.'

'No, no, Mr New. I'm Norwegian. You must be confusing me with someone else.'

'I'm so sorry, Lars,' said Paula. 'He does get very confused. Jack - that was a film you were watching about the Second World War.' Jack wondered if that could be true. Did he just imagine himself being tied up? Paula began fussing him to sit down. He'd better obey but he'd keep an eye on that German.

Jack sat down but looked around and again saw someone he thought he knew but couldn't work out who she was. Could it be Mary? He saw a young woman with long brown hair wearing a loose-fitting dress, rather like the hippy clothes he remembered. She was carrying something wrapped in a colourful Indian shawl. She was being very careful with it but Jack had no idea what it was. Paula seemed to know her and gave her a hug.

'I think they've invited her to try to get her to give up the child but her mind's made up. I told her she should keep to the agreement,' whispered Mary to Paula, who just smiled.

The young woman came up to him and unwrapped the parcel. What was that in it? It was alive. A tiny baby in a pink pair of what looked like long rompers, and wearing a knitted white bonnet. 'Meet your granddaughter,' she said. Jack stared in amazement, unable to take his eyes off the tiny form.

Jack was transfixed by the baby. 'Is it a thingy bob ... a Christening?' he asked. 'Is that why we're here?'

Just at that moment the Bondage Fairies were replaced by Tammy Wynnette singing 'Stand by your Man', and two men wearing identical white suits entered through the large double doors. One was tall slim and blond and the other was shorter, stockier and dark. Jack wondered who they were and what they were doing there. One did look familiar though. It must be a wedding but where was the bride? He looked around to see if he could spot her. All he could see were men.

As the music faded the registrar began his introductions. Jack turned back to look at the child again, wondering what it all meant, as she cooed and gave little windy smiles and baby coughs and sneezes. He hardly listened to the registrar as he droned on.

'We are here today to witness the joining in matrimony of James New and Christopher Beard who would like to thank you all for coming to celebrate the beginning of a new chapter in their life together. Family and friends have travelled a long way to be with them today; and it means a great deal to James and Christopher that you can be here to share in their happiness and witness their wedding vows.'

Jack began to pay more attention as he heard his son's name. It must be James getting married. He looked again, yes, he was the shorter one. But he still couldn't see the bride. He hoped he hadn't been jilted. He listened carefully as the registrar said:

'James and Christopher now wish to offer each other the security which comes from vows, sincerely made and faithfully kept, to bind themselves to each other till death do them part.

However, if any person here present knows of any lawful impediment to this wedding, then he or she should declare it now.'

What was the man saying about being bound? He couldn't let this happen to James. And that German was standing there too. He was a Nazi. James didn't know that. He must stop it.

There was a hushed silence as Jack rose to his feet. He could feel Paula's nails digging into his hands like sharp razors. She was grabbing at his sleeve now. He had to put his hand up to object. She was probably in on it anyway. 'Yes, I object, this cannot go on. I'm being kept against my will by my wife and don't want James to be tied up like me. You have to escape now, follow me.' Jack struggled up and took James' arm.

'No, Dad, sit down,' said James, pushing him off.

Why wouldn't James listen? Pushing him like that, yes pushing an old man when he was only trying to help. The other man in the white suit tried to get hold of him. Were they going to tie him up again? No, he couldn't stand it. 'Get off me, you can't do that to me!' He gave the young man whose name he had forgotten now a good shove. Getting hold of his arms so he couldn't move indeed. He ran through the doors down the corridors, towards the exit. He turned around. Where was James? That German was almost on his tail though and his mate in uniform,

'The Germans are after me,' he shouted. People would help if they heard that. He reached the outside and, blinking in the strong sunlight, saw a busy road in front of him. He ran across. One car almost got him and a man on a bike swore at him as he swerved. He was breathing heavily now but could hear people shouting. He had to get away. He'd have to leave James. Perhaps he'd found another exit. He spotted a black cab. He hailed it and in he got. Jack was panting and could only just get his breath.

'Where to, mate?'

'Putney,' said Jack. He'd be safe there. 'The golf club.'

The car started off and Jack saw the man in uniform shouting something at him. He must have been a friend of that German. Thank the Lord he'd escaped but what would Paula say? He sat back and began to relax.

'Whereabouts mate? I don't know of any golf club here. Is it near the Common?' asked the driver as they drove over Putney Bridge.

Jack thought. He must know that. He'd been going to her house for years. He felt in his trouser pocket. Arlene usually put her address there.

'Where are we going? We're in Putney now.' The man sounded angry.

He felt in his jacket pocket and found a slim notebook. He put on his glasses and looked more carefully, it was a diary and at the back was a section for addresses. The first one was Arlene's so at least he knew where he was going. He told the cabbie the address. It would all work out. Arlene would look after him.

'Twenty-five,' the driver said as they pulled up outside Arlene's.

Jack put his hand into his pockets again but no wad of notes emerged. No wallet. Arlene would have money though.

'Sorry, young man,' he said. 'I'll have to get my wife to pay. Seem to have come out with no money today.'

The cabby didn't look pleased. 'Who do you think you are? Bloody royalty?' he asked but unlocked the door for Jack to get out.

Jack rang Arlene's bell. There was no answer. Where was she? What could he do?

'If you can't pay I'm gonna have to call the coppers,' the driver shouted out of his window. 'Never thought I'd have this bother with a man like you – yobbos late at night are a different cup of tea.'

A haunted look came into Jack's eyes and his body crumpled as he collapsed on Arlene's porch. But a car stopped and Arlene emerged with bags of shopping.

'Jack,' she called, but before she could help him up, the taxi driver got out of his cab, leaving it double parked with the engine running.

He strode threateningly up to Arlene, shouting, 'Are you paying, missus? I can't wait all day. That'll be thirty quid.'

Arlene took some notes out of her purse, and the man snatched them from her. Jack felt tears welling up but the sight of Arlene strengthened him and he stood up tall. She took him by the hand and led him into the house.

Chapter 24

The Morning After

James examined his reflection in the mirror through a half-opened eye, still red raw but with rainbow bruises forming around it. His other eye was puffy; his unshaven jaw looked more protruding than usual, skin sallower and lines more apparent. Hair uncombed with some cake matted in it. Teeth stained with red wine and the putrid stink of his breath was overpowering. No wonder Chris found Adrian more attractive.

On the floor was his white wedding jacket stained red – was it blood or wine? He tried to remember what had happened, and gradually his befuddled mind became clearer. He looked over his shoulder to see Chris fast asleep. He looked so angelic despite the bottles of Don Perigon, Fitou and copious brandies he'd consumed.

He certainly remembered vividly his father's action. Dad had pushed him and then run out followed by Lars and a security guard. The Orangery had erupted while he was frozen to the spot but the registrar had called for calm. Eventually Lars returned to the hall.

'He got into a taxi,' Lars reported.

James was all for delaying the wedding but Chris was furious. 'Your fucking father, he's not going to spoil our day. He's safe enough in a car, isn't he?'

'Yes,' said Paula, 'he'll probably go home.'

'But can he get in and has he got any money?' asked James.

'You have to carry on,' his mother argued.

'You're suddenly keen on gay marriages,' James replied. 'The taxi driver is likely to dump him on the pavement if he can't pay.'

'Or call the police,' said Paula. 'Yes, perhaps we should go after him.'

It was good old Mary that saved the day. 'Shall I take a taxi back to your house, Paula, and see if he's there?' she said. 'Or even the train – that might be quicker. I'd need some money though.' For some reason they'd jumped at that, though to James now it wasn't logical. He supposed that no one really wanted to stop the wedding. 'I could bring him back to the reception,' she added.

'Oh Mary, you're wonderful,' said Chris, kissing her warmly, and between them they found a hundred pounds in cash to give her. James was still unsure, but agreed and they carried on with the service.

The registrar completed the ceremony, ignoring the *legal impediment* and the two grooms kissed. The usual photographs were taken while the orangery was transformed for the wedding breakfast. Everything had been fine at that point, he was sure. They'd smiled for the photos and he'd forgotten all about his dad.

When they returned inside James asked his mother to look at her mobile. 'No, nothing. Wait a minute; I've got a missed call and a voice mail.'

'It's probably from your friend,' Chris said. James gave him a disgusted look.

'It's Arlene,' she said. 'He's there.'

'Thank goodness, do you think she'd bring him to the reception?' James asked. He knew that was a mistake. But it would have been good to have his dad there.

'I'm not having that woman here,' she said. 'I think we should just carry on. Anyway, he'll be too exhausted with all the travelling.'

James couldn't blame his mum. Mind, he had to put up with having fucking Adrian there. 'But you will ring Mary, so she can come back?'

Canapés were set out on a long table while waiters offered champagne or mango and passion fruit juice. The overwhelmingly male guests formed an orderly queue, and Lars suggested bringing food to James and Paula. James steered his mother to a chair.

'I'm fine standing,' she said. 'Am I the only person here over fifty? Where are Chris's parents?'

'He's not been in contact with them for years. They don't approve of his sexuality, some religious sect. He never sees them.'

'So I've done well then, to come round to the idea.'

'Yes indeed,' and he kissed his mother affectionately. 'Oh Jenny, I'd better get her over too.'

Baby New was asleep in her Moses basket, ignoring the music, clinking of glasses, chatting, flirting, and wafts of warmed quiche, falafels and samosas. James carried the baby over and got a chair for Jenny. He still needed to keep on the right side of her. He was sure she'd agree in the end. He didn't want to go to court but he'd do it if he had to. And win.

Lars arrived with platefuls of Melton Mowbray mini pork pies, pigs in blankets, asparagus spears and salmon brochettes. Chris brought over several bottles of red wine and James began to relax and at last enjoy the occasion. Perhaps it was better his father wasn't there – one less thing to worry about.

Before the cutting of the cake, Lars made an amusing speech in the tradition of the best man. James wondered what his mother would make of some of the jokes. She'd not picked up on his quip the other day so probably the gay sexual connotations would be over her head. Then he had to listen to Adie's best man speech. He hadn't been looking forward to that. With good reason.

'As some of you know, Chris and I have been friends for years. This was when Chris used to like beautiful queens like himself but now he goes for bears. In fact I think I introduced you two. No, actually, I think James met Chris while he was cottaging – where he met most of his young men. Grindr hadn't been invented then.' There was tittering from the audience. 'But I know that James will keep him in the style Chris has become accustomed to. Chris will make a wonderful wife and care for your little daughter.'

James couldn't believe he'd said this. He'd been told not to mention Baby New or even the new baby. James looked over to Jenny. That remark might put her back up but he remembered she'd just smiled at him. Odd.

'And even the age difference will seem nothing as we can see how beautiful James' mother still is. And they do say – look at the parents.'

The parents indeed. The demented elephant in the room had now escaped. Chris had been so pleased to get shot of him. Paula rewarded Adrian with a beautiful smile. He'd even taken her in.

A band with a sexy blond female singer came out and the tables were cleared away for dancing. They belted out Dusty Springfield's, 'You don't have to say you love me'. To think how amazed Paula had been when he'd told her later on that the singer was a man. But not shocked. She'd improved so much since that awful day in the restaurant.

'Gosh, this is an old one,' said Paula. 'Even I know this. Are you two boys going to dance?'

Chris and James were still arguing. Fucking Adrian. And Chris thought that speech was okay. Still they'd better have the first dance. Everyone was waiting for that and it did feel great when their friends cheered as they stepped out together. Chris could dance so well while he was rubbish. He was lucky to have him. Perhaps he should put up with a bit of infidelity? He was glad when Lars took Paula's hand and she enthusiastically joined him on the floor. He didn't want to see her on her own

Adrian danced as close as he could get to Chris and James without tripping them up. He kept blowing big fat kisses at Chris. And fucking Chris was responding. James tried to ignore him; but the sight of them flirting while they were dancing the first dance was too much. That elastic band inside him which had been keeping all that anger in check became so taut that it snapped.

'Did you know what was going to be in that faggot's speech?' he asked, through gritted teeth. 'I didn't want Adrian as your fucking best man. I want you to ask him to leave.'

Chris looked at him with pleading eyes and clutched him tighter. He felt calmer. That was better. He shouldn't be such a prude. He must take after his mother.

There was now a crowd dancing and Adrian's presence didn't seem so threatening.

'Jimmy, sweetie, he's got to go soon anyway – flying to the States early tomorrow. Look, don't make a fuss. He's offered me work – we don't want another scene.'

The dancing and drinking continued; but later James saw Adrian carrying two drinks. 'You still here?' he said, 'I thought you had a plane to catch.'

'Just bringing Chrissie a big juicy cocktail before I check in. We've been having such a penetrating conversation, he's quite exhausted. But I'll be flying tonight.'

'Get the fuck out of my wedding,' James said. 'You fucking faggot.'

He remembered saying that but what happened after? Yes, Adrian calmly gave Chris his drink. But he was carrying two glasses and the next thing he knew he was spluttering, red wine dribbling down his jacket. The bastard had actually thrown the wine in his face. James remembered throwing a punch but missing, the red wine must have been in his eyes stopping him aiming properly or he'd have got the fucker. Then his mind went blank and the rest was speculation but there was no doubt there'd been a fight. You only had to look at his eye.

Suddenly he heard a disembodied female voice. 'James, how are you feeling?' James was disorientated. Who the fuck was that? He looked around – yes he was in his own flat. He grabbed for his robe and went into the kitchen, to find Jenny making coffee and Mary eating wholemeal toast with one hand and holding Baby New with the other.

'You haven't got any marmalade or jam have you?' she asked.

'Mum, shut up. Let me look at that eye. Sit down, do you want coffee?' asked Jenny.

Marmalade? Jam? He didn't think he had either. James sat down. It was all so confusing. Jack must feel like that all the time. Jenny came over and felt his bruised eye. Wow - just one slight touch and it's bloody painful. He screamed but it came out like a whimper.

'Sorry. You went right out. I can't believe he hit you.'

'I can't remember who hit me, what happened?'

God... Had Chris hit him? Surely not. They'd argued, of course, but it had never got physical. Not in that sense anyway.

'I'm glad your mother had gone, I wouldn't have liked her to see,' said Mary.

'See what?' asked James.

'You being knocked out, of course,' replied Mary.

'I can't believe you can't remember, you seemed better last night, or early this morning anyway,' said Jenny. Baby New then let out a loud squawk and Jenny took her to her breast. She sucked noisily, oblivious of everything else.

'Wasn't it the Norwegian that hit you? Anyway, it was one of them best men,' said Mary.

James was open mouthed, 'Lars – no Lars wouldn't hit me. He works for the Nobel Peace Centre.'

'No, not him,' said Jenny. 'Mum, finish making the coffee. I think there's some marmalade up there too, on the right next to the Lapsang whatever tea bags.'

'But wasn't Chris a hero,' said Mary, reaching for the Roses Lime.

'So he didn't punch me?' he said.

'No, of course, he didn't,' said Jenny. 'But he gave Adrian a shiner... didn't knock him out though. Then everyone threw him out of the wedding.'

What a relief. His sore eye didn't seem so sore now and his bruised feelings and sagging spirit improved. My God, Chris had defended him against Adrian. 'I think I remember, I tried to hit him, but missed. Then he knocked me out – I'd never have taken that Pansy for a fighter.'

'Well I think what really knocked you out was falling back and hitting your head on that pillar,' said Jenny.

Chris entered the kitchen wearing nothing but a Chinese black silk dressing gown, decorated with swirling red dragons and yellow bamboo shoots. God, he looked good first thing in the morning. He greeted James with a hug; but then went straight to the baby and took her from Jenny's arms. He carried the sleeping, satiated bundle over to James.

'You know she's yours and she's ours,' he said, examining James' eye. What was he talking about? It made no sense. 'We did tell you last night but Phil said that concussion can cause temporary amnesia.'

'Yes,' said Jenny. 'Your friend, the one who's a doctor, had a look at you and you revived a bit. He said to monitor you and you should be all right. So, we talked to you until really late. That's why we're here in case we had to take turns to sit up with you in the night.'

James was still befuddled, but it was the bit about the baby that really interested him. Did Chris mean that it was his sperm that had hit the spot, so to speak? 'The DNA test?'

'Yes I got the result the day of the wedding, she's yours. Paula was right,' said Jenny.

'Mum?' What was Paula doing interfering?

'Yes, the hair.'

James looked more carefully at his baby. He had thought she was practically bald but he looked closely. There was an auburn tint and the little hair she had was curly.

'Just like hers was apparently. She said it had to be her grandchild! I've decided to keep to our agreement. It wasn't fair on you two but I do love her.'

Her voice trailed off and she looked away blinking away tears. James stared open mouthed. His eye was throbbing, his head hurt, but it was amazing. He couldn't think of any better news.

'Fucking hell – my baby. Sorry Chris, are you okay about it? She'll be just as much yours as mine. I hope it doesn't put you off her - having Mum's hair.' James remembered his mother with her long wavy red hair though she often put it up in a sort of bun. It was rarely wild and free.

'No, I think she's beautiful and the next one can be mine,' said Chris.

But what about Jenny? Should they let her keep her? She looked so sad and dejected. But no, that would be stupid. He'd give her more money and she can see her as much as she likes.

'Thank you, Jenny. What made you change your mind?'

'Oh, I dunno, this and that. But I'll get to see her loads. We talked about it last night. I can't believe you don't remember. You're as bad as Jack.'

James looked at Chris and wondered if he was seeing the father in the son and even in their new daughter but Chris was staring at her, blissfully folding and unfolding her dainty hands. 'And Jenny's going to be your nanny,' said Mary.

'Your mum suggested it,' she said, but looked away not meeting their eyes.

Chris looked up and gazed directly at James, 'I thought it better. I wouldn't be able to do everything for her. I've got more work now and not all from Adrian.'

'And I'll sign the contract so she'll be legally yours,' said Jenny.

James frowned. How come Jenny had changed her mind back so easily? He knew Paula had something to do with it. Money must have changed hands but he couldn't ask Jenny straight out.

'And Jenny's getting a new flat nearer you,' Mary said.

Chris and James exchanged glances.

'How much are we paying you for nannying? Are you sure? The rents round here are sky high.'

'It was nice of Paula to say she'd make up the difference in cost,' said Mary.

'Yes it was,' said James. Trust Mum to sort everything out.

'And the name – are you still happy about her name?' said Jenny quickly. James looked blank. 'Christina Jemima Newby – pronounced Newbee - what do you think?'

James hesitated. 'Well I get the Christina, and Newby presumably was the best combination of New and Beard you could come up with; but why Jemima?'

'It's my full name. I'm not a Jennifer, I was called Jemima but it was shortened to Jemmy, then Jenny and I never liked Jemima as a kid, so it stuck. I like it now though – are you OK with it?'

'Fine,' said James, 'Except, didn't you know it's Mum's middle name? Are you OK with that?

'Oh yes,' said Mary. 'That's where I got it from. Didn't I tell you last night?'

James looked at Chris and Jenny. 'Even better,' they said in unison.

'I'll take her over to see Mum. She'll be thrilled with the name. I'll go tonight' said James. 'Do you want to come, Chris – see the family home? You always said you wanted to go over?'

Chapter 25

The Ex and the Wife

Dave's new top dentures were rubbing his gums but when he saw himself in the mirror he knew he looked better with them. The dentist told him they would wear in like a pair of shoes so he would persevere. He must look good to see Paula. The Steradent had whitened his bottom set so the tobacco and coffee stains were hardly noticeable. He thought he resembled an aging film star. Clint Eastwood? No, not tall enough. Dustin Hoffman, that was it.

He looked in his wardrobe wondering what to wear. It wasn't a normal conundrum. His clothes hung sadly, using up only a fraction of the space. He had an old suit he used for funerals, a tweed jacket Karen had bought him one Christmas, a few pairs of trousers and some shirts, many of which were stained at the neck and frayed around the collars.

He remembered Karen had bought him a new Ben Sherman shirt – that would be fine. Probably not up to Paula's standards but teamed with the tweed he would look very presentable. Anyway living with Jack in his condition, she must be a bit lonely, so to speak.

He thought he heard the phone so rushed to the hallway. His hearing had become worse and, though he was wearing his neat new NHS hearing aid, he hadn't switched it on. It was Karen, 'Dad, I've rung you several times, have you been out?'

'No, love, I've been in my room, didn't hear the phone.'

'And you're mobile's off,' she continued.

Dave hated his mobile and hardly used it. 'Sorry, love, I was just working out what to wear to Paula's. You know I'm going over later today.'

'Yes, that's what I'm ringing you about. You know what you've got to do.'

'Yes, you've told me. The money.'

'And you'll ring me if you find anything?'

'Yes,' he said. 'Don't worry, she'll be putty in my hands.'

Karen's grunt didn't sound as if she was convinced and, if the truth were told, he wasn't so sure himself. The memory of Jack and Paula's wedding was unclear in his mind but he had told the tale about his snogging the bride so often that it had become reality. It had been better than with Arlene - that was for sure. He was better off having a wank than with his own wife. It was always, *I'm so tired Dave*, or, *Get off, you're drunk.* Used to drive him wild, made him do things he regretted.

But Paula. He could still feel her open mouth and breathy sighs. The story had developed over the years; the white gown was ripped off, the virginal bride deflowered by the best man before the wedding night. It hadn't been like that but he was pretty sure she fancied him, at least then.

All doubts were suppressed after a shower, shave and rinse with the old mouth wash. Suited and booted he went to catch the train to Richmond, flowers and wine in hand.

But most important he also had with him the little blue pill. He'd not tried one before, but he'd got a pack from a young man in the Clapham Tavern.

He'd come up to him, while Dave was sipping his pint, Snatch sitting panting on the floor in front of him after a run on the Common, chasing sticks. 'You interested in these, mate?' he had said, and showed him a pack of strange looking tablets.

Dave was puzzled, didn't he look a bit old to be wanting drugs? 'Not me, I drink and smoke - just legal stuff. What are they anyway? Ecstasy?' He was proud of himself for thinking of their name. He had read about them in *The Mail* – awful stuff.

'No, mate, these are legal, just hard to get hold of, they're to help you with the women,' he lowered his voice. 'They help you get it up, stops the brewer's droop, do you think you need a bit of a hand in that department?'

Dave thought that was the last thing he needed, his hands were the only human contact his nether regions had had for many a year. But those pills, now they might be useful. 'Viagra?' he asked.

The young man winked and nodded.

'How much?' asked Dave, feeling in his pocket for some cash.

'Twenty,' he replied, 'pack of six.'

'A tenner,' replied Dave, and the young man had agreed so quickly that Dave thought he might have been done. They looked real, had the brand on them, but would they work? He'd need some led in his pencil if he was to compete with this young whippersnapper Paula was supposed to be seeing. He didn't have the stamina he'd had when he was young. He always got right excited. Found it difficult to stop. That time on the beach in Ibiza. With that Welsh tart. Jack had gone off with her friend. She'd been dancing wildly at this disco- short skirt, low top, out for a good time. Took her for a walk down to the beach. Merry from sangria washed down with lager, they started snogging. She was down his throat and he remembered her undoing his fly. He put his hands inside her; she was wet and ready for it. Then she'd gone on about her boyfriend back home and she wanted to go back to the hotel. But she'd let him go such a long way. He was excited, hard; she couldn't change her mind now – what a cock teaser. She struggled but he forced himself in and came quickly. He remembered calling her a bitch and she ran off back to the bar crying. He supposed those PC bastards would call that rape now but that wasn't true. She'd led him on. He'd been ready for it again too.

He wasn't like that now. And tonight, those little blue pills were safely in his pocket with his Pensioner's Freedom Pass and spare hearing aid battery, just in case. Dave put on his glasses and studied his A-Z. It had been a while since he'd been to Jack's house but he remembered it was off the Green. He could easily walk from the station. He was still pretty good on his pins, not like some of these old fellows you see hobbling along with their walking sticks.

Envy wasn't really part of Dave's nature but when he'd first seen Jack's house and new young wife there'd been a twinge, a small pang of jealousy. Dave's career, marriage and income had all been in free-fall while Jack seemed to prosper continually. But look at him now. He didn't know why Paula stayed with him. If Karen was right about her having a young lover she must be up for it. But, as for Arlene, what could she be thinking? She didn't even look so bad these days. She'd never been a beauty so had less to lose. And fatter women don't look so scrawny as they get older.

Paula opened the door looking rather flustered and examined Dave quizzically. 'Yes?' she said. She looked at him without even recognising him, as if he were a travelling salesman. And she'd known him years.

'Paula, it's me, Dave – we arranged for me to come round. I've brought some photos for Jack to see.' He hoped she'd not forgotten she'd asked him to dinner as he hadn't had much to eat for lunch. He still had a healthy appetite for food.

'Of course, I'm sorry. I've been a bit preoccupied, my son got married you know.'

She let him in, took his coat and ushered him into the sitting room. Jack was sitting in the armchair, staring into space.

'I remember James from when he was a kid, who's the lucky lady?' asked Dave.

Paula didn't respond but Jack suddenly looked interested. 'A man, he married a man and they have a baby.'

Dave was confused and looked towards Paula who had disappeared with his coat. 'I think you're getting this a bit muddled, Jack, aren't you?' But he could be right. He remembered now what Jack said about James and not to tell Paula. Sounded if she knew about it now.

Paula returned to the sitting room and she smiled rather fixedly. 'Tea, coffee or something stronger? It's after six?'

'Tell him, I'm not muddled. James is gay.'

'Yes, Jack, you're right. Would you like a whisky, and you too Dave?'

Dave nodded. 'With the same measure of water please,' he said. 'Don't want it to have too much effect on me.' He grinned and gave Paula a knowing look. He was sure that's why she'd invited him over.

Paula didn't respond but continued speaking to Jack slowly, pronouncing every syllable. 'Jack, Dave's brought some photographs from the old days. Why don't you sit on the sofa, both of you, so you can look at them? I'll get the drinks.'

When she returned Dave was showing pictures of their holiday in Ibiza, all in black and white, taken with his old brownie camera. He patted a space by his side, 'Room for a little one,' he said and Paula slipped in beside him. He could feel her warm body as she leant over to look at the snaps.

'My goodness, aren't you two young and handsome!' she said, as she looked at them He did look pretty good and what skimpy trunks they'd worn then. They were both tanned and, though he was a lot shorter than Jack, he was toned, muscular.

As Dave drank his Bell's he began to relax and was sure Paula was deliberately leaning on him and running her hand against his groin as she took the album from him to examine the blurry shots more closely.

Jack seemed to enjoy the trip down memory lane even if he sometimes got lost. He often mistook Dave for James, just like he had when he'd rescued him on the common. 'I'm hungry,' said Jack, 'I've not had my lunch. She starves me.' He looked accusingly at Paula as he got up, spilling his drink. He began pacing around the room.

'Jack, I've got some more photos here, sit down, mate,' but hoped that Jack's hunger would trigger Paula into getting some food for them.

'I've got the dinner on – Dave you are staying, aren't you? Meanwhile I'll get some snacks. Can you keep him in here? Jack, sit. Dave's come over specially to show you his albums.'

Paula sponged the carpet down, refilled the drinks and brought in a bowl of olives which Jack began to attack ravenously. Dave hated olives, couldn't see what people liked about them, but said nothing. Dinner would be ready soon and by the look of things Paula was nearly ready too. She'd better get Jack out of the way so they could be alone.

'Have you got your wedding album?' Dave asked.

'I'm surprised you, of all people, want to see those,' Paula replied, raising an eyebrow. 'After what happened....' She lowered her voice. 'Jack doesn't know, not that it matters now I suppose.'

She left the room to fetch the album from the study. Dave was surprised she'd brought that up. He was sure she must have forgotten about it after all these years. He began to think back. They'd both been drunk on champagne but she'd been willing, gasping for it. He remembered that much. They must have had a shag.

Anyway, she was being pretty friendly tonight, so he thought he'd better take his little pill. The lad in the pub hadn't given him any clear instructions and there were none in the packet. He presumed they'd need some time to work. Perhaps he should get some water - they might not work with alcohol. No, that would look a bit odd. He'd risk it and he swallowed one with the last drop of whisky. He had a whole packet so he could take another one if this didn't work.

When she returned he was glad he had as Paula had changed into a rather revealing black dress, slit at the sides. Mutton dressed as lamb. But Paula still had good legs; so was able to carry it off, and perfect for an old ram like him! 'You look fantastic,' he said.

'I like to change for dinner. I try to keep up standards, despite Jack's illness. Shall we go and eat? Jack'll probably go to bed soon, he gets very tired. Then we can have a good chat about the old days.'

Dave beamed, flashing his new dentures, his sore gums and his daughter's instructions long forgotten.

Chapter 26

Further Revenge

Paula led them into the dining room. She was having second or even third thoughts about this plan. She hadn't prepared herself for Dave's arrival. Her Brazilian had almost grown out and was itching badly in the process. Her skin had returned to its creamy tones, her Golden Kiss had got all over her sheets and stained her shower. She didn't really want to see him, let alone… She knew that Jack would be very jealous to see her with Dave. She wasn't sure what he'd made of Hot Rod. But if she went with Dave it would seem like she had enjoyed their encounter at the wedding. That was far from the truth. But she couldn't remember much and they'd both been drunk. It was as much her fault as his.

She'd hastily laid the dining table and was glad that she'd had that chicken in the freezer. It hadn't taken too long to defrost in the microwave. She'd found some candles too. She didn't look too bad without the main lights on.

'Arlene makes me coq au vin and spotted dick,' said Jack as he sat down at the table.

Paula was amazed. Was the Viagra working already? No, she'd only just put it in his drink! Perhaps what was left of his mind was transmuting his sexual desires into the names of food, his appetites getting rather confused?

'Does she indeed? More than she ever did for me,' said Dave, laughing in a rather embarrassed way. He lowered his voice and turned towards Paula. 'I don't know if you want to talk about it but did you know about Jack and Arlene? It was quite a shock to me and Karen.'

Paula hesitated, thinking how to reply, 'You know Jack always had someone on the go, but I hadn't realised he'd been seeing Arlene for such a long time.' Those letters and photos were burning into her brain.

She wondered if Jack could hear and how much he understood. Sometimes he appeared completely out of it but other times he knew she was talking about him. 'Is Arlene coming to fetch me? I'll pack my bag. Arlene feeds me.' He whispered to Dave, 'She's trying to starve me to death,' jerking his head in Paula's direction.

'No, she's not, we've got a good dinner coming up. What's on the menu, Paula?'

'Greek salad and some chicken breasts,' she said. 'I'll warm up some pitta bread.'

'See, lovely jubbly,' Dave replied. That was about Dave's level – a salesman - like some Northern barrow boy. 'Though I've always been a leg man myself and you've certainly still got some shapely ones, Paula!'

Paula moved her lips into a smile, served the food and poured three glasses of Dave's Cabernet Sauvignon. Jack ate his dinner quickly, noisily and messily. Paula frowned, she hated to see Jack eat and usually put him in front of the television with a tray.

'This is nice – I don't tend to cook much now, living on my own,' said Dave, picking the olives out of the salad. 'Sorry, never got the taste for olives, but the rest is really lovely.' Why was she going through with this? With this man?

'Thank you, it's nice to have one's efforts appreciated.'

Dave gave a leery grin. 'Oh I appreciate you Paula, always have. Shame we lost touch but when I stopped working with Jack, you know.'

'There's no need to apologise,' Paula smiled.

'If I'd known Jack was ill, I'd have got back in touch sooner. But me finding him wandering on the Common that morning, well it was like fate bringing us together again, after all these years.'

'Well it was certainly a coincidence, especially as he'd come from your ex-wife's. And, as I've said, I'm so grateful to you for rescuing him, you never know what could have happened.' She looked across to Jack who had cleaned his plate and was holding his dessert spoon, ready for his pudding. 'All right, Jack, I'll get you your dessert,' she said and turned to Dave. 'I know you haven't finished your main; but do you mind? He gets so tired. I can take him upstairs then.'

Paula went into the kitchen, and returned, apologising as she put a cake on the table. 'Sorry, M&S, I'm afraid. But they do make a lovely moist lemon drizzle cake.'

Both Jack and Dave licked their lips. Paula leant over Dave to cut Jack a large slice of cake. Dave had the view she intended. 'Would you like some later?' she asked.

'I certainly would,' he replied. 'And I hope you do too.'

'I'll just have a soupcon,' she said, making the words sound suggestive. Jack finished his slice and stood up, brushing the crumbs onto the carpet. 'Would you help me get him upstairs?' she asked, 'Jack shall we take you up now, you can sit on your massage chair and listen to some music?'

Jack might well refuse and from what Arlene implied those pills made him rather agitated. Paula hadn't noticed the last time she'd used them on him. Thankfully he accepted Dave leading him up to his room. Dave helped him into his armchair as Paula instructed. Paula picked a classical CD and put it on. She wasn't sure what it was but Jack was happy enough.

They both returned downstairs and Paula ushered Dave into the lounge. She poured him another whisky and sat next to him on the settee. She was beginning to relax; after all, if she could cope with Hot Rod, Dave would be a doddle, surely? Once she'd got him strapped in he wouldn't be able to do much anyway. She had slipped a Viagra into Dave's drink. He needed to be ready and willing to join in with her plans. She couldn't get her wedding out of her head though and wondered what he remembered of it.

'Did you look at the wedding photos?' she asked.

'We just started when dinner was ready. What did you mean when you said you didn't think I would want to see them?' he asked.

She looked into his eyes. 'You really don't remember, do you?'

'I'm not sure. I remember fancying you like hell. We had lots of champagne. We did a slow dance. Did I try it on with you?'

Paula didn't know how to respond. She didn't want to get angry with him, that wouldn't fit into her plan. But she could, she would, she certainly should be furious when she thought about what had happened. 'A bit more than trying it on! Don't you remember I went upstairs to the ladies and you were waiting outside for me? I was so drunk I had been sick in the toilet and my head was spinning.'

A look of recollection came onto Dave's face. 'Yes, I remember now, I said you should lie down for a bit and took you to one of the bedrooms.'

'That's right – need I go on? I've felt guilty ever since, despite Jack's philandering.'

'I'm sorry,' said Dave, 'for not remembering. Not for doing it – it must have been fantastic!' Paula's jaw dropped momentarily but she hid it with a hasty smile. 'I admire you, Paula; staying with Jack all these years and caring for him now he's, well, like he is. Don't you get lonely? I mean it can't be a proper marriage now, can it?'

'You're right, I do get lonely now. I can't have a real conversation with Jack anymore and the intimacy has gone.' Though she tried to remember when they had ever talked properly – not for many years in fact.

Dave slipped his arm around her shoulder and pulled her face towards his. 'You are still so beautiful,' he said and put his lips on hers. Paula responded; the bait was working well.

His hand wandered onto her thighs, quickly finding its way between her legs. He hadn't changed much in forty years. No finesse – straight at it but let's see what he'll be like later. She moved his hand away and whispered, 'Do you want to go upstairs? I think we'd be more comfortable.'

By the look of his trousers the pill was working only too well. Perhaps she shouldn't have given him one. She'd better get him into the bedroom pretty quickly. 'You get undressed, I'll just use the bathroom and check on Jack.'

She went into Jack's room. He was dozing, so she quickly bound his hands to the arms of his chair, but not too tightly this time – she didn't want to see that social worker back. She turned his chair to the picture which she removed from the wall. She shook him roughly – he mustn't miss the show.

When she returned to her room, Dave had stripped down to his underpants. He was shorter and stockier than Jack and, though he had a slight beer gut, he didn't look bad for his age. His slightly swarthy skin gave him a natural tan. Much better than her porcelain complexion.

She put the lights up and took some ropes from the wardrobe.

'What are those?' he asked. She was glad he'd not objected to the lights but that was a woman's thing.

'Don't you worry, you'll find out in a moment,' she said. 'Will you unzip me?'

Dave's hands were shaking as he stood up to reach the zip on the back of her dress. He pulled it down to reveal her black bra and matching lacy knickers. She made sure she could be seen in the mirror but Dave pulled her round to face him. He was getting very excited grabbing at her breasts. What an animal this man was!

'Not yet,' she said, pushing him away. 'Lie back and put your arms out against the bed head.'

He did as he was told and she tied his left wrist onto one of the bed posts. Dave's face changed and his voice hardened. 'What the, what on earth are you doing?'

Paula could hear the anger in his voice. He'd probably never done this sort of thing. But he must have seen it on TV or in magazines. She'd get him into the mood. 'Don't you want to be my slave? I thought you might be into a bit of S&M?'

Dave pulled his hand free, 'I'm certainly not. I don't want any of that purvey stuff.'

He dragged Paula towards him, roughly yanking off her bra and putting his hand into her vagina, his rough fingers searching for her clitoris. She was frightened, this wasn't going as she wanted. Memories of her wedding returned. Her head had been spinning as he pushed her into the hotel bedroom. She cried out that she was married as if Dave hadn't known that. He took off her going away outfit – a smart green suit she remembered she'd got from Biba. He pulled her tights off roughly and tore at her bra. She cried out but no one had come. What was she doing? Yet she'd let him carry on. The room was going round and round. She was going to be sick again. His hands were everywhere, his mouth was on her breasts. He pushed her head down towards his cock. She really was going to puke now. The smell of rancid sweat and the taste of stale sick. Her mind went blank. She must have passed out. God almighty, perhaps he was the reason she'd been put off sex with Jack for all those years.

Now it was happening all over again. She struggled but he was a heavy weight on top of her. He pushed her hand down to his prick while thrusting his stubby fingers into her. Like sandpaper against raw flesh. She dug her nails into his hands but he just kept on shoving them up her. Couldn't he tell she wasn't wet, wasn't ready? But she'd led him on, lured him there, fed him Viagra. What had Jack called her? A cock teaser. He'd been right. Her body went stiff and her throat dry. She tried to cry out and at first no sound came; but as he tried to enter her she screamed with pain.

Chapter 27

A Surprise Visit

Arlene sat down with a cup of Earl Grey and opened *The Guardian*. It was the first time she'd read the paper in days. The respite was snatched from her by the ring of her mobile. Her grandson had installed a deafening song for her new ring tone. 'You'll like it, Gran,' he had said and, when she discovered it was Rod Stewart singing, 'Do you think I'm sexy?' she regretted her outburst at Sunday lunch. She had no idea how to reduce the volume or change it to something more melodious.

She was tempted to ignore it but saw it was Karen. 'Mum, where've you been? I've been trying to get hold of you. You know Dad's gone over to Paula's today and he's going to try to find out what she's been up to and tackle her about the money.'

Arlene was glad Karen couldn't see the look of horror on her face. 'Karen, really, I think Dave will just make things worse. Paula promised that her son would write to me about it – it's much better to leave it at that.'

'But he hasn't written to you has he? And he never rang me back after I phoned him. We need to speed things up a bit.'

'He's been busy. He got married and well -'

'What?'

'Jack sort of disrupted it.' Arlene found herself explaining to her daughter what had happened, despite knowing that Karen's rock bottom opinion of her relationship with Jack would decline even further if that were possible.

Before she'd finished, Karen stated rather than asked, 'I'm coming over – I think we should go to Paula's anyway to see how Dad's getting on.'

Arlene had no chance to refuse but Karen's plan seemed completely barmy and she was determined to have nothing to do with it. She tried to concentrate on the paper but visions of her headstrong daughter bursting into Paula's elegant sitting room to discover what? Paula with this young lover Karen had found out about. Dave and Jack tied up. This was total fantasy she was sure. All Karen would achieve would be to anger Paula and make the likelihood of ever getting the money back even more remote.

Soon Karen was ringing the bell and, by this time Arlene had progressed to wine, and offered her daughter a glass. 'No thanks,' Karen replied, 'We'll probably have to drive over to Richmond. Dad's not answering his mobile – he doesn't hear anything these days. Anyway, you haven't finished your story about the wedding. What was Paula like when you took Jack back – must have been a sense of déjà vu?'

Arlene hadn't told Karen that she'd seen Jack since *The Great Escape* as Karen had started to call it and that episode was going to remain a secret.

'She was fine, quite grateful really that I'd got him. I'm not sure what that taxi man would have done otherwise. Apparently, the wedding went ahead without a hitch afterwards. So you see, I think she will help with the money, there's no need for you or Dave to get involved.'

Karen frowned, 'I think I should go - to explain what we want the money for. She has a son and I bet they paid school fees for him. And didn't you say Jack had his own business? So Paula should appreciate the problems Jeremy's having. I could say that I tried to ring Dad and was worried about him and have come to pick him up. I know, I could make something up about Snatch being found wandering.'

Arlene took rather too large a gulp of Chardonnay and her answer was distorted by her coughing and choking though she hoped the meaning would be clear. 'Karen, I won't be dragged into this ridiculous plan.' She began to feel even more foolish about how she had agreed to lending him the money in the first place. Karen must keep thinking it was a straightforward investment.

'Simon is very worried about having to leave that school. It might be different if he'd gone to a state school when he was younger; but he'd get bullied now – his accent, everything is so different from the boys at the local comp. Apart from the academic issues.'

Arlene could feel herself being manipulated, 'He's a robust boy and bright – it would be good for him. I can lend you the fees for this year without that money. I agree it's not good for him to change schools now. But he could do the sixth form in the state sector – I'm sure there are some good schools in your area.'

Karen frowned and Arlene could tell that she was going to try another angle. 'OK, Mum, but I won't be able to pay you back and I expect the house will be repossessed so we won't be in our area. Anyway you want your money back, don't you? Whatever you decide to spend it on. Why should she keep your money?'

Arlene had sometimes considered she owed Paula the money for sleeping with her husband for all those years but buried that thought. It certainly wasn't one to share with her daughter. And she didn't want to mention the fact it was really a loan which might have got swallowed up in the company. 'Yes, I do want it back; but I'm not sure rushing over now will help. And I don't want to see Dave again.'

Karen stared at her mother. 'I've apologised for that Sunday lunch but this is different. You don't have to come in with me. But our satnav has conked out so I would be glad if you'd show me the way. I'm not sure Dad will be persuasive on the money front. You never know, we might find your precious Jack tied up and we can save him from the Gorgon Paula.'

Arlene found herself putting on her tweed coat and sensible walking shoes and climbing into Karen's Land Rover. When they arrived in Richmond, Arlene watched Karen ring Paula's bell while she sat in the car listening to the dulcet tones of Radio 4. She saw a car drive up and stop outside Paula's. A man got out with a baby in a basket and went to the door. It must be James, she thought. Jack had told her a garbled tale about having a grandchild. She couldn't resist getting out of the car. James would be a much better person to tackle about the money and she would be the best person to do it. Not Karen or Dave.

When she reached the porch, Karen had introduced herself to James and, just as Arlene was about to explain why they were there, a piercing scream came from upstairs.

'I've got my key,' said James, and opened the door, passing the Moses basket to Karen. He rushed upstairs towards the noise, followed closely by Arlene. James burst through the bedroom door with Arlene just behind. She could hardly believe her eyes. Her ex was lying on top of Paula stark naked, Paula's bra was on the floor and her knickers were around her ankles. Arlene felt she should go out but stood transfixed.

Paula struggled from underneath and James averted his eyes as she grabbed her robe. She was crying and shivering and seemed unable to speak. James rushed over and looked as if he was about to punch him. He's probably never met Dave and thinks he's an intruder. Arlene knew she'd better say something but half of her wanted to see Dave get a bloody nose.

'Dave,' said Arlene, 'what have you been doing?'

James turned to her. 'You know him?' he asked.

Karen came into the room with the baby. 'Dad,' she said.

'Your father,' said Paula, 'tried to force himself on me, just like he did at my wedding.' Arlene stood open mouthed. What sort of man had she married? She should have put a stop to this stupid plan when she knew he was coming over to Paula's. Warned her what he was capable of.

The Bach concerto coming from the room next door suddenly stopped. She heard a cry – it was Jack. He sounded distressed. What had Dave done to him?

Arlene went next door to see Jack wriggling on his seat trying to get his arms free. They were tied to the arms of the chair. He'd said that and she hadn't believed him. Karen and James followed behind her. At first they all stared in amazement.

Karen was the first to speak. 'You see, I was right, she's not a fit person to look after her husband. And as for what she said about Dad…' Was that the truth? Had Paula tied him up?

Arlene tried to untie Jack but struggled. Her hands were a little arthritic but those knots were tight. Poor Jack – could Paula really have done this to her own husband? James helped and between them they untied him. Arlene put her arms around him and could see James looking in the mirror. His eyes widened and his face became grey.

'What is it?' asked Karen and also looked into the mirror. 'I can see into your mother's room. My God – mirror, mirror on the wall, who is the perviest one of all?'

'I don't understand. Is this for her to keep an eye on him – see he's all right?' asked James but his voice sounded unconvinced. He went back to his mother's room.

Arlene stared into the mirror and saw, not her reflection, but James' face. She wondered if he could see her. Her mind was whirring – what monster could do this to an old man but yet ...? She heard James' voice, loud, harsh and could see Paula sitting on her bed. 'You can't see Dad from your room but he can from yours,' he said.

Paula's voice was a hoarse whisper. 'Please, James, I can't cope with an inquisition now after the trauma I've just been through.'

'All right, but we'll talk later,' he said and came back into Jack's room.

Arlene wasn't sure she wanted to face Paula but she'd have to. She tapped on Paula's door and peeped round. 'I just wondered if you're going to call the police?' Arlene asked. 'I mean if he tried to rape you, then he needs to be punished – too many women don't report incidents like this.'

Though she said this quietly, Karen screamed from the landing. 'Mum, how can you suggest that? She set him up so her husband would be forced to watch it all - through that mirror, window thing. She's a witch.'

It was Dave's turn to look confused, as he came out of the bathroom, 'Jack watching, no, but she did want to tie me up,' he said.

Jack came out of his room to use the bathroom followed by James. 'Shall we go downstairs into the sitting room and talk about this quietly. I'll make us a drink,' said James, but then looking around frantically shouted, 'Oh, Christina, where is she?'

Christina? That must be the baby, Arlene could see she was still fast asleep in her basket in the corner of the bedroom - unaware of the discussion on rape, bondage, two way mirrors, threesomes and voyeurism going on around her. 'It's all right she's in here. I'll bring her down in a moment. I'm just having a word with your mum.'

But James came in and grabbed the basket with only a glance at his mother. Arlene swallowed hard as she looked at the tearful Paula. She shut the bedroom door. 'I was serious about the police, you know. Dave used to force me. I suppose he would have thought it was his right. I was his wife. But it was rape.'

Paula was staring through her tears and smudged mascara. Her words came out in sobs. 'Thank you,' she said. 'But I didn't behave well and I couldn't possibly report it to anyone. Thank you for trying to help though.'

'You shouldn't blame yourself,' she said, though she didn't entirely mean that. Though Dave was the real villain, if Paula was treating Jack like that, she had to get him out of there. 'Did you say he did the same at your wedding?'

Paula did not meet Arlene's gaze. 'Yes,' she said. 'We were both really drunk. I remember what happened though. I don't want to talk about it.'

Arlene decided not to press it. There was something else she needed to bring up with Paula. She sat down on the bed and talked.

Chapter 28

A New Father

James went downstairs, carefully carrying the Moses basket, followed by Karen. James could feel Karen's eyes on him and when he turned he saw she was staring intently at his face as if it was a piece of abstract art she couldn't quite understand. James began to feel his face colouring though his mind was on the scene he'd just witnessed. She must be wanting him to deal with this loan or whatever it was.

'I'm sorry I didn't ring you back,' he said.

'Yes,' she said, 'we do need to sort that out but you've got a lot on your mind just now.' She sat down and flicked through the wedding album which was lying open on the coffee table. She came to one particular picture and motioned to James to look at it. It was his parents' wedding photo of the happy couple, the bridesmaid and...? He looked again. It must be the best man but... He picked it up and peered more closely. He might have been looking at his own wedding photo except for the colour and style of the suit. They both stared at each other.

'So what Mum said must have been true,' he said. That bastard but that meant... Fuck, that was too awful to think about.

'What?' said Karen, 'he was probably having an affair with her. He was never very faithful but that doesn't mean he forced her into sex. She seems quite a goer. I understand she's had a young lover recently.'

Fucking Chris and now this fucking woman's seen all this. 'Please don't make unsubstantiated statements.' God, he did sound like a lawyer, but how could he defend her after what she'd done to his dad. Or not his dad?

'Well you saw what went on up there. But that's up to you. We should get to know each other a bit more as I'm your half-sister.'

James couldn't think of anything worse than having Karen as a half-sister except that this rapist might be his father. But he had no link with them. What did biology matter? Though they had wanted Christina to be their natural child, it wouldn't have worried him if she was Chris's. Jack had brought him up, read him stories, played with him, taken him on holiday, given him a bike for Christmas. He'd been his dad. Had he been infertile and asked Dave to provide sperm? No, that wasn't what people did; but he was Jack's only child and Jack had been married twice before. He must have known – or, at least suspected when his son grew up to look the image of his best friend. Yet he brought him up as his own. And his mum – it could have been an affair but somehow he doubted it. No, it was rape. She must realise that he was Dave's son. The wedding photos make it pretty obvious. My God... he was the progeny of rape and now his father had just tried to rape his mother again! Yet he was angry with her. Was it a bit like Hamlet's attitude to Gertrude or just the idea of his mother having sex with anyone? She shouldn't have wanted his Dad to watch though.

'What are you going to do about it?' asked Karen.

'Do about what?' James asked. 'I'm not sure it alters the situation - except perhaps we should get the police to investigate a case of historical rape.'

Karen opened her mouth to say something but no words came out. James heard his dad coming downstairs. He had put his dressing gown on and looked quite refreshed.

'Bit of trouble with the old water works,' Jack said.

'What was happening up there?' asked James.

Jack looked blank. There were some benefits to dementia. Perhaps what his mum had done wasn't too awful. Jack didn't seem to be affected by it now. Maybe he had wanted to watch? James couldn't think about it. The sexual activities of old people were not a pretty thought but when they were your parents as well, God Almighty. He wondered if his dad seeing the wedding photos would bring any memories back. But Jack sat down and picked up Dave's album, not his wedding one.

'James. Look at these photos of the holiday I went on the other year.' James studied them and, yes, he was the image of Dave in these photos as well. Couldn't his dad see that? Jack talked quite lucidly about the holiday he'd had until Dave came down looking rather shamefaced.

James wondered if he should confront him. He didn't want to distress Jack though. Even Dave was staring at James' face. Had he known about it too?

'I don't want you to get the wrong end of the stick about what happened today,' Dave said.

'What's the right end of the stick then?' asked James. 'Come into the kitchen if we're to discuss this.' James didn't want to talk about it. He feared he might get violent like with Adie - though surely that had been the drink?

'I think I should be involved too,' said Karen and followed them into the kitchen. 'Dad, look at James – can't you see? Had you and Paula been having an affair?'

Dave looked at James. 'Jack did mistake me for you. There is some resemblance to when I was young.' He stopped and his eyes widened. 'You don't mean. No, I would have known about it. Paula would have told me. And Jack, does he know? Did he think I could have been your father?'

'Dad, is it true?' asked Karen.

'Well, yes, we did have a bit of a fling. But I just assumed Paula was on the pill – I think it had been invented by then anyway. But that was before she married Jack. Paula's not the unfaithful type apart from, well ...'

James looked from one to the other and wondered whether he should believe this man but he knew what he'd seen upstairs.

'I don't know why you're defending her,' said Karen and proceeded to tell Dave about the mirror.

'Well, she certainly had some odd ideas up there; but you know she was happy to go to bed with me – for old times' sake, you know. I mean she doesn't have much intimacy with your dad now - with him being, well you know...'

James turned to put the kettle on and remembered the scream he had heard, like an animal's, worse than had come out of Jenny when she was in labour.

'She didn't sound very happy,' he said.

Dave coloured. 'I might have got a bit over-excited. It's been a long time since... and I got some of that Viagra stuff. I think it might have been a bit strong. Sorry, love, that you have to hear all this. I know you were upset about your mother and now it's me.'

James turned to Dave, anger surging through his body. His fists were ready but he couldn't hit an old man, his own father perhaps. Is that where he got this desire to thump people from? Jack had been powerful but never physical. He'd never smacked James as a child but he was sure Dave had packed some punches when he was younger.

Just then Christina wailed and they all turned to the baby. James picked her up gently and she stopped crying and nuzzled at his shoulder.

'That's your grandchild, Dad,' said Karen.

James' face turned as pale as Christina's translucent skin. 'Don't you dare even think it. In fact, I don't want any of this mentioned again.' It was strange how he had wanted to be Christina's dad. Now he wished she had been Chris's child. How could he have such an evil father and sister?

'You're not serious about this rape thing, are you?' asked Dave.

James knew his mother wouldn't want any scandal but half of him would like to see Dave in court. 'I'll talk to my mother and see it if she'll wants to press charges. If so, we'll want a medical examination and some DNA probably.'

'Now hold your horses,' said Dave.

'You can't be serious,' said Karen. 'I'm sure your mother would be pleased to see herself on the front of the Sun as the debauched duchess or perverted pensioner. No, Dad it won't happen. Will it bruv?'

Chapter 29

The Wife's Solution

Paula wanted to stay in bed, hide away from all the staring eyes. But she needed to tell them her plan or rather Arlene's plan. How come Arlene had been so nice to her? She didn't deserve it after what she'd done to Jack. She should have stood up to him when she was younger, not now when he was old and vulnerable. Arlene had been Jack's mistress for years and yet she was the only one who understood how she felt. It now seemed so obvious what the best thing to do was... She redid her face and tried to repair her dignity. She needed her mask more than ever. What would everyone be thinking? And James, she could hardly face him. As she followed Arlene downstairs she could hear Dave saying, 'I think it was those pills, they did make me go a bit wild, but she ...' He tailed off as he heard the two women come into the room.

'Go on Dad, you're right, she tried to seduce you,' said Karen. 'But I can't believe you took Viagra you bought from a bloke in a pub.'

Paula didn't find her voice, but her conscience told her she should confess to giving him another pill. Did that explain it? Would the double dose have that effect on a man? She thought not and it certainly didn't explain the wedding night. Arlene was right. He had raped her. Certainly then and he would have now.

She sat down quietly next to Arlene. She had almost forgiven her for all the years of betrayal. It was Jack who had been the main culprit after all. James brought in coffees and teas and Paula noticed his bruised eye. She managed to speak but in a husky soft voice. 'What have you done to your face?'

'Oh nothing, I'll tell you about it later. But can I have a word in the kitchen?'

Paula followed her son obediently, her heart thumping, trying desperately to think of a plausible explanation for bondage and two way mirrors. 'Mother, will you tell me what you were thinking of with this mirror – I'm not going to judge you.'

Paula looked down, 'It really was to keep an eye on him. And he did disturb me at night, wandering around all the time, so I began to tie him up'.

She looked up to see him staring at her. 'But you had a lock fitted and the mirror is a two way one. The wrong way round for you to *keep an eye on him*?'

Paula swallowed hard. She considered telling him about the photos and the letters that had fuelled her revenge. But compared to Jack being tied to his chair watching her, they seemed unconvincing so she said nothing.

'I know it wasn't the best marriage in the world but I don't know how you could treat my father like this, especially when he's ill.'

She couldn't confess all and beg forgiveness so she decided to say what had been on her mind in the last few weeks. It probably wasn't the best time to bring it up but anything to change the subject. 'He may not be,' she said quietly.

'What?' said James 'What do you mean? Not ill?'

'You know I got pregnant not long after we married and you know what I told you upstairs.' She dissolved into tears and James went over to her and put his arm around her.

'I understand, Mum, I know what you're going to say. Jack may not be my father.'

Her face was pale and her disguise was slipping, her eyes dark and smarting. 'How do you know? We always joked you didn't look like either of us, you were shorter and stockier. But we never thought you could be Dave's son.'

'Mum, I've seen pictures of Dave as a young man. At your wedding. It may be true but I don't care, not in the least.'

'I know I should have thought of it before but I think I'd blocked it from my mind until…'

James looked calm. How could he be when he'd found out that rapist was his father? Did he even believe she was raped? Perhaps he blamed it all on her. Should she explain what had happened? No, she wasn't up to talking about it anymore - at least not now.

'Mum, I said I don't care. Dave will never be my dad. Jack is. That's all there is to it.'

Paula noticed the baby in her basket on the kitchen table and went over to her. She was sleeping and, though she wanted to pick her up, she thought she'd better not wake her.

'I had come over to show you and tell her you're her granny.'

Paula was about to ask if she was her real granny but was unsure what that meant anymore. 'You've had a test?' she asked. James nodded. 'I knew she was yours all along. But it's nice you've named her after Christopher.' Like she'd named him after Jack but she had thought he was his son.

'She's Christina Jemima.'

'Jemima, oh James that's wonderful,' she smiled and a wail came from the basket.

'Oh my God, she probably needs feeding. I've been here much longer than I intended. I'll ring Chris to bring Jenny over,' said James, looking at his watch.

Paula picked the baby up. 'The poor little thing is wet through,' she said. She found a spare nappy in the bottom of the Moses basket and took her up to the bathroom. Jemima was wearing tiny Pampers, not terry towelling as it had been in her day. Now how do you work these things? To her surprise, she changed her easily. She felt a wave of love as Jemima looked up at her with her innocent blue eyes. She would always be Jemima to her. She brought her downstairs and joined the people in the sitting room, hoping the product of young copulation might put a stop to the talk about elderly sex.

James came into the room, 'I've rung Chris but, Mum, we hadn't quite finished what we were talking about.'

'No, James, but Arlene and I have decided something and we need to tell everyone.' The room fell silent. 'I know some of you will be surprised at what you're going to hear and my decision may seem rather sudden. But Arlene and I discussed it upstairs. You know I have been finding it hard caring for Jack.' She looked around anxiously, waiting for someone to mention *bruising, social services* or even *bondage*; but there was a shocked silence so she carried on.

'Arlene has kindly offered – do you want me to say, Arlene?' She was trying to stop her tone sounding too full of relief.

'Yes, go on, it's probably better coming from you,' said Arlene. Paula could see Karen mouthing *money*.

'It's all right, Karen, we'll get to the finance,' said Paula. What a detestable woman. She hated the daughter as much as the father. 'We have decided that Jack should live with Arlene. I know it might seem strange after we've been married for so many years but the marriage has been an empty shell for a long time – before Jack got ill, I mean.' She looked anxiously at her son who was staring at her as if this was the first time he'd been aware they had problems.

'You're going to let Dad live with Arlene?'

Paula looked at Arlene who was sitting next to Jack, his head on her shoulder and knew this was the right decision. Paula couldn't love him as he was now. Had she ever loved him or was it his status and wealth she had loved? James would realise this was for the best.

'But what about Dad – has anyone talked to him about what he wants?'

'I was thinking of residential care to be honest, James, if Arlene hadn't suggested this. He wouldn't want that.'

Jack raised his head but still appeared rather lost. 'I'll get my stuff. Are we going away?' he asked.

'Well, we might,' said Arlene. 'Would you like to come to stay with me for a bit?' He nodded enthusiastically. 'James, I would look after him. We could do it as a trial and, if it doesn't work out and he wants to return to Paula, that would be fine.'

'I can't imagine he would,' said Karen, 'but all this will cost my mother money. If you were thinking of a Home that would cost a bomb. My mother should be entitled to the equivalent. And, let's be honest, he can only get worse. Mum have you thought this through? Do you really know what you're letting yourself in for?'

'Yes, Karen, I have. I want Jack to live with me.'

'And I will be busy with little Jemima here,' said Paula as she looked down at the baby who was sucking her finger in lieu of a nipple.

'Jenny's going to be our nanny,' said James.

'I mean I would help Jenny – she wants to work part time in the homeopathy shop,' said Paula.

'You know you can't tie up babies,' hissed Karen.

Paula's eyes blazed but her voice was calm. That bloody woman again. She hadn't really worked it all out yet - but Karen wasn't to know. 'We have worked out the finances, Karen - your mother will not be out of pocket. And James is sorting out the money that Jack invested for your mum. She'll have it in a couple of weeks.'

There was a ring on the bell and James rushed to answer. He opened the door and showed Chris and Jenny into the sitting room. Everyone was sitting looking serious but Paula had regained her composure. She stood up, handed Jemima to Jenny and gave Chris a peck on the cheek. 'Do take my seat – would you be all right to feed her here? Or would you like somewhere more private?' she asked.

'Fine here,' she said and lifted up her top, undid her nursing bra and Jemima soon latched on like a vice.

'I'll make you a drink,' said Paula, escaping into the kitchen. 'James, will you help me?' She didn't really want to talk to her son alone again but all those eyes were burning into her and she had to know he didn't hate her. He might stop her seeing Jemima.

'James. I know you think I'm cruel and heartless but this is the best thing for your dad.'

'Certainly, if you're going to tie him up. Unless, I don't know how to say this. Did he want to see it? Was it a game you were both playing?'

Paula stared. Could she lie to James and say that he had agreed to it? Paula was shocked by her son asking that but could he be right? Had Jack enjoyed all this? Might her revenge just have been giving Jack entertainment? It could be true.

'He always wanted me to be more sexually adventurous,' she said. 'So I suppose it was my way of giving him a thrill.'

How could she talk to her son like this? Still, it was better for him to think that then anything else.

She turned away and was relieved when Chris came into the kitchen. 'What's this all about?' he asked. 'It's like a dentist's waiting room in there. How's your eye by the way? I can't believe Adie hit you like that. Lovely house, Paula, by the way.'

Paula's eyes opened more widely. She wished she'd stayed at the wedding longer. Her shoes had been hurting her so much and, to be honest, she'd felt a little out of place with all those gay men. Perhaps it wouldn't have happened if she'd been there. She wanted to ask more about it but decided that they had all shared enough secrets that day.

'Can you reassure that dreadful woman about the money? I asked you about it when we came for Sunday lunch,' she said.

James looked puzzled. Paula began to wonder if she'd mentioned it. Was she becoming like Jack?

'She asked me as well. I've been a bit busy though,' he apologised. 'But don't worry, I'll sort it. Oh God, my eye's really hurting now. Can we go after Jenny's fed Christina? Oh, do you want to see the house - now you're here at last?' asked James.

Chris glanced at Paula. 'No, it's okay. I'll see it another time.'

So Karen gave Dave a lift home. James took Jack and Arlene; and Chris took Jenny and Jemima. The house was so empty. She looked around her silent sitting room and images of happier times with Jack and James flowed into her mind. Jack had been a good father, a good husband in some ways. She looked at all their possessions. She liked her things, her clothes, her jewellery. The constant remodelling of the house. Jack had gone and things were all she had left. She supposed it hadn't satisfied her. Was she such a shallow person that this had been her life? Was she now going to get her life back? Fulfil herself at last. But how? A smile crept onto her lips. She had Jemima. She was the future. Jack was the past. And, of course, there was Mrs Robinson. Was she done with Mrs R? Probably... but if she were careful? There are plenty of young men out there waiting. Jack had finally made his escape. Arlene could have him – Paula had other fish to fry.

Acknowledgements

I wrote this novel as the final piece of my MA Writing at Sheffield Hallam University. I would like to thank my tutor, Linda Lee Welch, for her help and encouragement and fellow students for their robust but always constructive critiques.

My novel group led by Ann Grange also read many chapters and helped improve my style and characterisation.

I visited Darnall Dementia Care Day Centre for some of my research for the book and I would like to thank the staff and service users there for their time and support.

My friend, Rachel, read early drafts and was unstinting in her praise and encouragement. I want to thank my daughter Charlotte for working so hard at designing the cover in a very short time frame and, lastly, my husband, Mike, for putting up with me during the writing process.

Printed in Great Britain
by Amazon